OBLIVION'S DAWN
©2023 Dave Alexander/Drew Avera

This book is protected under the copyright laws of the United States of America. No part of this publication may be reproduced, stored in a retrieval system, or transmitted, in any form or by any means, without the prior permission in writing of the publisher, nor be otherwise circulated in any form of binding or cover other than that in which it is published and without a similar condition including this condition being imposed on the subsequent purchaser. Any reproduction or unauthorized use of the material or artwork contained herein is prohibited without the express written permission of the authors.

Aethon Books supports the right to free expression and the value of copyright. The purpose of copyright is to encourage writers and artists to produce the creative works that enrich our culture.

The scanning, uploading, and distribution of this book without permission is a theft of the author's intellectual property. If you would like to use material from the book (other than for review purposes), please contact editor@aethonbooks.com. Thank you for your support of the author's rights.

Aethon Books
www.aethonbooks.com

Interior design, print and eBook formatting by Steve Beaulieu. Cover layout and design by Steve Beaulieu. Artwork provided by Vivid Covers.

Published by Aethon Books LLC.

Aethon Books is not responsible for websites (or their content) that are not owned by the publisher.

This book is a work of fiction. Names, characters, places, and incidents are the product of the author's imagination or are used fictitiously. Any resemblance to actual events, locales, or persons, living or dead is coincidental.

All rights reserved.

ALSO IN SERIES

Oblivion's Dawn

Blood Lines

Artifacts of the Gods

PROLOGUE

BALA - 613 LIGHT YEARS FROM EARTH

THE GREAT ROOM HAD THE DISTINCT ODOR OF A RUNDOWN colony planet as human and Veshnian colonists filled the space. All around him, the whispers and cries of those confused by what was happening grew on his nerves. For the third time in less than a minute, the old mercenary felt the need to silence his prey.

"Sit down and shut up!" Garret barked. Spittle ran down his chin from this constant shouting as he wrangled his hostages into the atrium. Light streaming in from the overhead windows cooked the burn scars on the side of his face. They were still sensitive a year after he earned them on a mission gone horribly wrong. He wasn't about to let this one go awry under his watch, though. Live and learn.

Turning to avoid the discomfort, he leaned close to his lieutenant and spoke, covering his mouth to prevent anyone from reading his lips. "I need to go make a call. If anyone acts out, shoot them and leave the body for display. Nothing shuts people up like lifeless eyes staring back at them. You got it?"

"You mean the hostages or anyone?" Brady asked, an eyebrow raised mischievously. It was no secret the younger man hated their pieced-together crew. Typically, Garret used his own five-man-

DAVE ALEXANDER

strong team for jobs like this. But the stakes were higher and financial persuasion went a long way in getting him to agree to this so-called "assistance." Eventually, Garret took them on with less hesitation than Brady would have liked.

What could he say? Money talked.

Garret smirked as he watched the commotion of the hostages being led through the front entrance and ushered into position by strange faces. Only three of this crew were men he'd served with prior. He trusted them with his life. The rest were sewn together from other mercenary units exploited by the Bastia. He took note of them standing around, treating the situation like a lackadaisical training mission when the cold truth was that this was the real deal. Lives were at stake and either of them could breathe their last breath at any moment. A part of him resented the newcomers. In his experience they were a liability.

His overseer knew this, and casted them into the mission without Garret's approval. The disrespect gnawed at him like a raw nerve, but this was far from the first time. Still, he had to hope that this mission, and its success, would actually make a difference this time. There was someone at home who needed that hope as much as he did; assuming she could live long enough for him to succeed.

Garret spat, trying to get the taste that came with being a composite out of his mouth. He hated coming to and having to relearn how to be himself in a weakened state. In truth, he hated coming to at all. Each time he woke in a new form was because the universe was falling apart around him and needed a swift kick in the right direction. The highest bidder made the call as for what constituted right, but it was his size twelve boot iniating the course correction. That's what the customers paid the overseer for, a blunt force kill team to set things right. But successful kill teams had a history together. They weren; t just tossed out like dice onto the table and hoped for the best. Then again, this

OBLIVION'S DAWN

wasn't the usual mission. He knew that as soon as his eyes opened and the floodgates of his prescripted memory flooded into his mind.

He hated that part too. Almost as much as he hated the new faces on his team. Garret knew without a shadow of a doubt that they were just expendable pieces of meat cutting in on his profits. He could always mow them down for a richer cut, but you never knew who you might need until they were no longer breathing. *Later*, he thought, game for seeing just how tough these merc wannabes really were once things got less comfortable around here.

"I mean anyone. I don't care who. If they get too big for their britches, cut them down. Understood?"

"Yes, sir," Brady replied. A sinister sneer curled the younger man's lips as he gazed at the pantheon of unarmed colonists now under his control. "I'll maintain good order and discipline, Boss. You have my word."

Garret scoffed, knowing full well the lieutenant craved the action they left behind before they became mercenaries. For the first time in years, the opportunity to draw blood for money was back on the table, and bloodlust was not an easy fix to control.

"Don't shoot too many," he warned. "I want a decent payout." He knew his second in command would obey, but he had to scratch the itch, just in case.

Brady nodded, tapping his finger on the trigger guard of his rifle as he marched towards the other end of the room where their prisoners were corralled by the other men. "Walters. Get over here," he spat, his attention trained on one of the men standing around. Brady used his elbow to point to help maintain control of his weapon. He watched Walters jog over, his lips moving like he talking about him under his breath. Brady had been around the block enough to not be paranoid about it. It was simply an unconfirmed fact at this point. Let them say what they want so long as

3

they do what they're told – that was rule number three, or four, depending on who was counting.

"What's up, sir?"

"What's up?" Brady shot back. "What's up is that we have over a hundred colonists with less than a dozen of us. We need to secure this space to ensure no one acts like a hero. I expect this to get wrapped up quickly, but you and your buddies are being lazy with it. Put some fear into them. I don't care how you do it. You can put a few blunt strikes to the men, even the women if you have to. Just let them know we aren't afraid to hurt them. You got me?"

Walters stood there for a moment, looking like he had something to say, but was too afraid to speak up. It was an expression that wore thin on Brady's nerves. "I—"

"Is there a problem?" Brady asked, his cold glare calculating behind his cobalt eyes. There was nothing to prevent him from making a dramatic increase in his shares by killing the young merc where he stood. All he needed was a reason to pull the trigger. Being unfamiliar with the new faces was enough of an excuse in his book, but there was safety in numbers. And Garret wouldn't be happy if the first shots fired were against his own organization, despite the last order he'd given. At least not until the hostages were secured.

"No, sir. I'll make it happen."

"Be sure you do," Brady said, his default sneer returning. To say he liked watching people in pain was an understatement. The only thing he enjoyed more was inflicting it. Of course, both options paled in comparison to watching the light leave the eyes of his targets. It made him feel godlike. Control was an aphrodisiac, plain and simple.

Walters made his way back to his post, walking purposefully towards a lumbering Veshnian standing in line before the merc struck the alien scum with the butt of his rifle, splitting the man's head open like a melon. "When we say move faster, we mean faster. The next one of you maggots to not follow orders will be shot. Now, get in ranks and sit down."

Brady smiled at the enthusiasm Walters displayed. "Maybe I was wrong about him," he whispered as he pulled a double-shot bottle of whiskey from his cargo pocket and took a hit. Alcohol withdraws were already starting to hit him and he wanted to circumvent the situation by taking the edge off. Garret would be pissed to see him drinking on the job, but for all Brady knew, Garret's disappearing act was so he could self-medicate as well.

Secrets are inevitable in relationships like ours.

As he screwed the lid back onto the bottle, a commotion pulled him from his thoughts. When he looked up, he saw the largest Veshnian in the crowd grab Walters by the neck and heave him skyward, howling in rage. The beast-like alien squeezed, turning Walter's face blue in a matter of seconds while the other mercs circled him, too afraid to retaliate.

Brady ran over, his eyes wide with delight, and his rifle raised to deliver a reminder of why no one crosses an armed mercenary. At close range, he delivered said message with a splattering of blood painting the rocky wall behind the Veshnian. The dull report of the carbine reverberated off the walls before falling dead, the sound absorbed by the foreign, rocky surface. A hush filled the cavernous space as the alien's body drooped to the floor. Order restored.

Brady glared at Walters as the young man gasped for air. "Thanks, sir," he said, turning to look at the dead body before him. He slowly backed away, scooting on his backside as a pool of blood seeped towards him.

"You showed weakness, Walters," Brady said under his breath, stirring the other man's attention.

Walters looked up. "He caught me off guard is all. It won't happen again."

DAVE ALEXANDER

Brady smiled and knelt next to him, letting his rifle dangle from the shoulder harness, the muzzle forty-five degrees down and to the left of his position. "You're right. It won't," he said as he pulled the pistol from his hip holster, the sound of the snap releasing the weapon from its leather restraint and into his gloved grip drew Walters's eyes to it.

"You don't have to do this," Walters said, his voice high. For a split second, it looked as though the young merc was about to cry.

Brady said nothing as his eyes narrowed. He leveled the weapon and shot Walters in the face, the round tearing enough of its victim's flesh away to make him unrecognizable. The blood splatter was enough to kick back and cover part of Brady's face. The blast echoed in the large atrium from the large caliber weapon.

The crowd of hostages looked to Brady in horror. In less than ten seconds he had killed a hostage and one of his own men. He knew what they were thinking by reading the expressions on their faces. They thought he was crazy, capable of anything.

They were right.

Brady stood, a grin stretched over his face as he shoved the Bastian military pistol back into its holster and snapped the tab back into place. It was a superior weapon in every way to anything built by human means, and it made him appreciate this mission all the more. He took a deep breath as he surveilled the crowd, now deathly silent. He outstretched his arms and stepped forward, ready to claim his superiority like the commander he deserved to be. "Let that be a testament to all of you. Do as I say or meet your end in the same way as Mr. Walters and your fellow colonist. If I hear the rumblings of another uprising, I'll kill you all without question. If you want to test me, here I am."

He looked to the remaining mercs, their hands on their weapons and their eyes locked onto him. At any point, they could have fired on him, but fear had a way of paralyzing even the

6

OBLIVION'S DAWN

strongest-willed men. He'd seen it happen on more occasions than he could count. Sometimes the hesitation resulted in death. Other times it allowed cooler heads to prevail. He wondered which one it was going to be today. His actions had to get under their skin if nothing else.

Brady's finger began its dance along the trigger guard of his rifle as he eyed each man, taking a moment to try and get a read on them. Satisfied that no one was about to lift arms against him, he spoke. "Take a note on Walters's behalf. Neither Garret nor I will tolerate failure. You do the job, or you die. It's as simple as that. Any questions?"

"What's the plan now?" Jordan asked, taking a step forward as a show of respect as he spoke to the ranking member in the room. His dark skin contrasted against the stark whiteness of his eyes, where Brady saw no fear, only respect. Jordan was obviously a man who'd seen his share of combat and wouldn't buckle at the hard decisions that leadership often had to make. That, or he saw his stakes in the game rise as Walters bled out on the floor behind him.

Either way, Brady liked what he saw.

"By now, the Confederation should know we have hostages. They'll send an ambassador to negotiate their release and we'll get paid. Anything beyond that is above your pay grade. Any other questions?" Brady's jaw clenched, a habit he had when making a point.

"As long as I get paid, you won't hear a peep out of me," Jordan replied. The rest of the crew chuckled under their breath until the sound of bootheels at the entrance filled their ears. The ones with their backs to it turned on their heels, gripping their weapons until the intruder came into the light.

It was Garret.

"Easy, boys. I'm just returning to give you the good news. The call went out," he said as he made his way closer to them, not

7

DAVE ALEXANDER

looking at the two bodies lying in pools of blood. The old man was far from oblivious, he was just desensitized to the point that he did not stir easily.

That's what thirty years of mercenary work broke you down to; an unmoving, unfeeling shell of a human being. None of the men he ever worked with looked at it as a weakness. If anything, it was something to aspire to, to one day become a machine of death. He stopped in the center of the mercs' impromptu circle and smiled as he pulled a cigar from his pocket. He took a few moments to light it before speaking. "Now we settle in for the long haul, boys. Our payday is coming. Ten Million Shid per head or they all die. I'm pretty sure they'll see to our terms."

Jovial laughter emanated from the crowd of men. With that kind of money, each of them could retire to a remote location and never have to want for anything again.

Of course, the same could have been said for every other venture in their lives. But as far as Garret and his men were concerned, this was the first step towards newer and bolder opportunities. Retirement was the goal when death wouldn't take you. Not a single man in this room didn't wonder if they would make it to that point. Most never would, but for Garret, this was the final curtain call. He was done with this life and needed this to be the final mission more than he needed his next breath.

Garret just hoped the other side kept their end of the bargain.

ONE
GCS VERITAS IN THE BALA SYSTEM

MECHANICAL ARMS MOVED ACROSS THE OVERHEAD OF THE SHIP AS the constant chirp of the life support system stirred Ambassador Tella Spar from hypersleep. Without opening her eyes, the piercing blinding light made her head hurt. She lifted her arm to shield her eyes as she forced herself up. Like any newborn composite, her new existence was painful to behold, but experience told her it would pass.

Eventually.

"Lights," she croaked, the word sounding more like a guttural groan than actual speech. Thankfully for her, the onboard AI understood her displeasure, and the light levels were reduced to fifty percent. Not wanting to strain her voice, she swallowed, trying to wet her throat before speaking again. "How long was I out?" Tella asked, her voice tighter than she thought it would be, but lacking the slurring which generally accompanied the first words "coming to," as composites often described it.

"It has been four days since your consciousness was uploaded to the mainframe, Ambassador," the AI responded. The voice was distinctly feminine, but not based on any single human.

Tella sighed, still wincing from the light as she draped her arm back over her face and tried to sit up. Her muscles lacked enough control to risk standing, so she kept her weight on the bed as the mechanical arms continued about their work, scanning her for health data that she knew would come back as normal. She wondered why the AI even bothered. Every composite came to as a perfect genetic representation. Of course, faults could be programmed into the manufacturing process, but few would take the time to do such a thing. The creators of the technology boasted that God himself could not create a more perfect human.

Were Adam and Eve not perfect creations if they existed? Tella knew enough about the old stories to know the answer to that question. All creation has its faults.

Tella wondered if the creators of the composite technology would still feel that they outdid God after hundreds of years if they could see what their creation had led humanity to become. It was, after all, their technology that first allowed humans to travel the stars by transferring their consciousness across the galaxy. It was no longer the only method, but it had begun as an ambitious endeavor culminating in the same horrors the same horrors that humans committed when they merely crossed oceans to conquer other peoples.

Now the conquered weren't human at all, but alien races at the wrong place and the wrong time.

Or maybe it was the other way around.

"Give me a status report," she said, slowly letting her arm droop to see if she could handle the bright lights.

"Three killed and one injured since your last status update. Communications breakdown and resistance from the hostages has caused the mercenary force to act erratically."

"Do they still act as if they will release the hostages if we pay the ransom?" Tella asked.

"Affirmative. Though, frustrations have escalated. Analysis of recent outgoing messages suggests a breakdown in communica-

tions among the parties involved. It will certainly create a hostile environment for negotiations."

"Great." Tella sighed. This was what she was afraid of. If the mercenaries couldn't agree on demands, then anything she proposed would be met with opposition from either side. If it was as simple as paying the ransom to secure the hostages, then it would be an easy decision to make. But the moment the demands changed; she would be thrust into a position where neither side would come out as a winner. With so many lives hanging in the balance as collateral, this was a situation she wouldn't wish on her biggest adversary.

"AI, I need you to maintain my profile data just in case." She knew the data would be saved automatically, but compression of the files would delay another composite from coming to. If the situation dissolved on Bala, then she would need to act swiftly to calm the storm. Her job as ambassador put her in the middle of a possible escalation of violence, the absolute worst place to be if one did not want to be caught in the crossfire.

"Do you wish to update the memory storage to include recent information?"

"No, that isn't necessary. Once I'm prepared to disembark, I will leave a message for a future composite." Tella shifted forward on the bed until her feet touched the ice-cold deck of the *Veritas*. She already missed life on Earth, even though the composite version of herself had never stepped foot on anything other than the deck of this ship. It was a peculiar dichotomy, having memories one never truly experienced, but based on a very real life which spanned generations. Her selection as an ambassador of Earth on behalf of the Confederation afforded her the opportunity to live a life longer than most, but the costs were higher than she had expected when accepting the position.

"I have completed the scan, Ambassador. Your composite is free of defect." The mechanical arms lifted into the overhead and

relieved her of the claustrophobic feeling gnawing at her nerves. This was one of many side effects of being a composite. She felt like a ball of anxiety coming to on the ship; every movement and every sound unsettling. There were others she might discover the longer she wore this form, but none of them would be as bad as the chemical taste in her mouth.

She scraped her tongue against her teeth trying to brush it off as she rose. "Why am I not surprised?" Tella dared to put her weight on newborn legs. If animals can walk within hours of birth, then a fully formed adult human should be able to do so as well, based on previous experience. "Could you assist me in standing?"

"*Certainly*," the AI replied. A mechanical arm descended from the overhead and situated itself within Tella's reach. She grabbed it with one hand and slowly rose off the bed, closing her eyes as the room began to spin.

"Give me a moment to compose myself. I'm sorry," Tella whispered. The apology meant nothing to the AI, but it was a habit she formed when dealing with more advanced, sentient beings within the Confederation. The human was always wrong. That was the mantra her sponsor, a Veshnian ambassador, drilled into her so many years ago. If not for the Veshnians, humanity would have been cleansed from existence, but they saw potential where the rest of the Confederation saw a species too hellbent on destruction to be responsible for advancing civilization. Stunts like the one she was responding to now proved their point.

"*Ambassador, there is an incoming message from Chancellor Benoit. Would you like to hear it now?*"

Tella remained standing but kept her eyes shut. "Yes, it will give me something to focus on."

"*Very well. Commencing message.*"

"*Ambassador Spar. I do hope your coming to was not met with any unnecessary challenges. I'm sure the* Veritas *AI has briefed*

OBLIVION'S DAWN

you on the situation on Bala. From their perspective, they are in position to hold the negotiating power, but the Confederation is not interested in the negotiations, they want justice. Even our friends, the Veshnians, are applying pressure to resolve the situation and administer extreme prejudice in nullifying this mercenary group's existence. I realize you are not in a position to use force, but know that if the situation should grow worse, then the Confederation allies will hold humanity accountable for the loss of Veshnian lives. Ironically, they do not hold such esteem for any human casualties on Bala. I trust you will make the situation work favorably for all involved and forward data on the mercenaries, so we can begin operations to stop them. I wish you luck."

"Transmission over," the AI said.

"Yeah, I gathered that. It seems the pressure is on to keep these hostages alive against all odds. I highly doubt the ransom will be enough to secure their release."

"Do you have an alternative plan of action?"

Tella shrugged. "Besides pleading to their humanity? Not really. I don't think offering myself in exchange for the hostages' release will get me anywhere. Bala is a mining colony for hytocosic crystals. These mercenaries aren't just holding civilian hostages. They're holding the mining efforts for a very important resource. This was calculated to cause as much disruption as possible. In fact, it is probably already disrupting the economy." She opened her eyes and was relieved the spinning sensation had died down. Even the overhead lights no longer felt like they were searing her retinas.

"I ran a simulation based on current standing in the hytocosic crystal industry, and you are correct. Within a year, the market will plunge if mining is not restored. In fact, the market has already declined by four percent."

"See?" Tella felt better knowing her cognizance allowed her to think clearly enough to see the implications of the situation. If only her body would catch up to her mind, then she would be ready to do her job and meet with the merc leader. "I want to try walking."

"You must wait two hours after coming to before attempting to walk, Ambassador."

"Is that the rule?"

"Indeed."

Tella scoffed. "The rule is outdated, AI." She pointed to her neck where the number six was inked into her flesh. She now wore her sixth composite. "I've done this before."

"If you insist." A second mechanical arm dropped to her left to assist her with standing in the event she needed it.

"Thank you," Tella said, taking the mechanical arm in her hand and concentrating on the first step of her new life. "I need to be prepared to depart the ship in the next forty-eight hours if I'm to make contact at the appointed time. Waiting for each prescribed interval to attempt to gain control of this body is time wasted. Do you understand?"

"I understand you do not wish to be static in your physical therapy. Do you wish to neglect all prescribed intervals?"

Tella nodded. "Yes. Well, all but taking food for the first time. I think that interval should remain based on previous experience. I'm not fond of the cleanup for premature digestion," she joked.

The AI did not respond.

"Tough crowd," she muttered, concentrating once again on taking the next step, each time letting more weight bear down on her feet. Within minutes, she was confident enough to remove her hands from the ship's arms and stand on her own.

"AI, I need you to do something for me."

"What do you need, Ambassador?"

"I need you to initiate a scan for other ships in this system. Document each one and include planet of origin and military affiliation. These mercenaries had to arrive somehow, and if they planned on escaping, then their ride will be waiting in orbit."

"My scans have already been initiated based on previous orders, Ambassador. Currently, I do not detect other ships in this AOR."

Tella hesitated. "None at all?"

"Affirmative."

"That's odd. I figured there would be a freighter at a minimum. How can you transport resources without a ship?"

"Perhaps the shipping schedule occurs seasonally?"

Makes sense, Tella thought. She was unfamiliar with the exact process of mining the resources, but nonetheless, she understood how important operations were. In other operations, where hostages were kept, an escape ship was always nearby. It was unsettling to think that there was no means of escape for the mercenaries. What could it mean? Were they betrayed and left to fend for themselves, or was it deliberate? Either way, she didn't like the implications of it. "Keep scanning. Something doesn't feel right."

"Is it your legs? I warned against attempting to prematurely walk."

Tella smirked. "No, it's an expression I'm using to say how I feel about the situation on Bala. My legs are fine. Thank you."

"You're welcome," the AI replied.

Tella grinned. She enjoyed how the AI seemed to lack the communication skills to understand humor or sarcasm, which made its genuine responses hilarious. She stifled her laughter because she knew she would have to explain it, and the chore of doing so would spoil the situation.

"I need to sit down for now, but I want to be prompted to walk every hour. In the meantime, I would like to be brought up to speed on recent political events since I left Earth." She knew her physical body never left home, but her presence of mind certainly had. The moment her new composite began to be stitched together, the former composite was recycled. It was hard to not think about it as a form of death, but luckily no composite ever came to with memories of those final moments. It simply felt like waking from a long sleep.

"I will prompt you for the exercises as you asked. In what way do you wish to experience the latest reports?"

"Visually and audibly," she said. "It helps when I see faces with the names."

"Very well. I have downloaded most of the data. All I am missing is the last twelve hours, but I have a scheduled download via tight beam daily. I can catch you up at that time."

"Thank you, AI." Tella made her way to a cushioned chair in the corner of the medical bay. Now that her eyes had adjusted, she noticed that every surface of the room was stark white and sterile. It made her feel uncomfortable. "Can you dim the lights more?"

Without a response, the overhead lighting dimmed to a more appealing level.

"Forty-eight hours," Tella said, reclining in the chair to take in as much of the newsfeed as possible before returning to her physical therapy. By her calculations, she was already three hours ahead of the proposed interval for a fresh composite returning to the world of the living. Now, if only she could maintain that headway, she might regain enough of her strength to not look weak before the mercenaries she was sent to negotiate with. Weakness was, after all, what made the likes of such men feel that they could get away with these actions.

She swallowed hard, realizing how dry her throat was from speaking without having consumed any water. Looking at the time, she knew she had to wait at least another ninety minutes before putting anything in her stomach, water included. So, she resolved to not speak until she could replace the fluids lost.

Luckily for her, she didn't need to speak to catch up on current events and formulate her negotiation plans.

Pressing the red button on the armrest of the chair, she manipulated the feed with the scratch pad beside it, scrolling her fingers along the surface until something caught her eye.

"Bastia Leader Declares Human Hostage Situation an Act of Terror. Recommends Immediate Cut in Supplies to Bala."

Interesting, she thought, her eyes catching on the image of the Bastian leader, Supreme Commander Freist, his yellow eyes standing out from his pale, reptilian skin. *What would cutting supplies to Bala do when there were enough supplies on the surface to last several months?* It struck her odd that his plan of action did little to change anything about the situation. "Just trying to get your picture on the feed," she mumbled, forgetting she wanted to save her words until she could drink something.

She clicked the red button again, saving the report for a later time, before continuing to scroll. She had no idea if the report was relevant but giving herself time to ponder it was better if she had more information to accompany it. She stopped once again when she saw Director Cantor on the feed. As she read through the report, she was struck by the fact he echoed some of the same sentiments as the Bastian leader. Director Cantor did say he had sent an ambassador to negotiate the release of the hostages, hence her presence on the *Veritas* now, but the fact he would suggest the same course of action if negotiations failed was a slap in the face to their own people.

"What are you getting at, Director?"

An alarm blast stirred her from her thoughts as she looked up in a groggy panic. "AI, what is it?"

"A surface missile launched from the Bala moon. Someone turned on the orbital defense countermeasures. Prepare to evade."

Tella groaned and pulled over her shoulder harnesses. *This is a stall technique*, she thought, gritting her teeth as the ship acceler-

17

DAVE ALEXANDER

ated. *They think if I miss my window, then we will concede in their favor.*

"Not on my watch," she said as the *Veritas* deployed its own countermeasures. The rapid report of projectiles caused the deck to shutter hard enough to make Tella's teeth chatter. She could see on the monitors that the ship banked hard in both directions, attempting to confuse the incoming missile. The only thing Tella felt was increased pressure in her seat as the ship accelerated quickly. "Did you miss?"

"The countermeasures were ineffective. I am attempting to increase the distance between us and the target before trying again," the AI replied with no concern in its voice. It was almost humorous if not for the fact Tella knew she was seconds from death if the second attempt failed.

Another hard bank and turn later, the deck erupted once more as the *Veritas* launched another wave of countermeasures towards the incoming missile. This time, the monitor zoomed in on the threat just in time for Tella to see it explode at a considerable distance. Unfortunately, debris from the missile continued its trajectory and struck the hull of the *Veritas*. The sound of it reminded Tella of hail falling on the roof of her childhood home, but her thoughts were interrupted by another alarm. The piercing wail of the ship's pressurization system.

"What now?" Tella spat, already pulling off her shoulder harness to reach the oxygen mask descending from the overhead once the alarm was triggered. She pulled it to her face and held it there, not wanting to waste the air as long as the ship's environmental system was still contained.

"The hull was damaged by debris. Standby. I may need your assistance."

Tella shook her head, feeling powerless as a flash of anger befell her. Her memory returned to the only successful assassination attempt, which claimed the life of her third composite. The fact it too happened on a ship unsettled her more than she would like to admit. But for as long as she still breathed, she would see her job through to the end. Assassination attempt, or not.

She rose from her seat, ignoring her shaky legs, and rested the oxygen mask atop her head. "What do you need me to do?"

TWO
BALA

WHAT BEGAN AS AN OPPORTUNITY TO STRIKE IT RICH WAS FAST becoming a babysitting chore as Brady took a seat on a wooden crate filled with explosives. The smell of newly manufactured weapons had a distinct odor, one that made him think about the past in much the same way certain perfumes reminded him of his no-good mother. It didn't make him feel uncomfortable, but it did cause him to wonder how many lives he would have to live to fully disassociate himself from his past. It seemed to follow him like a lost puppy.

Brady kept his eyes on the hostages as he took another pull from his cigar. It struck him odd how comfortable the expressions on their faces were now that several days had passed. The familiarity between captors and prisoners did not sit well with him, but whatever the boss said, went. If it was up to Brady, he would tug on the captives' heartstrings a bit more and remind them of what they had to lose. Most of the mercs hardly kept their hands on their weapons anymore. The entire situation felt too casual to be intimidating any longer.

"Is this seat taken?" Wyatt, one of the new guys, asked as he stopped next to the crate, an MRE in one hand and a bottle of water in the other. The man's last name brazened on his flak jacket looked like someone forgot how to spell "Apple." It was a source of joking among the man and the crew he was familiar with. For Brady and his crew, it was hardly worth mentioning. The number thirteen etched into his neck denoting how many composites he'd bore was of much more interest. It appeared that Wyatt was either new to the business, or stayed hidden away in his off-duty time to avoid getting captured by the authorities. Neither boaded well for Brady wanting to trust the man.

"Depends," Brady replied. "You have one of them for me?"

Wyatt smirked and dropped the MRE on the crate before pulling another from his cargo pocket. He was the youngest merc on the team, and also the one that expressed the most courtesy. It was one of the things that made him stand out. It may have been desperation on his part, but Brady could forgive that, considering the rest of the crew seemed more focused on themselves than maintaining any semblance of team unity. Of course, Brady killing Walters, one of their longtime friends, probably skewed him out of their favor. Still, it made an impression on Brady that the young man would make the attempt despite the rest of his crew.

"Thanks," Brady said, acknowledging the MRE on the crate, but not grabbing it.

"The selection leaves a lot to be desired, but it beats eating what counts as Veshnian food." He plopped down on the crate next to Brady and let one leg dangle towards the ground as he opened the package with his teeth. "I've seen dog food more appetizing than that mess."

"I've had worse," Brady said nonchalantly. "Me and the boss took a job into Montat territory years ago. We ran out of supplies on-world and had to eat local foliage while we waited nine days for a recovery ship to snatch us out of there. I'm guessing the pamphlet on edible plants was outdated because I didn't shit right for a month after that."

Wyatt chortled, almost choking on what was ostensibly a cracker but had about as much flavor as cardboard. The texture was equally faithful. "The things we do to survive in places we weren't meant to live." His words hung in the air for a moment, the closest thing to philosophy that Brady had heard since their arrival.

"Yeah, no kidding. So, what brought you into this line of work? Are you a runaway like most of us?"

Wyatt shrugged. "Not really. I guess I was born into it. My dad was a merc and worked a few jobs for the Confederation as a bodyguard. It was the most honest work he'd ever done. He said everything else he was paid to do required night ops and loose morals. I think the loose morals is how he met my mother." The last sentence sounded like resentment to Brady's ears.

"Not very close to her, huh?"

"Nah," Wyatt said, letting the conversation die as he shoved another bite of cracker into his mouth and broke it off with his teeth as crumbs rained from his mouth like hail. "What about you?"

Brady hesitated to answer, not knowing what might get used against him later, still not wanting to trust the hired help. "I guess I'm not close to anyone aside from my mother and maybe Garret," he answered. It was vague enough to not reveal too much and had the added benefit of being mostly true. The list of people he trusted was shorter than he often admitted, but it kept him alive, somewhat.

Wyatt nudged him with his elbow as he chewed. "I meant what got you into this work?"

"Oh," Brady said, shaking his head before looking back to the dozens of hostages on the other side of the atrium. "I needed money, and I didn't have much in the way of people skills."

OBLIVION'S DAWN

"You seem to be doing all right. You're Garrett's right-hand man."

Brady knew Wyatt was trying to pay him a compliment, but it cut him the wrong way. "Don't get too familiar with me, boy. Like I said, I don't like to get too close to people."

Wyatt rubbed at his chin, a few days' worth of stubble cutting through in splotches of red and brown. He cut his eyes at the lieutenant. "Yeah, I got you. It's probably for the best, right?"

Brady nodded and turned his back on the other man. "Watch after the hostages. I have something I need to take care of."

"Roger that," Wyatt said as Brady walked away. He needed to escape to get his head right. All the idle chit-chat got Brady's mind thinking about the things that could go wrong. It was a thought process he often couldn't back out of, even if he wanted to.

Brady found Garret leaning against a pillar on the far side of the atrium, his arms crossed and a scowl on his face. Despite the youthfulness of his composite, Brady could see the aged weariness in Garret's blue eyes. It was a look that reflected his own sordid past.

"Is everything all right?" The old man asked, letting his right foot drag down the side of the pillar as he stood straight, towering over his lieutenant.

"Yeah, Boss. Everything is fine. I just wanted to check on you," Brady replied, falling in next to Garret against the pillar and matching his stance. The emulation was meant as a joke, but he didn't think Garret was in the right headspace to pay any attention to it.

"We have thirty-eight hours. I didn't think they would wait until the last minute to send their ambassador," Garret said under his breath. It was the way he confided with his men without letting outside ears listen. Even from the distance between them

23

DAVE ALEXANDER

and the rest of the mercs, he maintained his quiet tone, more so out of habit than anything else.

"When you give the government a deadline, they'll ride it all day," Brady replied. "What's new there?"

Garret shrugged. "I don't like it. It makes me think these mines aren't as valuable as we were led to believe."

"So, you think this is going to be a bust?" Brady watched his tone, not wanting to let it sound like a complaint, but he had a lot riding on this gig.

"I don't know. But it doesn't feel right. The longer we're here, the more paranoid I get that things are going to fall apart at the last minute. Almost like Gantor. You know what I mean?"

The mention of Gantor hit a soft spot in Brady. They had almost died because of a setup. Three days on the run from hordes of militant locals and a Perusion special ops team claimed two of their men, neither of them patched into the composite program. Their deaths were final and unjust. It was the first mission where government oversight got in the way, paving the way for a long string of failures which led Garret to believe all of this was merely a test for something darker. He could have refused, but they were under contract, and it was either get paid or get dead – a simple decision. The revenge mission later made things better, but for a while there, he was certain they were done for.

This situation lacked the immediate danger of an incoming army to mow them down, but you never knew where the next threat waited to get you when you least expected it. Brady nodded. "Yeah, I didn't want to say anything, but I've felt like that too. I can't tell if it's the new faces or the fact this colony is so small that it doesn't seem to be worth the effort. Add to that the fact the last shipment departed days before our arrival, and the threat of shutting down the market won't feel as imminent. Either the intel involved in mission planning was sorry as hell, or this isn't the mission we thought we signed on for."

24

OBLIVION'S DAWN

Garret exhaled loudly from his nose, a subliminal way he voiced his agreement without speaking. His eyes darted from side to side before he spoke again. "It's the psychological game. Desperation only strikes when you feel the end coming. We're a long way off from that point. Maybe they aren't taking us seriously?" The leader turned to his confidant and lowered his voice more. "Maybe we need to send a message."

Brady grinned from ear to ear. This was what he liked to hear. "I'm game, Boss. You know me."

"That I do, Brady." Garret leaned back against the pillar, his eyes narrowing as he glared at the mass of hostages on one side of the atrium and the small pile of bodies on the other. Each death was a result of a hostage stepping out of line. Once you defined the barriers, the prisoners would feel comfortable in their little boxes. He felt it was time to shake things up, to disrupt the feeling of ease and strike fear into them once more. "Maybe we can kill two birds with one stone."

"How so?" Brady asked, his palm casually resting on his weapon.

Garret looked at his lieutenant with a smirk. "Any of these men you don't trust?"

"Half of them I don't know from Adam. Other than our crew, I wouldn't want to turn my back on any of them," Brady said. He knew it was a sentiment shared by the rest of Garret's men. Those who fight and die together create a bond. Sometimes that bond rejected outsiders. This was one of those times.

"Agreed. Have a couple of prisoners leave the atrium to gather supplies and set them up with escape accusations. Have the new guys handle the situation and charge them with setting up a mock trial. We'll toss a little mockery at our hostages on some bogus charges before taking a few heads for display. If these men don't follow the order, then they become the display. The only thing I hate worse than not getting paid is insubordination."

DAVE ALEXANDER

The chance to cut a few men down was just the right amount of bloodshed to make Brady's heart beat a little faster. It was like a teenage boy's first time, but with brutal finality. He patted his boss on the back as he leaned off the pillar to execute the command. "You got it."

"Oh, and one more thing."

Brady turned. "What's that?"

"If my gut is right, this is going to be all for nothing. You need to make your peace with not coming out of this the way we thought."

"You mean coming to with no memory of this exchange and being dead broke? I already made peace with that. As long as I make it out the other side, I can fight another day."

"That's the kind of soldier I expect to lead this force one day," Garret replied with a grin. "Sometimes the sacrifice is worth it to know where you truly stand."

"You never have to question my loyalty, sir."

"I know," Garret said, pulling a cigar from his shirt pocket and lighting it up. "But sometimes I question why you so willingly follow when the men look to you for leadership." He puffed the cigar as he looked at the lieutenant.

Brady gazed back, a puzzled expression on his face. "I don't understand, sir. What do you mean?"

Garret shrugged. "Nothing. Just take care of what I asked you to do. The boredom is about to kill me. I'd like to let off some steam."

The devilish grin returned to Brady's face as he turned back to the task at hand. His mind was already formulating the plan before he left Garret's side.

"Wyatt, I've got something for you," Brady half-shouted across the atrium, causing several sets of eyes to peer in his direction.

Wyatt, still seated on the crate, looked up mid-chew. He

26

slowly dropped off the crate and met Brady in the middle. "What do you need?"

Brady crossed his arms and half-turned, keeping his back on the hostages as he spoke. "Take a few Veshnians on a supply run ten klicks east. They're running low on food and the boss doesn't want to elicit a riot. But on your way, make sure you give them space enough to run for it."

Wyatt looked cross at Brady, his eyebrows raised. "I don't understand."

Brady leaned closer. "We want a little action. Give them an inch and let's see if they go for the mile. You got it?"

Wyatt shrugged. "So, just let them go?"

"No. If they run, drag them in and we'll take care of it. But encourage them to run by lollygagging on the mission. Pretend you don't care."

Wyatt's eyes darted up to Garret, the older man still leaning against the pillar, his eyes piercing as they stared in his direction. "This feels like a setup."

Brady chuckled under his breath. "I don't care what you think it feels like. Take care of the situation as you were ordered." His eyes narrowed. All friendliness evaporated in a sneer as he looked at the younger merc.

Unsettlement spread on Wyatt's face. "All right. Do you want me to take anyone with me?"

Brady's glare eased, and he patted the man on the shoulder. "No. we'll be monitoring the situation and will chase them down on rovers if needed. We just have an itch we need to scratch."

Wyatt's eyes peered back at Garret, all the pressure of the situation falling onto his inexperienced shoulders. "You got it, I guess."

"There you go. Just don't take the big ones, if you know what I mean?"

Wyatt nodded. He put his hand on the stock of his weapon and

DAVE ALEXANDER

made his way to the seated hostages, identifying three Veshnians who didn't look too intimidating. "You three, get up and come with me. Line up right here," he barked. The change in his voice surprised Brady, who nodded approvingly.

The three Veshnians rose slowly, making their way out of the small containment area and before Wyatt.

"Yes, sir?" One of them asked as they settled into line.

"You three are retrieving supplies ten klicks from here. I'll escort you. Don't try anything or you know what will happen." Wyatt patted his weapon with a gloved hand before looking back to Brady who no longer appeared interested in the situation. Wyatt pulled at his flak jacket to relieve the pressure on his body as stress crept up with a stranglehold. Trying to fight it off, he took a deep breath.

"Yes, sir," the three Veshnians replied solemnly, not taking notice of how uncomfortable their guard was becoming.

"All right, then. Let's go." Wyatt led the men out of the atrium, alone on a mission he did not agree with and was powerless to do anything about.

THREE
GCS VERITAS

The face shield of Tella's oxygen mask fogged over as she worked to plug the hole in the hull. Working from inside the ship presented its own barriers to generating a good enough environmental seal, especially with less than thirty percent visibility. She canted her head to one side and peered through a thin line in the mask she could still see out of and held her breath to keep the fogging down.

It was futile.

"How's that?" She asked, pulling the tube of liquid weld from the bulkhead and eyeing it warily. Perhaps it was the shaking of her hands, an amalgamation of fear mixed with her newborn composite still developing basic motor skills, which made her work appear sloppy. Or maybe she wasn't cut out for shipboard maintenance. Either way, it was the best Tella had to offer.

She felt the ship pressurize again to test the seal, this time the loss of pressurization alarms did not sound. *"The patch appears to be holding, Ambassador."*

Thank God, she thought, pulling the mask from her face and inhaling pungent air. "Why does it smell like that?"

"I had to secure the environmental controls system while you

worked. You're smelling the chemicals used in oxygen generation."

Tella rolled her eyes, almost preferring the confines of the mask to the odor currently assaulting her nostrils. "How long before normal?"

"*I calculate two hours before normal operation, but your senses should grow used to the smell before that.*"

If that was the AI's attempt at making her feel better about the situation, it wasn't working. "I spent the better part of an hour working on the seal. How far behind am I on my intervals?"

"*I tracked your movements, and it appears your motor functions and cognitive abilities are exceeding the milestones set forth in the intervals. If anything, you are fourteen percent ahead of where you should be.*"

"Well, at least there's that," Tella said under her breath as she made her way back to the chair in the corner of the room. Her body was weak from the stress of exercising newly formed muscles and the lack of sustenance. The discomfort was centralized in her neck and between her shoulders which made sense considering that was where she typically contained her stress. A new body did little to manipulate her personal physiology, it seemed. "I would like to take a break until I can refuel."

"*Understood, Ambassador. Would you like me to alert you when sufficient time has passed?*"

"Sure," she answered, falling into the chair and closing her eyes. This was her sixth time coming to as a composite, and she always forgot how easily she grew tired on the first day. Her mind demanded much from her, but physically she was unable to meet the standard she had set for herself. Some people would call her an overachiever, but she didn't look at it that way. She pushed herself because people's lives were at stake, and she didn't want to live with the burden of regret. Her focus did not come from selfishness, but selflessness. At least that was how she viewed it. "In the meantime, please continue with the newsfeed."

The monitor sprang to life with more images flashing past in a flurry with headlines sprawling above. If not for her enhanced cognitive skills, it would have been a mess to try and decipher, but she managed well enough. She noted the lack of feed coming directly off Bala enough to speak up. "AI, are there any sources reporting directly from the mercenaries on Bala?"

"Negative. All source data is coming directly from the Confederation."

"Odd. Can you intercept any outbound signals from the colony?" *There should be something,* she thought, narrowing her eyes as she watched the feed zoom past.

"Yes. I will begin tracking now."

"Thank you," Tella said, her words slurring from her lips as she reengaged the newsfeed. Her eyes darted across the monitor in a way that would give a normal, non-augmented human an epileptic seizure. She lost herself in the stream, allowing her surroundings to fall away until the cold, stark-white bulkheads of the *Veritas* became virtually nonexistent.

In the background, the AI spent the better part of an hour continuing to monitor Bala, allowing the ambassador to immerse herself in her work. It was nothing more than preprogrammed servitude to a representative of the Confederation. Easy to take for granted, but necessary to keep the member up to date on the latest intel. It was this kind of work that revealed an unsettling truth.

"I apologize for interrupting, Ambassador, but I believe I have found something."

Pulled from the stream, Tella regained her focus on the real world. "What is it?"

"There is a relay hub that just came to life on the other side of Bala. I believe it is about to receive a transmission."

DAVE ALEXANDER

Tella rose from her seat on shaky legs. "From Bala, or from another source?"

"I won't know until the transmission begins. But it does raise a question as to why a sleeping relay hub would orbit a mining colony. Does it not?"

"It does," Tella said under her breath. "If anything, a relay hub would constantly monitor for transmissions in case of an emergency. Perhaps this one is designed to receive information at predetermined intervals, which means its focus is operationally directed."

"Like a military operation," the AI suggested.

"Exactly. I want to know exactly what kind of transmission the hub receives. Might reveal something our enemies won't expect. Something I can use against them." She didn't want to get her hopes up, but she was in the business of negotiating and it helped tremendously to have an upper hand. Knowledge was power, after all.

"I'll keep you abreast of any developments."

Tella nodded her consent and looked at the time. It was finally safe to put food in her stomach. She knew better than to gorge herself, but she felt the hunger pangs sharp enough to make her want to eat her body weight in pasta. Unfortunately, all she had were prepackaged protein meals which had the consistency of cottage cheese. They were the least appetizing thing she had ever consumed, but they were all she had available to her. She doubted the food on Bala would be any better. It would mostly consist of heavily preserved Veshnian cuisine and human MREs. Neither of which were appealing.

She pulled a tube of food product from the storage container and opened it with her teeth. It was far from her first time living in space, but the first taste of "sustenance" was a hard thing to swallow. Even after spending the better part of a decade of her fourth composite living on a ship in space, the taste and consistency of the food jarred her.

"Better to not take the time to taste it," she said to herself before emptying the tube into her mouth, squeezing it out as she pressed the tube closed from the far end, dragging her fingers closer. She closed her eyes in hopes it would help with the terrible taste.

It did not.

Once consumed, she washed the taste out of her mouth with water. She craved something stronger. Especially with the scenario on Bala growing worse by the minute.

"How do you feel, Ambassador?"

"The feeling that my body was about to eat itself has subsided, so that's a little better than before," she answered while pacing the room. She did not want to sit as her newly formed body digested what she had just eaten.

"That is good news."

"Indeed," Tella replied. "Can you provide an image of the surface where the hostages are being kept?" Changing the subject back to the task at hand seemed like a better use of her time than contemplating how she felt. At the end of the day, her feelings meant little while lives were at stake.

The AI produced a grainy image on the monitor. After a few moments, the surface came into view in full detail. The atrium where the hostages were being kept was the tallest building on the small colony planet. It once served as a temple for an archaic religion. Now, it was nothing more than a social hall, and currently a prison.

"Magnify." Tella leaned as close to the monitor as possible, her nose nearly touching it before the static of the screen tickled at her nose. "What is that structure?" She pointed to a box shape north of the atrium with a large, orange flag-like object waving in the breeze.

"It appears to be a storage container. Presumably, one which was air-dropped to the surface."

"Like a military airdrop?"

"Possibly. Though it has no markings as such."

"How large is it?"

"It is difficult to determine as the parachute obscures part of the structure, but the dimensions appear to be more than half the size of this ship."

"This must be how the mercs arrived," Tella said. "I assumed they had a ship, but I see no evidence of such on the surface and we have no readings in the area. I assume that is still the case?"

"It is. But it is not feasible for a shipping container to be used to drop people to the surface. It is difficult to guarantee safe landings using only a parachute. Not to mention that the containers cannot land on precise coordinates. There is no way to control the landing once it is in atmosphere."

Tella realized she had been holding her breath before letting out an audible exhale. "I don't think the mercs were alive during the landing. I believe their composites were formed after landing."

"That would be impossible," the AI said. *"Remote operation of that kind of equipment at such a scale is impractical at best. Someone, or something, would need to be on the surface to monitor the situation. I don't see how a dozen mercs could be composited with no one on the surface knowing."*

A sneer formed on Tella's face as a sudden realization formed in her mind. "What if the hostile takeover was not orchestrated remotely? What if the person running the operation was already on Bala?"

"That is possible."

"That's what I was afraid of. I need a manifest of everyone attached to the colony; Veshnian and human."

"I will compile that data for you, Ambassador. Is there anyone in particular you are searching for?"

"Begin with anyone with military or mercenary backgrounds. We'll start there," she replied. Her fingers curled into fists as the data populated on the screen. To her surprise, no one matched the search criteria. "Something's not right. I'm not seeing what I expected."

"Perhaps this operation was not military in nature?"

Military made the most sense to her, but it was not the only motivator for an operation of this magnitude. She drew in a sharp breath, not liking where her thoughts were going. "Perhaps not," she whispered. "Scan the colonists for ties to political organizations. Broaden the search to include three generations of family members. We need to find something."

The data came back nil. *"There is nothing matching your search criteria, Ambassador."*

"What the hell?" Tella spat. Her brow furrowed in frustration. She knew there had to be a tie to something that she just was not seeing. Whatever that tie was, she was determined to find it. She did not come halfway across the galaxy to fail.

"Keep scanning, and broaden the searches as needed. I want something tangible to work with," Tella said.

"Yes, Ambassador. Might I suggest aliases as part of the search criteria?"

"Obviously," she answered. She had assumed the AI would have picked up on that without asking, but this ship was generations old. It was unfair to assume it was as capable as the AI she generally worked with on Earth.

"It will take some time to complete the scan. Perhaps now would be a good time to exercise your legs?"

She didn't want to, but neither did she want to sit there staring at a screen while the AI worked. Tella paced the room until her feet hurt. She had hoped for something to come up by then, but nothing did.

This was proving more difficult than expected.

"Wake me when you find something," Tella ordered as she lay back in the chair. The AI acknowledged, but she was already drifting off to the hum of the air recycler.

FOUR
BALA

FOUR KLICKS AWAY FROM THE ATRIUM, HIKING UPWARD ON ROCKY terrain, the sound of a revved rover engine caused Wyatt to turn. The entire time he'd escorted the Veshnians to retrieve the supplies he'd wondered how he would carry out the order Brady had given him. Now that the time had come, he couldn't shake the impotent feeling of failure as he realized what would happen if his hesitation to act was witnessed by his superior. He had seen what happened when someone in the unit openly opposed Garret, or his henchman, Brady. Neither man would care if he disagreed with the orders. Moral dignity meant nothing to them. Action did.

I never should've signed on for this, he thought, his grip on the carbine tightened as if he was desperately clutching a security blanket. Part of him wished the white-knuckled grip was him wringing Brady's neck for sending him out here. His heart flittered as guilt riddled him. Wyatt wasn't a killer, not like the men coming towards him now. They craved the stench of blood and fear while Wyatt desired something else entirely.

As the sound grew closer, his desperation built up like a rising tide. He glanced back, eyes wide as he dared to watch the small vehicle approach. It was too late to let this operation manifest on its own. With his back against the proverbial wall, he took the only action he could muster from his growing pit of despair and rampant fear.

"Run!" Wyatt shouted, startling the Veshnians as they walked slowly in line.

Three sets of eyes looked back at him questioningly, muted confusion their only response.

"Do you not understand? These people are coming to kill you. Run!"

They stared back, frozen in time that was rapidly running out.

Wyatt's desperation swelled as the sound of the rover grew louder. With clammy hands he fired his weapon over their heads, screaming like a banshee under the report of gunfire.

It was effective enough to get all three Veshnians to sprint away, their long legs carrying them faster than any human could run. Even on the hard, rocky surface of Bala, their feet kicked up dust as they ran eastward. Why they would choose to go in the same direction as one another was lost on Wyatt, but he was relieved that the aliens ran, allowing him to not look like he couldn't follow Brady's orders. He hoped the approaching men didn't see how badly he messed up the plan, but his heart ached at the fact all three Veshnians would be caught easily. What would happen once captured was an image he did not want to dwell on.

Pulling him out of his depressing thoughts, the rover leaped over the hill and accelerated past Wyatt. One driver and one gunner from the crew he'd previously deployed with were on the chase. He was surprised not to find Brady onboard as he made eye contact with the gunner. When the man looked back at Wyatt, he recognized disappointment in the other merc's eyes.

The feeling Wyatt got from the man's cold gaze could have been a manifestation of his mind, but it certainly echoed what lay in his heart.

"This isn't what I wanted," Wyatt said under his breath,

knowing no one could hear him, but hoping the truth would put his mind at ease. Unfortunately, it did no such thing and his guilt raged like a furious, all-consuming fire scorching inside of him. He tried to shake the feeling as he scaled the hill. He watched over the ridge as the rover sped closer to the Veshnians. They had stopped and huddled together. Each one had their fists raised as if they had the capability to fight against armed soldiers. It was a noble attempt for a last stand, but anyone who saw it knew they were in no position to fight. It was simply the last act of defiance in the face of impending doom.

Once the rover was in range, the gunner launched a net, capturing all three captives with one pull of the trigger. The heavy net closed around them, clamping tightly on one end and slamming the Veshnians to the ground. The rover spun around in a cloud of grit and dust. Even at a considerable distance, Wyatt heard the Veshnians scream as the rover dragged them back towards the atrium over the rocky ground that cut into their skin like dull daggers.

This wasn't justice. This was a game, and it made him sick.

The cold truth was that things would only get worse and then they would die. He knew it like he knew the back of his hand. This was a ruse to give evil men an opportunity to blow off some steam. He'd seen it before and had hoped he would never witness it again. "Why do I find myself in these situations?"

The answer was simple, but not easy.

The sound of screaming Veshnians and the screeching rover motor failed to articulate the answer for him. Perhaps nothing could and that was the problem. He did this for no other reason than because it was available to him. No, it was expected of him, and it was what his father would have wanted.

That was his excuse anyway, though it fell flat as reality barreled into him, nearly taking his breath away at the horrific role he played in such cruelty.

DAVE ALEXANDER

When the rover passed, the driver signaled for Wyatt to turn back and follow. There was no sense of comradery as he made eye contact with the driver. He wondered if the merc knew this was a setup, or if he indeed believed Wyatt failed to keep control of the hostages. Either way, it didn't matter now. As he turned to follow them back, his eyes fell to the ground where he saw the trail of blood left behind as whimpering Veshnians tried to escape the net and their pain.

"I should have just shot them," he muttered under his breath as he reluctantly followed. But he was powerless to do anything now other than follow along with the plan. He felt like a coward, and he didn't know how he could escape the shame, save for a bullet to the brain and hope to forget all of this.

The iron smell of Veshnian blood was similar enough to human blood to make his stomach turn as he reflected on how it would feel if he was in the same situation. It could have easily been human hostages chosen for this fake mission, it was just the hatred he knew Garret and his men felt for the Veshnians that brought this on them.

It was a wicked thing to do to anyone, regardless of species. If a man could do that to someone powerless to defend themselves, then what would they do to anyone who opposed them? It was that thought that led Wyatt Appel to believe there was no way he was getting off this world in one piece.

And it was his guilt that made him think he didn't deserve to, anyway.

Wyatt placed his hand over his neck, feeling the slight rise of his skin where the number three was embossed. Somewhere, out in the ether, data comprised of his last upload waited for his heart to stop beating before it would begin to stitch him back together. That meant he wouldn't have to remember any of this if he didn't make it.

Small consolation for taking part in this horror, he thought,

40

kicking the rocks beneath his feet as he descended the hill leading to the makeshift prison.

He hadn't been raised to be like this. He never wanted to be a heartless cog in a machine of death. Wyatt always looked at his father as a hero, a paid soldier who took men like Garret and Brady out. Was he wrong about that the whole time, or were these bad seeds simply multiplying in a universe Wyatt hadn't known existed?

His hand tightened on the grip of his weapon, now at half capacity after wasting bullets to chase away prisoners too stupid to run. They never had a fighting chance.

He wondered if the same would be said of him when the shady mercs finally turned their focus on Wyatt. "That's how this mission ends," he muttered to no one. "They kill everything, and everyone, until they turn their guns on us. You don't have to split profits with the dead, or the ones that can't remember that they were ever here."

With that thought, Wyatt finally understood what was happening, what he was too stupid to realize over the last several days as he watched the mission go down faster than a ship on fire.

This was indeed a suicide mission. But not if he could help it. He just needed a way out.

FIVE
GCS VERITAS

"Tell me more about Steven Chancey," Tella said moments after waking to see the lone name on the monitor. She didn't realize how tired she was before drifting off but stirring awake sent her immediately into a panicked state. It was nothing more than the side effect of waking in a different body when your previous thoughts echoed from an Earth-bound subconscious. It would take time to get used to, just as it always did, but knowing that did little to make it easier.

"*Steven Chancey is the stepson of deceased former Director Artimus Chancey of the Galactic Confederation, who adopted him when he was two years old. His mother, the late Gwen Chancey, passed when Steven was seven. Steven spent the next decade in military school to be groomed for service, but prior to graduation, he disappeared without a trace.*"

"And you're sure Steven is on Bala? Could there be a mistake or someone with a similar DNA pattern?"

"*If it is not the man, then it is a direct composite, yes.*"

Tella craned her neck, popping her vertebrae, a welcomed relief after falling asleep in a bad position, especially considering how hard the muscles in her new body had to work to keep her

42

OBLIVION'S DAWN

mobile. If not for electrical stimulation, her muscles would have been too weak to support her before coming to. "It doesn't make any sense. Why would you run away from Earth to come to a colony in a nowhere sector of the galaxy? Life on any colony this far out must be more difficult than the military would have been. Especially considering that there hasn't been any real conflict involving humanity for over sixty years."

"Perhaps that is a question you can ask when you land?"

Tella scoffed. There were bigger things on her plate than that line of questioning. Still, Steven's was the only name to appear in her inquiry. If he had something to do with the mercs being on Bala, then maybe he was precisely the person she needed to question. There was no such thing as a coincidence in her line of work.

"How much time do I have before I'm in the launch window?" Tella asked. Anticipation was the most difficult thing for her to manage. She refused to call it anxiety, though clinically, the term was appropriate. It was all in the mind either way.

"Twelve hours and nineteen minutes. But you should consider taking more time to train your body according to the prescribed intervals."

"I don't have time for the intervals. This isn't my first time coming to, I don't need you to babysit me." She groaned at the thought of regimented training when the bigger mission lay ahead of her.

"As you wish, Ambassador. I will add that launching once you are in the window will mean you will have to be in the drop capsule for the most amount of time. If you wait an additional twelve hours, you can minimize capsule time by seventy percent."

Tella bit at her lip without thinking about it. All she wanted to do was get the mission over with. With so many lives at stake, she was concerned that the ticking of each second drew them all closer to inevitable death. She wasn't wrong. Death came for everyone. But by whose hand would the end be administered?

43

DAVE ALEXANDER

"Very well. I want to be prepared for dispatch in twenty-four hours. In the meantime, I need to know as much information as possible. Were you able to intersect the transmission coming from the satellite?"

"*I was. I think you will find the information interesting.*"

"How so?"

"*It was not a message, but one of the composites uploaded an encrypted personnel profile. I believe it was one of the mercenaries, but I cannot be certain without decrypting it.*"

"That is interesting," Tella replied. "Begin decrypting it immediately. I want to know who it is. If they are trying to upload their profile, then perhaps things aren't going according to plan down there and they want to ensure they're recycled once everything falls apart."

"*I will begin that process now. I must say that this is a military-level encryption, it could take a day or more to work through it.*"

"That's fine. Do what you can. Do you have any more information on Chancey?"

"*Not for Steven Chancey, but I found some files on his stepfather, Artimus.*"

"Let me have it onscreen. I'll cycle through it at my own pace. I could use some recreational reading." Tella reclaimed her seat, careful not to get too comfortable in order to stay alert. There was something about the coldness of the room and her weak body which made her prone to falling asleep. It was not a luxury she could afford at the time. Not with all the data to sift through for clues.

The screen filled with information, most of it biographical in nature. The early life files mostly contained official records, birth certificates, marriage licenses, life insurance policies, but the data shifted towards news articles within the past ten years. The closer to the end she read, the darker of a person the information painted,

44

OBLIVION'S DAWN

especially considering the mounting information compiled more than a decade after the older man's death.

"It says here that authorities believed Artimus had his wife killed to claim the life insurance money, but there was no way to prove it. The coroner signed off on the certificate of death as her dying of natural causes, but I remember seeing reports about an assassination attempt years ago. Even if those reports were false, I can't find information that supports the claim that her death was a conspiracy to commit fraud. Can you perform another broad search for Artimus Chancey?"

"*That is everything, Ambassador. I completed five full scans for data. All other records are lost or sealed with a higher clearance than you are authorized.*"

"Figures," Tella said under her breath as she continued to read the screen. She hated having to rely purely on speculation, but this rabbit hole practically screamed that knowing the story would help her formulate a plan to deal with the mercenaries. Her acuity was the deciding factor in the Confederation choosing her as an ambassador in the first place. They must have had confidence in her ability to do the job given most humans were looked upon with disdain.

"*I can provide more family information, though a preliminary search reveals nothing of interest in your current inquiry.*"

"It's fine," Tella said. "I might have to go in blind, but it's not the first time I've negotiated with limited information. I think it's time for another interval, isn't it?"

"*I scheduled a reminder to alert you in three minutes.*"

"I'll do it now," she said, rising to her feet, relieved that her legs weren't as wobbly as they had been. As much as she hated doing the intervals, she recognized the necessity, even if she wasn't willing to say it out loud. "Do you mind assisting me with a simulation?"

"*As you wish.*"

45

"Match the gravity of Bala as I walk around the space."

"Gravitational forces are already matched."

Tella canted her head towards the screen, her lips moving as she read the readout. "I expected it to be more."

"I increased it slightly over the course of the last twenty-four hours. I took the liberty when you decided to escalate your intervals."

"I appreciate the thought," she replied, walking to the far bulkhead and resting her hand on the cold, white surface. The darker shade of her hand stood out in contrast, giving her something to focus on to gauge whether her vision was blurring from the exertion.

"I wanted to remind you that you have waited a sufficient amount of time if you desire to eat again."

Tella paused, contemplating what may have been a hunger pang...or gas. "I'll wait. I don't want to overtax this body prematurely." She sounded like a hypocrite, but she didn't think the AI needed to know she was concerned about the results of an upset stomach. It was better to wait and ensure she could hold it together before stepping over a ledge and setting herself back. She smiled at the thought of the report she would have to file if she missed the launch window and how much grief her boss would give her when the excuse was that there were no toilets on pods.

She walked to the opposite side of the room; each step more confident than the last. She was thankful to be barefoot, feeling the cold tiles beneath her feet to help her maintain her balance, but she knew she would have to dress appropriately before departing for Bala. That meant suitable footwear and the potential to trip over herself if she wasn't prepared.

The things we take for granted when we have the luxury of muscle memory and not relearning everything in foreign bodies, she thought.

"AI, I would like to practice with boots on," she said, a frown on her face as the image of her falling over in front of a merc unit and dozens of captives flooded her mind. *That would be worse than not having access to a bathroom,* she thought. *It's hard to negotiate with people when you get toppled over by your own feet.*

"I have limited availability, but these are in your size," the AI responded as a hatch opened on the bulkhead revealing three pairs of shoes.

Tella approached, disappointed by the options, but grabbed the pair that appeared the most comfortable, equipped with ankle support and a higher sole. They were practically combat boots, but what better to wear on her current mission? "What do you have for clothing? I don't want to dress feminine. This is as much a military operation as it is a humanitarian effort."

Another hatch opened in response, this time revealing an assortment of outerwear. Her eyes fell on the dark gray utilities near the back. She pulled them out and let the pant legs fall towards the deck to reveal the whole outfit. It was plain, with only the Confederation flag adorning the left sleeve. It didn't scream military, nor did it suggest that she was an ambassador, it was wholly as neutral as she was going to get and still afford a level of comfort.

"I'll take this one," she said, tossing it onto the bed. "I may as well dress for the job and get used to it."

"*Very well,*" the AI replied. "*You are currently twenty-three hours from your launch window.*"

Right, Tella thought as she reached down to remove her shirt. *Twenty-three hours from descending into madness.*

SIX
BALA

THE ATRIUM WAS A MADHOUSE AS WYATT ENTERED FROM THE south side. The team of mercs dragged the net of Veshnians by hand, their piercing wails reverberating off the high, domed ceiling. Wyatt paused and took a deep breath. Guilt plagued his mind as he took a cautious step towards the action and what he knew he had to do to keep suspicious eyes off him.

"You think you could run away from us?" Jon said as the net sprawled open, revealing the prone and bleeding captives. The man pressed an electric prod towards the nearest Veshnian, sending more than one-thousand volts into the alien's body. The man barked laughter as spittle ran from his chin down onto the flak jacket where his last name "Baker" had faded from his compulsive picking at it.

Wyatt winced at the blood-curdling scream. A wave of nausea threatened to overwhelm him. He stopped and turned away, unwilling to look at what he had allowed to happen until he heard a voice bark his name.

Wyatt turned to see Brady staring at him, a smirk of satisfaction stretched across his face. "Why don't you join the party with us, Wyatt?" Brady asked, his voice booming and taunting. On the

48

OBLIVION'S DAWN

far side of the atrium, Garret looked on, skepticism chiseled into the old man's face. Garret was the man on the team who held the most mystery to Wyatt. He could read most of the others, but reading their leader was like reading a foreign language.

Wyatt wanted to decline, to run away and pretend none of this cruelty was happening, but he was smarter than to reveal his hand. That way led to death at the hands of these monsters. Wyatt stiffened, drawing another breath in hopes that it would strengthen his resolve. "I'll take a whack at it," he said, extending his hand for the prod as he stepped forward. Wyatt fought the urge to make eye contact with Brady or Jon as the other man handed him the weapon.

"I've always wondered what one of these would do to a Veshnian if you got them between the eyes on full power," Brady said, his words an order disguised as musing. "Maybe their heads explode into brain confetti? What do you think, Jon?"

"I don't know, Brady. Maybe Wyatt here should find out for us. He's the scientific-minded one."

"How about an experiment, Wyatt?" Brady croaked, urging the young merc to give into the game.

Wyatt recognized the question for what it really was; a test to gauge his loyalty to the team. *Damned if you do, damned if you don't*, Wyatt thought as his thumb increased the output voltage of the prod. The blue electrical arc sizzled, scorching the ozone surrounding it, and making the exposed hairs on his arm stand on end. There was enough power surging between the two metal points to kill a human, he had no doubt about that, but the Veshnians were stronger and more resilient. Still, he questioned their ability to withstand this magnitude of assault.

"What are you waiting for, Wyatt?" Jon taunted. "Fry this Veshnian's brain like an egg."

Laughter filled the room and Wyatt felt every one of his fellow mercenaries' eyes on him. The Veshnian lay on his back, its

49

wide, pleading eyes filled with terror. Wyatt couldn't deny the understanding glint in the alien's eyes or the hopelessness etched in its face. The sentiment echoed in Wyatt's heart as he did what he was told.

The prod struck the Veshnian between the eyes, the metal points digging into the reptilian's skin. The jolt of current coursing through the body was enough to produce a kick that ran up Wyatt's arm, pushing him back before the involuntary seizing of the Veshnian propelled him forward again. Wyatt held on with a death grip, unwilling to let go until the gathered mercs were satisfied that the Veshnian had had enough.

Wyatt's eyes never left the Veshnian's, though he doubted the alien could see him since the prod liquefied anything on the other side of the prongs. He kept the prod dug in until the Veshnian seized, stiff as a board and the smell of burnt flesh filled the air around him. Still, he didn't let go for fear that Brady or Jon would demand he do the same to the next victim.

"That's enough," Garret barked as he approached. The man's booming voice pulled Wyatt from the terrifying place his mind went to avoid the confrontation he knew was brewing. He couldn't tell if he had succeeded in winning Brady's trust, but the satisfying expression on the man's face as his eyes moved past him on their way to Garret suggested something positive at least. It was enough to turn Wyatt's already churning stomach. "I don't want to smell boiled alien brains when I'm trying to sleep tonight."

The mercs gathered around the Veshnian captives and moved to provide a space for Garret to stand as Wyatt pulled the prod from the alien's skull. He noticed two dark holes cooked into its head and the repulsive image wouldn't go away, even as he watched his superior approach him.

"You passed the test, kid. Maybe you were a little overeager with the duty, but it was a satisfying climax I would say." Garret took the prod from Wyatt and handed it to Brady. "You chose well. Perhaps a little too well."

Brady grinned as their leader walked away. The other mercs applauded Wyatt, but he was too on edge to understand why until Brady approached him.

"You're one of us now, kid," Brady barked, clapping the younger man on the back with a heavy hand. "Now all that's left is to finish off the others, but you should probably just shoot them you sadistic sonofa—" Brady stopped midsentence and stared as Wyatt's face turned green. "Are you planning on puking boy? You better get that weak nonsense out of here."

The men surrounding them burst into laughter, but Wyatt wasn't concerned with them. He was more focused on getting out of there and into the open, to suck in the closest thing Bala had to fresh air, in hopes of composing himself after what he'd done. Wyatt turned on his heels, the grips of his boots squeaking against the stone-worked floor before he bolted for the door.

The sound of his compatriots joking with one another at his expense wasn't lost on him. He knew in the back of his head what awaited when he returned. A good ribbing was expected with hardened men, but Wyatt knew that beneath the façade of the mercenaries' human flesh were monsters that salivated for more.

Oddly, what Garret did in taking away the prod was a show of mercy. It might not have appeared so to the other mercs, but Wyatt recognized it for what it was. Unfortunately, it came too late.

The evil deed was done and done exceedingly well.

Wyatt let all of it go as he burst through the double doors. The heat of the Bala sun cooked against his exposed neck as he heaved, pulling away the facemask before his lunch escaped. The putrid splatter on the ground was reminiscent of the smell the prod made as it cooked into the Veshnian's head. He couldn't stop the smell from violating his senses no matter how hard he tried.

What was worse was the company the smell invited – it brought forth the image of the prod pulling from the dead alien's skull. Overcome with the grief of what he did, Wyatt's knees buckled, forcing him to the ground, weak and remorseful.

"Let it all out," a voice said after several dry gasps emanated from Wyatt's throat.

The younger merc glanced back to see Garret watching him skeptically. The man's brows furrowed with equal part disdain and indifference, causing Wyatt to catch his breath a moment before speaking. "That's never happened before," Wyatt spat, his throat raw from the stomach acid cooking the tender flesh of his weeks-old esophagus.

"It's not a good look for anyone, but I would be lying if I said the smell didn't get to me too. These Veshnians are a disgusting race. Personally, I'll be glad to be rid of them."

Wyatt nodded, not in agreement, but to delay the need to respond until something of substance came to mind. "The odor packs a punch, that's for sure," he said after a long silence, his stomach turning and twisting under his flak jacket.

"Yeah," Garret replied, his gruff voice tighter as he craned his head back to peer at the sky. "What's worse is that we're running out of time."

Wyatt glanced in the direction his leader did and squinted into the light. "The ambassador is coming?"

"Any day now. The boys are getting antsy and I'm not sure this is going to pan out as I expected. Keep this to yourself, but I wouldn't be surprised if this all goes to hell minutes after the ambassador arrives. You might want to make peace with that."

Wyatt gawked at the older merc, the cigar still protruding from his lips. He took it as the leader revealing a secret that no one should have heard, and Wyatt couldn't help feeling that it was another test. "Are you at peace with it, sir?"

"Absolutely not. But I haven't known peace since before you

were a wet spot in your mommy's drawers. Just know that when the time comes, I'm going to expect you to be stronger than what you displayed just now in front of your peers. I'm sure you heard the old adage about a chain only being as strong as its weakest link. I prefer to say that a team is only successful when they all feel that they are working for the same cause. I recognized your hesitation in there. It might have only been for a split second, but there was no denying it. Are you still with us?"

Wyatt shook off the chill forming down his spine as his gaze met that of his leader. The cold, cobalt-blue orbs appeared lifeless when the man glanced down at him, dissatisfaction splayed across his crooked face. "Uh—yes, sir."

The reply was weakness and Wyatt gulped at the quizzical stare reflecting back at him. *Don't let him know*, Wyatt pleaded silently in his head. Stale air in his lungs escaped in a pitiful groan.

Garret pulled the nub of a cigar from his mouth and flicked it out into the open sand. The butt rolled downward, smoke rising in twisted columns before the gusting wind swept it away and out of view. "I'll hold you to that," he growled before turning back for the door, leaving Wyatt with haunted thoughts and morbid regret. The last image of the Veshnian flashed in his mind once more, the scorched hole in its head an exclamation mark on his evil deed.

"I have to get out of here," Wyatt whispered before attempting to spit the rancid taste from his mouth. The urge to leave only got stronger after Garret confided in him. Total annihilation was coming for Bala, if Wyatt understood him correctly. That would include the team as well, not that they didn't deserve it.

His heart thudded in his ears as he turned his gaze skyward. With Garret running the operation, any hope of salvation was in vain.

SEVEN
GCS VERITAS

TELLA SAVED THE VIDEO SHE HAD MADE FOR HERSELF IF EVENTS on Bala went the way she thought they would. It was her job to sacrifice herself for the common good. It may not have been a human ethos, but in the larger universe within the Confederation, self-sacrifice was just part of another day ending in "Y." It took years of grooming for the human ambassadors to be on board with the philosophy, but once you understood that you were but a speck of dust, the mindset to do the right thing was simple.

It also helped to know that death was not a permanent construct for those with means.

She pulled a hard breath of cold air into her lungs and she stepped out of the room into the passageway leading to the airlock. The EVA suit fit her like a glove, but it had a tendency of bunching while she walked. She tugged down at the fabric closest to her knees and turned a tight circle to look back in case she forgot something. The inner door of the passageway closed automatically, cutting her off from the safety of the *Veritas*.

Tella was in the launch window. It was time to dispatch. The second-guessing of her preparedness was just her own anxiety. The Director's words echoed in her mind as she ran a gloved hand

54

OBLIVION'S DAWN

along the bulkhead towards the escape pod: "Have faith because you will know what to do when you arrive." It sounded too much like hokum, but it was all she had.

It would have to do.

The pod waited like a hot bath, the wave of heat rushing past Tella's exposed face as the hatch swooshed open. "I didn't expect to step into an oven," she said, pulling back a moment, reluctant to step foot into it without knowing the precise temperature.

"The heat will dissipate in a few more seconds. The pod has been in preservation for close to two decades. It required a cleanse to kill any bacteria which could contaminate the surface of Bala," the AI informed her.

Tella knew the science behind it, but kept her mouth shut, lest having to hear more dribble from the ship's computer. She didn't want to further distract herself from the task at hand. "Let me know when it's safe to enter."

The airlock was grave quiet, with even the static from her helmet muted in the depressurized chamber. The suit she wore was precautionary, a form of redundancy to keep the liability down for the manufacturer. The pod was designed to carry a single person from orbit to the surface, and back, with no environmental suit at all. But the Confederation enforced a strict policy, unwilling to risk the loss of an ambassador when other lives were on the line. That sacrifice was only acceptable on their terms, not fate's.

"The internal temperature of the pod is thirty-seven degrees Celsius and falling, Ambassador. You are safe to enter it."

Tella closed the face shield of her suit and stepped in, holding her breath as if the heat might penetrate the layer of thermal coating she wore. "It's not as bad as I expected."

"The environmental suit is designed to protect you in temperatures exceeding eighty degrees or dropping to negative fifty degrees."

"Fahrenheit or Celsius?" Tella asked with a smirk, her thoughts reflecting on a childhood joke her mother used to ask when their family relocated to the American continent. Tella always wondered how a single hemisphere could justify an entirely separate unit of measurement to the rest of the world with their day-to-day lives. She was relieved to discover that units she was familiar with were used in the sciences, but it still made the first year a difficult adjustment. She hated it at the time, but once she grew used to the idiosyncrasies of life on the American continent, she was saddened to leave it.

"*Celsius*," the AI responded, its voice void of any sarcasm, or life.

She rolled her eyes as she stared out of the tinted acrylic shield and prepared for the pod to pressurize. "How long will my descent be?"

"*Approximately twenty-seven minutes before the thrusters engage. You will land five minutes later at the prechosen coordinates.*"

"Thirty-two minutes would have sufficed," Tella muttered.

"*Thirty-two minutes*," the AI added. "*Are you ready, Ambassador?*"

Tella craned her neck, trying to stretch one last time in the closed-in container which tickled at her sense of claustrophobia. The suit wasn't helping, but she remained calm. Relatively.

"I am."

The pod's hatch closed, sealing and pressurizing to the point that Tella felt it in her middle ear despite the helmet's own seal. "*Ten seconds until deployment*," the AI's voice sounded muffled until Tella reminded herself to swallow, relieving the pressure with an audible pop in her ears. "*Five seconds.*"

Here we go, she thought, clasping onto the handholds near her shoulders.

"*Three. Two. One. Deployment engaged.*"

OBLIVION'S DAWN

A jolt of mechanized movement rumbled beneath her seat before inertia slammed her back, her head pressed at an angle against the headrest for several seconds until the forces let off. "I didn't expect that," she groaned.

"The forces necessary to carry you away from the gravitational pull of the GCS Veritas *may feel extreme at first."*

"No kidding," she grumbled, trying to stretch out her arms to see how hard it was against five times the gravitational forces as was on the ship.

"You can expect a shift in forces when you breach the atmosphere."

"I can't wait," she said with obvious sarcasm, already wishing she was back on the *Veritas* and that the negotiations were over. It was wishful thinking, but anything was worth keeping her mind off the feeling that a large boot was slowly crushing her to death.

Tella focused on the view outside of the thick glass as she breathed slow, deep, full breaths. Bala was little more than an orange, marbled ball haloed in rich, purple hues as rays of light from Bala's star hugged tightly around the gaseous atmosphere. She knew the upper atmosphere contained high levels of noxious gas, fatal if breathed by a human, but it was effective at diffusing the UV radiation before it reached the surface below. "Habitable" was the only word humans needed to hear before coming to this world in hopes of mining a resource that wouldn't destroy their own planet. They found it, but at a greater cost than anyone realized. Now, centuries later, Bala was nothing more than a cohabitated colony near ruins.

That did little to offset the demand for the Hytocosic Crystals, though.

She blinked as the pod was enveloped by the refracted light. Even with the tinted face shield, the beams were piercing. Tears welled under her eyes before spilling over, cascading onto her cheeks before their salty trails met her lips. Tella continued to breathe, her grip on the handholds growing weak from the strain, but her stubbornness unrelenting.

"How long before touchdown?" These were the first words she spoke in what felt like an hour. Her throat dried to the point her voice sounded like a croak.

"*Drogue thruster deployment in less than three minutes,*" the AI announced, the boom of its voice startling her. "*Eight minutes before touchdown.*"

Tella didn't respond. Instead, she shifted her focus away from the blinding light and onto her plan. When the pod landed, she needed to be focused on the mission. The hostages below needed her to do her job as effectively as possible. The radicalization of the mercenary's demands made her question what she could possibly do to defuse the situation, but she buried her doubts lest they corrupt her path.

"I will negotiate the release of the hostages by declaring parley as per Article Eighteen of the Galactic Confederation Treaties Act." Tella repeated the words half a dozen times, each time she annunciated the words as clearly and articulately as she could manage with the pod jarring under her. Article Eighteen was nothing more than a blanket law used to elicit momentary peace. If the mercenaries knew Confederation Law, then she hoped they would comply. But the sad truth was she only saw the declaration prevent one slaughter in the last century. Five other occasions resulted in massacres, one effectively annihilating an entire colony.

This one had the same potential if the mercs weren't willing to negotiate.

The pod cleared the upper atmosphere, and the drogue thruster deployment immediately snatched the pod into deceleration to the point Tella felt her spine compress from the force. She winced, biting back tears as her newborn body suffered from a lack of developed muscles to counteract the impact.

She mumbled the closest thing to a prayer that her mother taught her in a different life. She didn't have an ounce of faith in a higher power, but she uttered the words in hushed tones out of habit, hoping that the familiarity of reciting them would ground her enough to regain her composure.

"Drogue thruster deployment successful."

No kidding, she thought, rolling her eyes and wishing this could all be over.

The horizon unfolded below her, waves of sand rolling against the surface, capped with pointed stone. The terrain was unforgiving, and she hadn't yet stepped foot on it. But it wasn't the location that caused her heart to tremble.

"The mercs must have seen the pod enter the atmosphere," she said flatly. "They've assembled their captives near a clearing in anticipation."

"I will maintain comms with you to provide a detailed recording of the confrontation. Unfortunately, the video array was damaged during entry, and I only have audio now."

"Audio is better than nothing," she replied, her knuckles going white as she squeezed the handholds. "Don't forget my last order. If I don't return to the ship for any reason, I need you to escape, evade, and create another composite. She will need to relay everything to the Director."

"I have not forgotten," the AI said.

Tella knew that, but she felt the need to repeat the plan to comfort herself as the growing panic inside of her stifled her breathing. As her view of the people below drew closer, she held her breath in anticipation of a rough landing. Instead, it was pleasantly smooth, though the dust kicked up from the impact created a thick haze between her line of sight and the lead merc standing twenty meters in front of her. A cigar jutted from his mouth with a plume of smoke dissipating above and behind him as he sneered at her.

DAVE ALEXANDER

She recognized his face from the initial reports. Garret Cushing. This wasn't the first time she heard his name implicated in some form of dark ops event. He was the leader of the Splays, a covert ops team which spent years undermining the Confederation, and promoting terror across the galaxy. He was the one leading the team when the raid on a Terraman colony almost brought the humans and Bastia to war. He had been a relative newcomer to the media until what the humans declared an act of heroism cemented his legacy. How murdering a colony in their sleep constituted heroics, Tella was unsure, but it appeared that he rode his new-found fame for as long as he could. The last time she saw his face in media, it was without the burn scars, but it was hard to forget those deep-set eyes.

The pod settled and depressurized before the hatch opened, exposing her to the enemy. She swallowed hard, hoping that her exercises had prepared her for the gravity on Bala so she didn't fall facedown before negotiations began.

She placed one foot in front of the other, slowly leaving the protection of the pod, with only her comm link to the *Veritas* to protect her. If this went sideways in any way, she was doomed, but that was also what she was here for. Her death sacrifice could mean salvation for the less fortunate. A life for many other lives was currency when money and power weren't enough. It was a foreign concept for humans, but very much a common theme for other species scattered across the galaxy. It often made her wonder if humans valued life too much.

"Welcome to Bala, Ambassador," Garret said with the cigar still shoved into one side of his mouth, disregarding respect for authority.

Tella raised the visor and squinted from the piercing light. The mercs positioned her facing the light as a power play to unsettle her, but she wasn't going to show weakness if she could help it. "Thank you for agreeing to meet with me."

OBLIVION'S DAWN

This was protocol and she knew he would have agreed to meet anyone if it meant he got what he wanted out of the situation.

"I'm sure you know that we lost a few hostages along the way."

"My last report was of six deaths," she replied. "It's unfortunate."

He smirked. "I still expect one hundred percent of what we've asked for."

"An escape ship, ten million Shid per head, and a pardon from all of your crimes. I'm aware of your demands, though I'm not sure this was the best means to obtain them."

Garret shifted his weight as he pulled the cigar from his lips and eyed her. "I didn't ask for your opinion, Ambassador. I simply told you my expectations. If those aren't met, then I'll dissolve this transaction and this entire colony."

Tella glanced from side to side, the fear and trepidation she read on the captives' faces spoke volumes. They had seen death, and each of them expected the same if she failed them.

"I have a ship orbiting Bala as we speak. We are prepared to meet your demands." Her words tasted bitter in her mouth.

"You expect all of us to use a single-person pod to get to the ship? Have enough pods deploy to transport my men, and then we'll talk," Garret said, his tone biting. He turned, about to address his men when Tella replied.

"That's not happening without a sign of good faith on your part," Tella spat as she stepped forward, exposing herself to the flanked, menacing mercenaries.

Garret spun on his bootheels, grinding dirt and rock beneath him as he stalked back to confront her indignant response. "Good faith? Ambassador, I am at the precipice of destroying this rock and halting further production of hytocosic crystals. What'll happen when the markets fall? They'll see how wicked humanity really is and cut Earth from the Confederation's roster. How long do you think Earth will last without the allies' protection? You want good faith, how about I not carry through with my plans because you meet my demands?"

The air left Tella's lungs as she considered his position. It was no secret that the future of humanity was in the balance. But having it dangling over the edge by their own kind spun it with loathsome hypocrisy. "You know I can't do that. You already murdered citizens. Doing so restricted my legal right to concede to your full demands without orders from the Director of the Galactic Confederation. Considering the gravity of the situation, I am evoking parley in accordance with Article Eighteen of the Galactic Confederation Treaties Act. You will give in to the demands of the Confederation in exchange for your request, or you will be eradicated."

Her final word hung in the air like a feather whipping in the wind. She watched as Garret bit down on his bottom lip, his eyes narrowing to slits of anticipating rage. "If the Confederation wants a sign, I'll give them a sign," he replied. The merc leader took hold of Tella and slammed her to the ground, pulling his sidearm from its holster and placing the barrel against her forehead.

Tella panted, desperately trying to keep the fear at bay, but failing. "Don't do this." Her words were nothing more than a whine.

"All you political puppets are the same, Ambassador. You come on your little trips, nothing more than a composite further removed from the humanity you swore to protect, and what is the endgame, peace?" Garret spat the word, putrid hostility flailing from his lips as it wafted under her nose. "There'll come a time when the wars against humanity are at the forefront, not buried by the posturing of people like you. You want to know what my demands are? I want the people to know how humanity was sold into bondage, enslaved to be the laborers of the known universe

OBLIVION'S DAWN

by vindictive species seated on thrones built on the destruction of those too prideful to kneel. I want the truth revealed. I want humanity to have a fighting chance."

Tella lay on the ground, her heart pounding like a war drum as the barrel of his weapon shoved harder onto her forehead. In less than a minute, her own view of the situation shifted as Garret revealed his hand. It wasn't about money, or power, or political protection. Garret sought something that only a madman would provide, a means to an end. What was worse was that he knew more than most men should know about the way of the world, of the galaxy. How did he come by that information, and how could he manipulate it in such a way to bring about such a dastardly cause? She knew that what he said wasn't a lie, but what he demanded would bring a desperate, final cry to humanity as they knew it.

As near as she could tell, Garret wanted the extinction of humanity. Those weren't his words, but that was precisely the path he was dead set on taking. Humanity would never have a fighting chance if they broke from the Confederation. Surely, he could see that. He argued for the same thing she was trying to preserve, but his actions would guarantee failure.

He was misguided. Somehow, he had it in his head that the Confederation kept them in bondage when the reality was that their status as allies kept them free. He was willing to destroy an entire colony to condemn their species.

But the question she couldn't answer was why?

EIGHT
BALA

Everything falls apart sometimes.

It was taught as a universal truth when Tella became an ambassador. Of course, at the time, it came across as a sardonic statement, a metaphorical phrase that fell from the lips of someone with authority, but with no real-world experience in the matters of negotiations.

The idea sounded ironic at the time, almost laughable, but she wasn't laughing now as she viewed the current situation from her prone position on the ground with rocks digging into her back. With her eyes wide, and her body full of trepidation, she watched fearfully as the armed mercenaries marched around the perimeter, the cold steel of their barrels tilted menacingly towards their captives. All the weight of their lives, or deaths, was on her shoulders.

Keep it together, she thought as she turned her attention back to the mercenaries' leader perched above her, the barrel of his gun still resting against her head. "The pods have been deployed," Tella stated, an air of uncertainty for the future etched in her voice that she couldn't control.

"Good," Garret responded coldly as he rose off her. She

OBLIVION'S DAWN

watched his eyes dart from side to side, the calculating gesture of a madman. It was more intimidating when lying only a few feet away. Since her arrival, she watched as his men moved about, bullying and tussling with the locals as if all of this was a schoolyard game, and the stakes were not dozens of lives in the balance. She wondered if their leader would call an end to it, knowing that the pods were coming to sweep them away and take them to the *Veritas*.

It was doubtful, increasingly so when he turned away from them with a smile and returned his attention to her. She expected a snide comment, or pontification of his righteousness, yet he said nothing as he gawked at her.

Tella averted her eyes from the man's steely gaze. There was a coldness to him that made him come across as even less human. She knew his history, at least enough to paint a picture in her mind of the hardships he endured in his line of work. Admittedly, what he suffered sounded hellish.

Tella was brought back from death many times, each time with the purpose of negotiating peace, of brokering the next steps toward a brighter future. This man was brought back just to end the lives of others in a vicious cycle, repeating the horrors to the point she could read it on his face like a map.

"You do realize that even if the colony lives, it's only temporary?" Garret asked as he knelt beside her, the crunching of the rocks beneath his boots stirring her more than his voice.

"That doesn't have to be the case," she replied, refusing to match his gaze. "Your men could disappear for centuries with the number of Credits that the Confederation deposited into the account for you. You can live in total freedom."

Garret scoffed. "You still think this is for the money, don't you?"

She glanced back at him involuntarily, but it was too late after her eyes met his. "When is it about anything other than that?

DAVE ALEXANDER

You've built your career on the premise that every mission ends with a paycheck. How could this one be any different?"

He grinned, the pull of his lips tugging at the pot-marked scars left from the fires of Terraman, the retaliation for his team's slaughter of the colonists. "Sometimes a man takes a road in life not knowing where it will lead. Sometimes he takes the one with the destination clearly marked, only to discover everything he thought was true, was just a lie of convenience. The fast lanes are clearly marked, but seldom hold up to their promises. That's what my life became in this line of work. You think you know me because your database tells you the bullet points on my profile, or at least what is made available. But until you've lived in these boots, you will know nothing of who I truly am."

"The same can be true of anyone, though I'm not the one pontificating on a colony rock with my captives held at gunpoint," she spat.

Her response served only to widen his grin.

"Boss, we have incoming." The man she came to know as Brady approached with his eyes skyward while he held his weapon at low ready.

Tella thought it ridiculous, as there was no threat to any of these men in this colony. The entire display of power was overkill, a means to terrorize.

Garret shielded his eyes with his hand as he peered up. Tella didn't need to be told what they saw – she had ordered the pods herself. She was aware of what was coming beyond the delivery vehicles from the ship. "Get the men ready and line up the hostages," Garret ordered. "I want to be ready to go as soon as the pods touch down."

Brady stalked off, leaving Tella with the ringleader hell-bent on destruction despite the myriad of alternatives at his disposal.

"You don't have to kill them," she hissed, trying not to stir the attention of the others.

"I know," Garret replied as he rose to his feet and stared down at her like a child. "But it's always come down to this. Don't think of it as a failure on your part, you performed flawlessly, but the cold, hard truth is that we can't have loose ends whipping in the wind. All that'll do is leave a thread for someone to pull later down the road. No one wants that."

Her jaw fell slack as he marched off towards his men, leaving her to wallow in the dark thoughts running through her mind. She had the power to deliver these people to safety. Instead, she felt complicit in sentencing them to die.

Where was the honor in that?

The first pod touched down behind her, drawing numerous sets of eyes towards it, towards her.

"Round them up and lay them down," Garret ordered his men.

"No!" Tella shouted without thinking about it. She knew acting out would cause the situation to further disintegrate, but she was not about to watch these people be slaughtered. "If you fire one shot at them, I will redeploy the pods and you will have nothing. Your brutality will not be rewarded so long as I draw breath."

She slowly rose to her feet and stared them down, but her defiance elicited little more than smirks from the band of killers.

Garret nodded to Brady, whose smile widened as his lumbering frame stalked towards the ambassador. "You can't redeploy them if you're dead, sweetheart. Thanks for the ride." Brady pulled the Bastian sidearm from his hip and planted the barrel firmly under her chin.

Tella held her breath with anticipation, knowing that a simple squeeze of the trigger was the only thing keeping her brain matter inside of her skull. She refused to blink, to give him the satisfaction of not having an eye-to-eye connection with her before he ended her life. Tears welled, blurring her vision, but she stood fast until she could no longer contain herself.

DAVE ALEXANDER

It wasn't a blink that disturbed her impromptu execution. It was movement from her left as a dark-clad man slammed into Brady, sending the larger man to the rocky ground with a crunchy thud.

Tella blinked away her tears so she could see, but all she saw was a blur coming towards her, grabbing her by the hand and yanking her towards the pod she had arrived in.

"Redeploy the pods," he said, his voice somewhere between a frantic shout and an angry bark.

"Deploy evacuee pods," she said, her voice trembling.

She glanced at the dark-haired man as he grabbed her and shoved her into the pod a split-second before thunder clapped. But it wasn't a weather system growing in the distance. It was the abrupt firing of automatic weapons. The report echoed in the distance, screaming into Tella's ears as she watched the young merc slump before her, blood seeping from the corners of his mouth.

"No, no, no." Tella pulled herself from the pod and grabbed the man by the arm, spinning around on the rough, rocky ground and pouring him into her pod before his life faded from him. "Initiate emergency life support and deploy the ambassador pod, now."

"*You are not in the pod, Ambassador*," the AI's muffled voice said into her helmet. Static crackled from what she could only assume was due to damage and not interference.

"I'm not coming back. Keep him alive. You know what you need to do."

"*Affirmative*."

The pod launched to regroup with the empty pods streaking skyward towards the orbiting *Veritas*. The thrust tossed her backwards, but Tella kept her eyes on the only good thing she could do in the moment. She had just sentenced herself to die with everyone else on this rock. She prayed to whatever power the

68

OBLIVION'S DAWN

universe might hold over this world that she made the right decision to bring justice. But her faith was weak, and her knees buckled. It was the sharp rocks digging into her shins and knees that drew her gaze downward. That was when she saw the blood seeping from her EVA suit.

They got me, she thought, unable to resist the faintest of grins from forming on her face.

"That was a stupid thing to do, Ambassador."

Tella cut her eyes up at Garret as he lit another stubby cigar and let the smoke rise to the ether. "I told you that you didn't have to kill them. I would have let you go," she said, the remorse in her voice reserved only for the innocent lives she knew would be wasted in this tragedy.

He knelt next to her and glanced at her wound. "The word of someone working for the Confederation means nothing to me. You could have given me the entire galaxy and it never would have changed my plans. That's the problem with people like you; you're too willing to give the things you don't own in order to elicit an outcome that is beyond your control. Where does your authority begin and mine end?"

"Are you a philosopher now, or still just a murderer?" she asked, her vision blurring from the loss of blood.

"Maybe in another life," he grumbled as he rose to his feet. She hadn't noticed the gun in his hand until he turned slightly, the barrel pointed downward until he spoke again. "But you know how that goes."

Garret pulled the trigger and ended the composite's life on his terms. It was the last thing in his control before he laid waste to the colony.

And then his team.

DAVE ALEXANDER

Garret stomped away from the bleeding corpse of the Ambassador's composite, holstering his firearm as he spat with derision. Inside, a thousand curses tingled at the tip of his tongue, but he had to keep it together for a little while longer. The gnawing sense of failure ate at him, and he hated himself for giving into the emotional response of taking the Ambassador's life. She was right, there was another way, but agitation and desperation created a mixture of hopelessness that he could hardly put into words, much less communicate to his men.

The mission was over and that was all she wrote.

"Brady, I need a word," he grumbled.

"Sure, Boss," Brady replied, leaving the other mercs to deal with the whimpering hostages.

They stepped in tandem away from prying ears. He knew the smartest of the bunch would gather enough information from his demeanor to know where things were headed, but he capitalized on not hiring the best or brightest. He sought the ones who blindly followed. The ones not as green as Wyatt Appel had been.

"We've reached the end of the road," Garret said when satisfied that prying ears were no longer within earshot. "We need to scrub the place clean and move out."

Brady's brow furrowed and his fingers toyed with the grip of his carbine. "They could send another ambassador," Brady suggested, but his tone insinuated that even he didn't believe it.

Garret would have laughed if not for the boiling of his blood. This was supposed to be the easy part, but now he had to depend on Plan B, the plan he never put his full effort into because he was sold so well on this one. With a sigh, he responded, "We don't have the time to wait. Our supplies are low and unless you want to resort to cannibalism, then I think we should cut our losses."

Brady glanced back at the men waiting for their next order. "How do you want to handle them?"

"Let them do the dirty work, we will do cleanup after. I'll get in contact with you after this is over and we can reassess from there." Garret moved to step away, but Brady grabbed his upper arm, holding him fast.

"I haven't uploaded my memory to the server since we arrived. I planned on doing it on the ship."

Garret patted his number one on the shoulder. "I'll give you time to do it before we end this. See to the task at hand and then meet me in the atrium."

"Roger that," Brady replied, the worry in his voice eased ever so slightly.

Garret lumbered towards the atrium, heart heavy at what was about to happen. He took no pleasure in it, but orders were orders, and this was out of his control. In his private, makeshift quarters, he powered on the computer and waited for it to connect to the satellite. Once the connection was available, he placed the scanner over his temple and allowed the recovery data to upload. A light beep alerted him that the data transferred successfully, and from there he chose to send the data across an encrypted tight beam to a transfer station.

"That'll do," he mumbled, his voice overpowered by the report of automatic weapons fire. The first wave was over, the captives dead and all that was left was the final purge of witnesses. That was Brady's job. Garret had more pressing matters to contend with.

He pulled the comm from its perch atop the computer and recorded a final message to his employer. "The mission failed. I have no other choice but to resort to Plan B. I understand that this is not ideal, but it is what must be done to further your cause. I'm sure you will understand. My next composite will brief you after it is constructed. Give my regards to my mother," he said solemnly. He returned the comm and fell back into the chair, letting his head rest against the cushion as he listened to the final gunshots ring out over the horizon.

It was done and they were dead.

All but one at least.

Garret pulled his sidearm and checked the chamber. Locked and loaded, he was ready to bring about the finality of the worst mission of his life.

"It's done, Boss," Brady said as he stepped into the room. The younger man was bleeding from a wound on his arm. Garret knew it was because Brady opened fire on the other mercs and one of them had time to react. There was no need to ask about it.

"I appreciate your service to the cause," Garret croaked.

"Of course, sir. I believe in it. I believe in you," the man replied.

"Do you trust me?"

"Sir?"

Garret rose from his seat and lumbered towards the lieutenant. "It's a simple question. Do. You. Trust me?"

"Of course, you've never done wrong by me, Boss," Brady replied.

Garret nodded, his lips pulling tight as he forced a grin. "I'm trying to keep it like that," he said before raising his gun and blasting a hole into Brady's head. If the young man saw it coming, he didn't let on for a second. It reminded Garret of their last mission.

I'm slipping with my old age, Garret thought as Brady's body slumped to the ground, the hollow thud of lifelessness a stamp on the failure of Garret's leadership.

"I'm sorry that it came to this, but I can't afford for you to know how this turned sideways under my leadership. I need you to believe in me in ways that no one should. I'll see you on the other side." It was the closest thing to a eulogy Brady was going to get and with those words, Garret turned the gun on himself and fired.

NINE
GCS VERITAS, OUTSIDE OF THE BALA SYSTEM

THE PRINTER HUMMED AND THE SMELL OF ELECTRIC HEAT WAFTED in the *GCS Veritas* as the ship's AI printed the final layer of Ambassador Tella Spar's seventh composite. It was a rush job, but as the alarm dinged, the freshly completed composite came to, a newborn life on a hardly familiar ship.

"Are you alert, Ambassador Spar?" the AI's voice boomed, stirring Tella from her sleep.

As her eyes opened, she tried to speak but was unable to find the motor skills needed to open her lips. Panic enveloped her as the muteness persisted and her extremities floundered, seeking purchase for anything that would help bring her back from the brink of obsoleteness. *I'm defective* her mind screamed between her ears, forcing her to hyperventilate involuntarily.

"Please, remain calm, Ambassador. Allow yourself time to adjust to the new composite," the AI said. The hiss of a chemical sedative sounded above her, and eventually Tella stopped flailing, but her eyes remained wide, fearful orbs as she panted heavily. *"The composite was constructed as a Level Five. There are, of course, side effects when constructing a composite in a severely*

restricted timeframe. Do not fret, the coming to process will complete in a few minutes and you should regain full control of your faculties."

Tella forced herself up, trying to lean back on shaky arms that hadn't had the opportunity to experience electrolysis to develop her muscle twitch fibers sufficiently. She worked her jaw side to side, trying to relearn what six previous versions of her had already known upon waking, how to talk. Somewhere in the cobwebs of her mind, she knew what a Level Five composite meant, but she couldn't quite grasp the meaning in her foggy state.

The AI spoke again, "You left me with explicit orders to produce a new composite if the previous version was killed. I lost connection with Composite Six three days ago. We are now outside of the Bala System with no one tracking our whereabouts. There is, however, a member of the mercenary team onboard."

Tella glanced around the large, stark-white room, searching the space for a notable threat. "He is in a refugee pod in preservation. The mercenary has several near-fatal wounds. I took the opportunity to preserve him for questioning at your convenience, though I suggest going through your intervals first."

The ambassador rolled her eyes. "Yeah," she muttered, the word sounding more like a moan than anything intelligible. She reached for a mechanical arm jutting from the wall and pulled herself up and let her feet dangle over the side of the printer's top surface. "How soon before I'm well enough to see him?" her ability to speak returned as the AI suggested it would, but her voice sounded strained, like it was someone else speaking.

"Approximately twenty-four hours if you factor in the intervals and appropriate rest. I advise not rushing through them this time."

Tella scoffed. She had no memory of the last time, but she had no doubt the AI had her pegged for how she viewed the training.

OBLIVION'S DAWN

Of course, this was the first time she came to as a composite drafted in such a short period of time. Typically, a week to ten days was standard with the technology available to the Confederation. There were concessions for military operations that allowed for faster and better composites, but budgetary constraints were like a flu that never went away; it ultimately weakened the whole body.

Her new composite was constructed in less than half of the standard time, which meant there were likely errors. She just hoped none of them would impair her ability to do her job. A new composite after all of this was over would be the easy part. Getting there might be problematic, though.

"What is his health status?" she asked, pleased that her verbal acuity increased exponentially each time she spoke.

"*Serious, but not critical, at least for the time being. I think that will change once he is removed from preservation.*"

"Here's hoping he stays that way," she muttered, wincing as she placed weight on one leg before aborting her plan to stand up. "What happened down there?"

"*The mercenary leader did not take to the parley, despite your efforts to meet his demands, and he decided to kill the colonists. You tried to intervene, but a firefight erupted. Though my camera was damaged, it appeared that the mercenary onboard tried to save you. That is when you shoved him into the pod and ordered me to redeploy it to the ship.*"

"Were all of the colonists killed?"

"*Affirmative.*"

Tella's face paled and she nearly slumped over. The burden of so many lives lost because she didn't have what it took to save them weighed heavily on her heart. "Then I failed them." She didn't need the AI's affirmation to know the truth. Her previous composite went down to negotiate for the lives of the colonists, if

75

they were dead, then her failure was the only reason why. "Where does that leave us?"

"You left a video for yourself in the event the mission failed. Would you like to view it now, or after your first interval?"

"You mean in the event that I failed."

"That is not how your previous composite justified the reason for leaving it."

Tella groaned. "Perhaps the previous composite lacked the hindsight of failure to base her reasoning. Still, I would like to see the video." She let herself fall back onto the medical cart as a monitor shifted above her. It illuminated in bright light as the screen powered on. She squinted against the brilliance until she grew used to it, refusing to ask the AI to adjust it for her. Seconds later she was met with her reflection, though it was not truly hers.

"Ambassador Spar, I assume if you are seeing this, then the mission did not go as I anticipated. The situation on Bala has deteriorated since my coming to, and despite my best efforts to resolve the situation within my rights to do so, I can only assume that it was not enough. Tragedy is not how I want to look at my failures, but the loss of any innocent lives when I was there to protect them is hard to justify as anything otherwise. I trust that you can relay the information gleaned from the mission to the Director and find a way to make things right. The question at the forefront of my mind right now is, "Who is Steven Chancey, and why is he on Bala?' The ship's AI can piece together why this man is suspect number one if I fail. I hope that you have better luck than I did."

The screen went black, and numbness washed over Tella as she lay back. Her eyes welled with tears as she contemplated the loss of innocent lives that were her responsibility. Failures happened, but this was volumes more than she had experienced in the past.

"Do you have an answer for who this person is and why he

OBLIVION'S DAWN

was there?" Tella asked in hopes to get to the meat of the situation and work it through in her mind.

"I have no record of the previous composite asking that question after her arrival, so it is still an open investigation."

Great, Tella thought as she wiped the tears from her cheeks. "Get me up to speed so I can interrogate our prisoner," she ordered.

"Would you like to begin your intervals now and I can transcribe everything the previous composite knew while you train?"

"Sure," she replied. Tella groaned as she pulled herself off the medical cart and onto her feet. Her legs were limp noodles and she struggled to remain upright until the AI shifted a harness towards her to help facilitate her training.

"Place your arms through the device and it will help support you," the AI told her.

Tella did as she was told and immediately felt relief as she no longer had to support all her weight with underdeveloped legs. She took the first of several awkward steps before she grasped the mechanics of walking, a sad display for someone who had lived several mini-lifetimes over the course of a century. Starting over was as frustrating to her as failing, and here she had to come to terms with both.

Tella wondered if the news had made it back to the Director, or if she would need to debrief him. *I'll ask later. I don't want to get involved when I'm feeling so weak and powerless*, she thought as she placed a shaky leg in front of the other. Tella bit her lip to stifle the whine she felt coming on as her knees buckled from the strain. This was going to take time and that wasn't on her side.

Steven Chancey, why is he important? If he was down on that rock, then he was already dead. Maybe he had been a composite and would eventually come to with no memories of what had happened. Or worse, maybe he would remember. If so, then that meant he was behind the massacre, at least in part.

DAVE ALEXANDER

Not wanting to focus all her attention on what she couldn't do, she decided to put it where it would do the most good. Data analysis and coming up with the next step to try and make things right, if that was even possible. "I'm listening," she said, ordering the AI to begin the transcription.

"*Very well*," the AI replied. "*Let's begin*."

TEN
UNDISCLOSED LOCATION IN THE BASTIA SYSTEM – 27,890 LIGHT YEARS FROM EARTH

GARRET DOUBLED OVER IN THE FETAL POSITION, DRY HEAVING AS he came to. The side-effect of coming to in another composite body typically sent him into shock, a byproduct of the process used to recreate himself in a minimal time, so this was a welcomed relief.

"I didn't expect you to fail, son," a man said flatly. Garret couldn't see him with his newborn eyes incapable of focusing more than five feet in front of him. He glanced down at his hands to see the pasty white skin of his knuckles flexing as he tried to throw up with an empty stomach. "Then again, you are your mother's child."

"Get out," Garret barked, but it sounded more like a whimper despite the vitriol with which he spat the only two words he could muster between crippling spasms.

"Bold of you to try and order me around, Steven. Has my generosity not been gracious enough for you after you flunked out of military school?"

The sing-song cadence of the man's teasing grated on Garret's nerves, but he knew the old man was right. He was a loser before he was even born and his mother marrying up did little to change

DAVE ALEXANDER

that fact. Taking his deceased father's name only further perpetuated his shortcomings in his stepfather's eyes. But it also made it less likely for anyone to trace him if no one knew who he was.

At this point, he was nothing more than a ghost, albeit one with stomach acid burning the back of his throat.

"Don't call me that name," he said after gathering his bearings, or at least enough of them to maintain some semblance of composure. He hated this part, and having *him* here to bear witness to his weakest moments only made things worse. His stepfather was a coward with power, but he had his head too far up his own backside to notice.

One day he would come to the same realization Garret had. Then all of this would be over.

Artimus chuckled under his breath and stepped towards the newborn composite. He placed his hand on Garret's shoulder and cleared his throat. "Whatever name you go by won't affect your legacy or mine," he said as he guided Garret to his feet. "Your mother wishes she could be here for you, but you know how the disease has taken a toll on her." His words softened, though his stoic expression remained as if chiseled in stone.

Garret held himself as straight as possible, his will in open defiance against his wobbly legs. "Has it spread more?"

"Indeed, it has. The Bastia are doing everything they can to make her comfortable, but a cure is looking far less likely as her days are numbered."

Garret winced as he tried to take a step forward, but Artimus held him back.

"They needed you to succeed to help your mother. You do know that, right? This failure has set us back several months."

Garret shrugged his stepfather's hand from his shoulder and hobbled towards the door, grabbing hold of the wall for support as he refused help from the man he'd grown to fear, and then to hate.

80

OBLIVION'S DAWN

"You're a real piece of work, you know that? You concocted a scheme under the false pretense of making her life better, by giving her an extended life at the bequest of a species that hates us, and you think that jumping through impossible hoops will make all of this right?

"They don't care about her, they just want to rig the system against their political adversaries, and they'll use you and anyone else they can get their claws into to get what they want. You say they have her best interest in mind, that you're subservient to them on her behalf, but the more composites you cycle through, trying to hang on to her one diluted version at a time, suggests you don't care about her either."

Garret didn't see the hand swinging towards him until it was too late. The crack of flesh against his face rang long after he found himself collapsed onto the textured, stone tiles. "Speak against me one more time and I'll see to it that you never wear your scar-free composite again."

Garret hadn't noticed that the pain from his facial scarring had been absent until that moment. When he glanced towards the full-bodied mirror across the room, he saw the version of himself that had been saved before real life collided with his youthful exuberance. He rubbed his cheek where his stepfather had struck him, kneading it until the sting subsided. "Yes, sir," he said through his teeth.

"Good. Get yourself together. We have business to conduct tomorrow. You best hope that we can get back into the Bastia's good graces...for your mother's sake."

Garret clenched his jaw, biting back the flurry of curses he felt towards the sardonic old man. His mother's life dangled in front of him like a carrot. Eventually, Artimus would no longer have that control over Garret. Once she was safe then the gloves would come off. He just needed to bide his time...for now.

"Did my men come to yet?" He asked as he picked himself up

off the floor, ignoring the urge to rub at his cheek where he was struck.

"About that. The Bastia insisted that we terminate the contract with them," Artimus said nonchalantly.

"Meaning what exactly?"

Artimus took a step towards the door and rested his hand on the frame. Glancing back over his shoulder, he said, "Meaning those men have been expended for the last time."

"You killed them?"

"Don't take it so personally. It was strictly a business decision."

"Those men risked their lives for me...for you. How could you just dispose of them so heartlessly?"

"That's the problem with you. You're too scared to do what needs to be done that your first step is to play the victim," Artimus sighed. "You push the blame onto me, but it was your lack of leadership that killed them. Don't forget, I kept a watchful eye over the situation. You let your friend do the bulk of the leading while you sat back and let the mission go sideways. You can't be friends with the help and expect them to follow you."

"Brady followed me to hell and back on numerous occasions. He deserved better than that!" Garret snapped.

"Perhaps. But let this be a lesson to you: Failure comes at a cost, and it was high time you paid for your share of the mistakes made. Maybe next time you will factor in those losses when you're sent to do the Bastia's bidding. The next price paid might come at a cost too high...your mother."

Artimus left Garret alone with the weight of dozens of lives on his heart. What he did was for one purpose, to save his mother, but each time he lost a part of his soul in the process. How long before there was nothing left of him that was human at all? That was the question he asked himself in those quiet moments, as few as they were.

OBLIVION'S DAWN

But for now, his mind drifted not to what he would become, but to what he had lost.

One day I'll get revenge for everything you took from me, he thought, but dared not say out loud for fear his stepfather would hear him. The older man had ears all over this place, this veritable prison. Garret would escape one day, but for the time being, he needed this weathered, traitorous, vile human. As long as the former Director controlled the well-being of his mother, Garret was powerless to stand against him, but he knew those days would likely come to an end, and he would be ready.

Until then, he would play the part of loyal stepson. After all, his mother deserved that much, at least.

ELEVEN
GCS VERITAS

TELLA MADE HER WAY TO THE AIRLOCK WITH A TODDLER'S GAIT. Despite obsessively sticking to the interval training over the past twenty-four hours, she still felt she was running at only half capacity. The medical scans suggested she was healthy and developing at a normal rate, but it was hard to believe that when her legs wobbled like loose strings.

"What are his vitals?" she asked as she crept closer. She kept to her schedule, asking the AI to thaw out the mercenary halfway through the interval training. She would have preferred to be stronger before the interrogation, but time was running out, for him at least.

"*Stable, for now. His pulse rate is approximately fifty-five beats per minute and his blood pressure is creeping lower, but he is alert.*" Tella sucked in a breath, trying to maintain her composure as pain shot down her legs. "*I can continue to preserve him until you are capable of walking unassisted,*" the AI continued.

"No," she hissed between twinges of electric nerve pulses making it feel like she was walking through an earthquake. "This is time-sensitive." She stopped and held herself upright, breathing in and out meditatively as she waited for the pain to subside.

OBLIVION'S DAWN

"As you wish, Ambassador."

The airlock cycled to reveal the drop pod door opened with the weary, forlorn expression of a dying man welcoming her. She wanted to feel resentment, but it was hard to do so knowing what he did for her previous composite. He may have been an enemy combatant, but he was dying for doing the right thing in the end. At least, as far as she could tell. How far his second chance at redemption went was up to him.

"Ambassador?" He shuddered, teeth chattering like cymbals as the preservative fluid continued to thaw. His face was as pale as death, and it unsettled her to look at him. This man was broken, yet he was the only person who could give her answers. The ship's AI had zero success finding anyone left alive on Bala.

"What's your name?" Tella asked as she stopped short of the airlock just in case the man feigned weakness. She doubted he could come out of preservation ready to fight, but she wasn't about to risk it. She had seen too many soldiers come from the brink for one final assault.

The mercenary shivered for several seconds before answering. "Wyatt Appel, Ambassador" he replied.

"Are you lucid enough to tell me about your time on Bala?" According to the ship's AI, the mercenaries had been on board for nearly one Earth month. She expected him to have at least something to share about his mission. She hoped it was enough to answer the long, lingering question at the tip of her tongue.

He nodded, following the expression with a sizzled, "Yes."

"Who were you working for?"

"Garret Cushing," came the answer, but she already knew that name.

Garret was a familiar name in many dark circles, and he was responsible for more black ops missions than were probably on record. How the man seemed to pop up still breathing after so many years was beyond her imagination. One would think

DAVE ALEXANDER

someone would have found and wiped out the database storing his memories; leaving any composite created from his file a living vegetable. She wished that she could remember seeing the man in something more than just a grainy image on the screen. She wondered if her previous composite had seen him up close enough to commit his image to memory. The fact that he had stayed at an angle that obscured the pod's camera from getting a good look at him made her think that he had years of experience avoiding detection.

"A mercenary force doesn't work for itself," she scolded. "I want to know who hired you."

Wyatt coughed, the hacking harsh enough to force blood from his mouth. As his spasms settled, he lifted his eyes to her, his notable plea for mercy piercing her soul. "I wasn't privy to that information."

Tella stepped closer, her heart breaking as the man slowly faded. His would be just another wasted life. "Do you know anyone named Steven Chancey?" she asked with a heightened sense of urgency in her voice.

He shook his head. "That name doesn't ring a bell. Should I know him?"

She pulled a tablet from the bulkhead and showed him the only image of Chancey that existed. It was decades old, from when the young man was in military school, but it was all she had. "The ship discovered a DNA signature matching him. He had political ties several years ago, and I'm trying to figure out why a Director's kid would be this far from home after disappearing close to thirty years ago."

Wyatt glanced at the image before doing a double-take. "I do know him, but not by that name," he said, his voice faltering as he panted for air.

Tella had noticed his breathing had grown shallower and it

OBLIVION'S DAWN

gave her pause. These were his final moments as the sands of time quickly ran out. "What name did you call him?"

He looked back at her, his eyes looking past her as his last words escaped his lips. "Garret Cushing."

And then he was gone.

"I thought I'd have more time," Tella said under her breath. A part of her felt sorry for the man, while logically she thought herself foolish for taking pity on a hired gun who volunteered to terrorize an entire colony. Still, she hoped what good her previous composite saw in him was worth the effort, and the sacrifice.

"He was in preservation for several days. There was only so much that could be done for him due to his condition," the AI replied.

"I know," she said, biting her bottom lip as she reached to the bulkhead and commanded the pod door to close. "Deploy the pod. It's the closest thing to a burial that he's going to get."

"Yes, Ambassador."

The airlock closed behind her as she stepped back into the passageway of the ship. The dull thump of the pod being ejected into the bleak darkness of space rumbled under her feet, and she muttered a quiet prayer to the deaf ears of what she believed was an antiquated god.

"We now know that Garret Cushing and Steven Chancey are the same person, but what am I supposed to conclude with that information?"

"Name changes are common for criminals. Perhaps he felt that using an alias would make it more difficult for the law to track him. His relationship with the former Director would only complicate things, wouldn't you think?"

"Hmm, perhaps, but why would he care? Any backlash would reflect poorly on Director Chancey for raising a criminal. Somehow, I doubt that would be at the top of Steven's mind. I have a feeling that this might go deeper. You said that several records were classified beyond my clearance regarding Director Chancey, but what about Steven's biological father? What do we have on him?"

Tella plopped into the chair and let her head fall back, relieving the sore muscles in her neck and back from standing during the interrogation. If she had any choice in the matter at all, she would never be brought back as a rushed composite ever again. The limitations of the newborn body were too much given the severity of the situation for which she was responsible.

"Steven's biological father is not listed on his official birth certificate, but I did find a possible link in an obituary record tying his mother to a man named Garret C. Foley."

"Isn't Foley his mother's maiden name?" Tella asked, seeming to remember seeing that name in her brief the day before.

"It was her surname before her marriage to the Director, but it was not her maiden name."

She scoffed with an exhausted sigh. "So, she married someone else before falling for the most powerful man in the GC? Color me surprised. Even with the known history of arranged marriages, this family situation is getting weirder by the moment. Give me everything you have on Garret Foley and Gwen's marriage. I'll review it when I wake up."

"Do you want me to wake you for your next interval, Ambassador?"

"No. I'll wake on my own. Maybe I'll dream something that will help put the pieces of this puzzle together in my mind."

"That is highly unlikely."

"I know," she said as her eyelids closed like heavy curtains.

She meant to say something else, but her thoughts slipped away just like her consciousness.

TWELVE
UNDISCLOSED LOCATION IN THE BASTIA SYSTEM

SHE LAY THERE, TUBES PROTRUDING FROM HER BODY LIKE A dried-out squid. Gwen was once a beautiful woman, with worlds of possibilities ahead of her, but now she was riddled with a disease slowly eating her away.

Garret watched over her, taking note of the shallow rise and fall of her chest with his heart in his throat as he stepped into the room. Any day now, she would be gone, another dead composite in a long line of them as her husband, and the former Director of the Galactic Confederation, spewed more empty promises to the Bastia in exchange for help in saving her. The prodigal son's heart broke for her, his powerlessness a slap in the face for the life she tried to provide for him.

"Hello, Mother," he whispered as he took hold of her hand. The chilling touch of her skin served as a reminder that death was only a heartbeat away. Garret refused to believe that she wasn't aware of his presence, that she simply existed in suspended animation until the machines could no longer pump blood through her veins. The scan of her brain function revealed the lack of capacity to even know that she existed, but reality did little to

DAVE ALEXANDER

curb the budding hope within his heart. "Artimus said you wanted to see me."

The obvious lies that they told one another to play make believe that she was still the wife and mother from decades before bordered on ridiculous. They began in his formative years and only perpetuated into the present because neither he nor Artimus was willing to let go of the past. There was much to hold onto, though. Each composite provided a new opportunity for healing. Each time she came to, she was the version of herself who still had months of life left to enjoy before succumbing to the disease targeting her nervous system.

The number forty-two etched in ink on her neck was the only reminder Garret needed that she had but days left before yet another funeral. The courtyard was a mausoleum of headstones dedicated to her memory. One day they would be evidence of what the family endured to save her, but for now, they were a collection of failures stacking up against them, mounting like the growing debt Artimus Chancey owed and held his stepson accountable for.

Garret sat next to his mother, the hum of the machine breathing for her the only sound in the room. The solitude and silence screamed in his head as his thoughts drifted to how his failure was another setback at his mother's expense.

"She spoke to me three days ago," Artimus said as he entered the room. Garret sucked in a breath, wiped tears from his eyes, and rose from his seat, gently dropping his mother's hand back to her side. "It wasn't much more than eight jumbled words, one of them was your name, so I think she was asking about you."

"Are you trying to make me feel guilty? I can do that on my own," Garret replied sardonically. He didn't want to hate his step-father, but his rage only had so many places that it could be directed, and Artimus made himself a good target.

"Not at all. If anything, I'm hoping to inspire hope in you that

90

OBLIVION'S DAWN

the Bastia are doing as they said they would. The treatment, while not yet a cure, has done more to extend the quality of life for her composite than anything else has. I think you would agree that is a good thing." The older man took a seat across the bed from Garret and crossed his arms over his chest. "Perhaps she'll live a full life in another decade or two."

Garret let the words fall deafly in the room. He knew where Artimus was going with this. There was another request from the Bastia. Another impossible mission with his mother's life held as collateral, and Artimus sprang onto it like his own life depended on it. He looked at his mother, the once jaunty face of a loving person was replaced with the sunken cheeks of a withered and battered warrior. There was no doubt that she was a fighter, but all battles were eventually lost, and this one would be no different.

"Do you plan on acknowledging what I'm telling you, or continue hiding behind your remorse for your dying mother?"

Garret swallowed the biting words forming behind his teeth, not wanting to unleash his fury in front of his mother, whether she could hear them or not. "Where am I going this time?"

"The good news is that you aren't going far. The bad news is that you won't be here for your mother's services."

He glanced at his stepfather, the lines in his forehead creasing as his brow furrowed. "I don't understand."

"The Bastia believes that the mercenary who escaped on the pod may reveal information tracing back to your true identity. They no longer have confidence that you were not compromised," the man said as he rubbed his thumb along the toe of his shoe to remove a blemish.

"This is ridiculous. That man was as good as dead when the pod departed. There's no way I've been compromised," he replied. His heart pounded hard enough to ring in his ears.

"They believe otherwise, and I'm inclined to agree with them."

DAVE ALEXANDER

"Of course, you do, you're in their pockets like a leech on a jugular. Why would you go against them when they're funding your private war against the Confederation?"

"I don't have a private war against anything other than this disease that they infected her with. What I do is for your mother, not myself. She deserves better than to rot when I was their target," Artimus shot back. His vitriol stunted the resolve in his stepson's attack. The young man stood there, his shoulders rising and falling in time with his breathing, but he said nothing. "They have a place for you to stay. You'll be well taken care of until this passes. I'm sorry it came to this, but there's no avoiding the situation. We can't afford for this to get traced back to us here."

"If that's true, then what makes you think I was compromised?" Garret asked, his voice tinged with defeat. He was careful when selecting his team. Then again, he was always careful, but that didn't make him immune to other people's complacency.

"The ambassador who was sent to Bala has been digging into information about you, and not just the name you go by now. The Bastia believe she was given information she otherwise wouldn't have had access to. I'm not saying that it's true, but if she's connected those dots, then it's only a matter of time before she connects you to me and expands her search. The Confederation thinks I'm dead. If they discover the truth, then we're all dead. Are you satisfied with that assessment of the situation?"

"Well then," Garret sighed, knowing he would lose the argument no matter what he said. "When do I leave?"

Garret flipped the collar of his jacket up to protect against the cold, stiff breeze as he walked towards the Antikuo. It was an upscale place, with all of the amenities afforded to the wealthy. *Not a bad place to lay low*, he thought.

The Antikuo was situated atop a hill overlooking a city that Garret hadn't stepped foot in since his family arrived three decades prior. It was no secret that the Bastia disliked humans, mostly for their inclusion in the Confederation. The fact that they opened the door to his stepfather when he sought help for his mother had always puzzled Garret, but as long as the help was offered, he felt an obligation to accept it.

Garret entered the abode, the massive archway leading inside reminding him of the atrium on Bala. His hands trembled, a sensation that shook his upper body as he made his way inside. The marbled stone flooring glistened under the bright lights, and he saw someone seated in the center of the room, his back facing him.

"Hello?" Garret said as he approached.

The man turned, a Bastian in the presence of a human, not a common practice given their disdain. "Steven," the man said solemnly.

Garret considered correcting him on the name but thought it unwise. The last time he spoke to a local it wasn't under the best of circumstances. The fact he was being ushered into hiding painted the current situation in a similar light. "Yes."

"My name is Morta, and I am here to ensure that you are not found by the Confederation during their investigation. Please step closer."

Garret moved an inch closer but stopped short, a sudden strike of dread giving him pause. "How do you plan to keep me hidden?"

The Bastian smiled, the curve of his lips revealing daggered teeth.

That wasn't an answer, but it was all Garret needed to know.

DAVE ALEXANDER

He turned on his heels to run, but two more men stepped from behind pearled, polished columns, blocking his escape.

"There's nowhere for you to run that we won't find you, Steven," Morta said as he stepped behind the human. "My people have extended a great honor to you, but you have snubbed them more than once. The disrespect with which you performed your missions was a great disappointment to us. We regret that it has come to this, but we have no other choice. Your involvement must not be traced to us. I'm sure that you understand."

Garret's eyes widened and a flash of despair crept upon his face as the two men before him leveled weapons in his direction. The yawning barrels of instant death gaped at him, and he knew the end would come with a simple pull of the trigger. Dozens of pleas formed on the tip of his tongue, but these men were not ones to extend forgiveness, so those words faded like the exhale of a final breath.

"Will you accept your fate like a man of honor? It is the last spectacle of dignity that we can extend...in your mother's honor."

Those last four words rang in his ears mockingly. He turned to face his accuser, his shoulders squared despite the lack of strength due to his newborn composite's construction. "You dare to mention her to me while pontificating about honor? You lured me here to assassinate me instead of pressing formal charges. Why is that?"

Morta didn't answer.

"That's what I thought. This isn't official. This is *his* doing," Garret seethed. He finally understood what was happening and his hatred swelled. "If you're going to shoot me, then do it. Just quit talking about it with your self-righteous sense of honor."

Morta nodded his consent to his men, the grim expression of an executioner.

Two blasts erupted in the inner chamber, the report of gunfire shrieked as Garret fell backward, the projectiles narrowly missing

OBLIVION'S DAWN

him. Both rounds pumped into Morta's chest, violently ripping through his torso as the shooters' eyes looked on horrifically.

Garret didn't have time to assess the situation, to think about his next move. All he could do was act.

He spun, flailing his legs as he swept outward, striking the man nearest him just above the ankle. The kick sent the man howling to the floor, and the bone in his leg snapped and protruded from his skin. As the shooter crashed down next to Garrett, the human snatched the weapon from the Bastian's failing grip, rolled over the alien, and popped off two rounds towards the lumbering attacker.

The man stalked closer, his eyes targeting Garret with angry precision. "You won't get past me that easily," the man seethed as he stepped over his fallen comrade still wailing as he held onto his wounded leg.

Garret skidded back on his hands, pushing himself to go faster, but Morta's blood slowed him down as the warm, slippery liquid stalled the fleeing human. He raised the weapon again and fired wildly, the projectile striking the ceiling above the Bastian's head, but the man did not flinch.

Slow down and focus your shot you idiot, Garret thought as he scurried back. The Bastian returned fire like a tiger playing with its prey. Each shot crept closer to Garret, teasing him with his imminent demise.

"Stand still and die like a man. Where's your honor?" The man spat and he took aim once again.

"My honor is right here," Garret seethed as he rolled himself over Morta's corpse, popped to his feet, and leveled his weapon at the Bastian. The other man smirked and pulled the trigger.

Click.

It was Garrett's turn to smile as he returned the gesture. The barrel exploded with fire as the primed projectile exited. The round pierced the other man's head before Garret could blink, scattering brain matter and skull fragments across the pristine, white walls of the Antikuo.

Sobering to the fact that he narrowly defied death, Garret lowered the weapon and stumbled forward as his racing heart made him light-headed. Across the room from him, the Bastian with the broken ankle scurried towards the door, trying to flee, presumably to call for help and descend more killers on their human target.

Garret crawled on his hands and knees, trying to maintain consciousness long enough to dispatch the threat.

"Not so fast," he said, panting from the effort. The gun scraped against the tile as he pushed forward, closing in on the alien.

"It was only business. There's no need to take it personally," the man said, surprisingly void of emotion.

"Funny, I've heard that before," Garret replied as he lifted the weapon and fired. The Bastian's head disappeared in a cloud of spewed crimson painting the wall and door behind him. As the man's body slumped, Garret's face widened with a satisfied grin.

"How's that for doing what's necessary?" The question was directed at his stepfather whom he hoped was watching as he said he always did. Garret had only one more thing to say to him. "If you're seeing this, know that I'm coming for you, and when I do, you're dead."

He plopped onto the floor, weak and needing to rest, but time was running out. He groaned as he pushed himself up, his heart racing, pumping with adrenaline. It was the only thing that could propel him forward and he planned on using as much of it as he could to get out of there. Where he would go, he wasn't sure, but he had one idea that was just stupid enough to work. If not, he was dead anyway.

He was going to let the ambassador find him, and then he was going to tell her everything.

THIRTEEN
GCS VERITAS

"YES, DIRECTOR," TELLA SAID TO THE HOLOGRAM VERSION OF her superior. The image made him look portly, most likely a disruption in the reception stemming from how many routers the call had to go through.

Director Cantor's grim expression gave her pause, but he was the boss. She was to euthanize her current composite and reanimate at the GC's Citadel to continue her investigation on-site. It was a waste of time in her opinion, but the decision was made well beyond her pay grade.

"I'll upload as much data as I can and secure the composite within the next cycle." That gave her less than two hours on the ship, not enough time to do everything herself.

"Roger that. Listen, I have a pressing meeting that I'm running late for. I appreciate your efforts. I'll see you when you come to."

"Thank you, Director."

The display went blank. The call was over.

"That sounds like a pressing matter, Ambassador. What can I do to help?"

"I don't know. Unless you can compile all of the data and

DAVE ALEXANDER

submit it without my being conscious." Everything was digitized already, but it required authorization from someone with the appropriate clearance. If her composite was not alive to give the authority, then access to the data would be lost. It wasn't like she could give the order and then dispatch herself.

"*I'm ready to begin the transfer if you can provide initial authorization,*" the AI replied, prompting her for a retinal scan on the screen.

She stepped forward as the infrared beams scanned her pupil. She fought the urge to blink, knowing it would waste precious time that she didn't have.

"*First upload has begun with files marked 'Wyatt Appel'.*"

It wasn't much information but sending the data across tight beam and confirming receipt would still take several minutes at best. The most she could hope for was to declare the top three files in her investigation and hope that she could piece the rest together when she came to. The fact that dozens of lives were already lost with no way of bringing justice weighed heavily on her heart. She salivated at the idea of tracking down the men responsible and ensuring that they never reanimated again. Permanent death was the only justice the mercenaries deserved for what they did.

"*Receipt confirmed,*" the AI said, but it had to be premature. There was no way the data reached the GC already.

"How—" Tella began but was cut off by the AI.

"*Ambassador, there is an emergency message being sent to your private channel. Do you authorize receipt of it?*"

"Uh," she paused a moment, the perplexity of the situation gnawing at her. How could anyone reach her on her private channel? "Yes, open it."

The screen illuminated and there stood a man, vaguely familiar, yet unknown to her. The image quality was spotty, suggesting the delivery method was encrypted, decrypted, and encrypted again to prevent a data breach. "Ambassador Spar," the man said as she watched his eyes dart from side to side, a panicked expression etched on his face. "You may not know me, but you've certainly heard of me. My name is Garret Cushing." Tella held her breath and her jaw fell slack.

"I've done many terrible things in my life, and I know that the Confederation wants me dead. I'm sure that you have similar feelings considering what happened on Bala. I won't waste time defending myself. I want to surrender to you in exchange for immunity. I'm involved in something much bigger than the Confederation is aware of. I'm willing to give myself up if it means it'll save more lives. I'm delivering a separate message with coordinates for where to meet me. I'll be there, in hiding, anticipating your arrival. If you're not alone, then I'll leave and this opportunity will be lost to you. I hope that I can trust you." Garret paused a moment, leaned forward, and touched something out of frame, before returning. "If it's any consolation, I'm sorry for the part I played in all of this. I think you'll recognize that I had no choice when we communicate again. I hope to see you there."

The image went blank. Tella realized she was getting light-headed from the lack of oxygen. She sucked in a gulp of air and braced herself against the bulkhead. "That was him?" she asked, but the emphasis wasn't on the question, it was on her dismay.

"*It appears to be, though the composite looks much too young based on the images collected recently. This composite is void of the facial scarring that disrupted many of the images I have on file.*"

"Then he must be utilizing more than one composite mold. That's the only thing I can fathom," Tella said.

"*That is a high crime from the Confederation. That technology is not supposed to exist in the private sector,*" the AI replied.

"Maybe he doesn't work for the private sector," she muttered.

DAVE ALEXANDER

"His stepfather is the former Director. Could it be that Garret seized the technology before the Director passed away?" Tella paced the room, her mind working out the details as the second message was delivered.

"Receipt confirmed."

"Is it from Garret?"

"It is. Would you like to view it now?"

"Yes."

The message appeared and Tella almost lost her balance as she read the meeting location. "That's in the Bastia System," she spat. "They don't like humans. How can he be there?"

"Perhaps that is a question you should ask when you meet him."

"How fast can you get there?" She asked, not wanting to waste precious time that she didn't have.

"Two days if we jump. It takes twelve hours for the ship's jump drive to repower after use."

"Do it," she ordered.

"But the Director expects you to return to the GC for the investigation, Ambassador."

"That's going to have to wait," she grumbled as she returned to pacing. She didn't need the AI to tell her that disobeying the order was a criminal offense. She was well aware of the law, but she also knew that following this lead might save lives which would otherwise be lost. It would be worth the risk if she was right. If not, then she hoped she didn't have to suffer for it.

"Do you plan on forwarding this information to the Director?"

Tella stiffened, knowing that acting without a valid reason would appear as if she'd gone rogue to her superior. The risk was a matter of counting six in one hand and half a dozen in the other and she was stuck having to make the decision without backup, or a safety net.

"No," she said finally. "But I do want you to monitor and

OBLIVION'S DAWN

record everything. If I die and this investigation is lost, there needs to be some record of it."

"*Yes, Ambassador.*"

"One other thing," she continued, "Continue to upload the data to the GC database. I don't want the ship to go dark despite what I'm doing. That will only further aggravate things later on. I'll ask for forgiveness instead of seeking permission. I hope my past successes will grant me at least that much."

Hopefully, she thought. But that was a lot to ask for. If she was wrong, they would label her a traitor and she would be recycled permanently. She shook off the thought and focused on her new plan.

"Nothing," she replied. "Just continue the data transfer in silence. I need time to myself."

The AI didn't respond, not that she expected it to. It was created to obey orders; the complete opposite of what she was about to do.

FOURTEEN
BASTIAN SYSTEM

GARRET KEPT HIS EYES ON THE WINDOW, NOTING THE PEDESTRIANS skeptically as they moved past. No one knew he was there, at least for the time being, and he hoped the halo he wore around his neck was enough to fool the security cameras that his stepfather would undoubtedly use to try and find him. It was a crude technology, but effective in areas with dense populations to help defeat facial recognition computers. Still, he was only tricking the cameras with this tech. The locals met him with a standoffishness typical of Bastia, who lost no love for humanity.

Where that sentiment came from was beyond him. It had just always been that way, but he held onto the hope that their utter disregard for him would translate to their not mentioning him to the authorities either. Humans were, after all, nothing to regard in their eyes. Despite this, all it would take is being seen by the wrong person and he would be made. It was best to be careful even if that slowed him down.

"If you aren't going to eat something, then get out," a gruff voice said from around the other side of the doorway.

Garret canted his head towards the owner of the establish-

102

OBLIVION'S DAWN

ment, who was standing over a customer, arms crossed, with a fierce scowl on his face. If there was one thing that Garret knew for sure, it was that crossing these people was a bad idea. He returned his gaze to the window as the altercation settled to a dull roar. It wasn't his fight. It wasn't even his planet.

He patted his foot in time with the thrum of his heart and calculated his next stop. He chose to settle for no more than an hour per location. Staying on the move would benefit him in evading capture, but how long he could keep it up was a mystery. Once night fell, this place became much more dangerous.

Garret recalled previous missions, traipsing through the jungles of some forsaken world for weeks at a time, doing unfathomable things to innocent people. He could hole up practically anywhere for the long haul, but this wasn't necessarily the place he wanted to do it. He needed somewhere with multiple escape routes and a bit more security. Otherwise, he wasn't going to get any sleep, and without that, he would slip up.

Knowing your own weaknesses was important to survival.

"Hey, get your filthy hands off of me!" The shout came from the same origin as before, and when Garret glanced back, one of the Bastian men was grabbing the other's throat. An eruption of cheers and pleas roared in the small space and the escalation of violence was a threat that Garret couldn't afford.

"Time to skin out of here," he mumbled to himself as he rose slowly from the chair, staying close to the wall to avoid drawing attention to himself. If the authorities arrived, and any of them were part of Artimus's crew, then he would be done for.

Garret made his way out into the alley as a cold breeze threatened to take his breath away. He sucked in, wheezing at the bitterness as he tucked his chin to his chest and walked away. The attempt on his life had changed his timeline and he still didn't know where to go.

103

DAVE ALEXANDER

Thankfully, the bustling township ignored his presence as he stepped out onto the main thoroughfare. Above, personnel carriers hovered quietly, a serene image not unlike the paintings of birds he once admired when living on Earth. He missed those days. Life had been easier then, before his mother's death, before he was shipped off to military school. He still looked on those earlier times happily, though that life felt like someone else's memories and not those of a hardened mercenary.

"You buy?" A voice asked as a woman tugged on the arm of his coat. Garret pulled away, unnerved by the fact he hadn't noticed her until she was within arm's reach. She scurried back once she saw his face, his humanity.

"I'm not interested, sorry," he said, acknowledging her quiet nod as she slunk back behind her table of handmade goods.

He shoved his trembling hands into his pockets, taking comfort in the firm grip on the weapon he had used to kill his would-be assassins. Being armed was like having a blanket in the winter. It was necessary for survival regardless of how cumbersome it was.

Garret took a sharp left turn into an alley and sighed a light reprieve as the gusting wind settled to something less harsh than being out in the open. The stone walls rose like a prison cell, disappearing in the shadows of the overhanging roofs which cut off the sunlight. It was cover, but far from secure. He wound his way through the twists and turns, trying to find something useful. He hated being closed in. One way in and one way out limited his escape options. There was nowhere to run if they came for him.

The alley gave way to a courtyard shared by adjoining apartments. It was empty, save for a few household items left unattended. It was also deathly quiet. A small commodity when hearing your enemies approach was a necessary defensive strategy. He surveilled the area, noting three doors and windows for each apartment. Two windows were equipped with bars, but the third one was unobstructed, and slightly open, with a curtain wafting into the alley from the slight breeze.

"It's better than nothing," he muttered as he slumped into the corner, out of view from any of the doors or windows. If he had to use the window for an escape, he might as well be close to it. "Let's hope it doesn't come to me needing to use it."

FIFTEEN
GCS VERITAS

THE SHIP JUMPED FROM ONE POINT IN SPACE TO ANOTHER, THE action flexing the hull as it reappeared several thousand light-years closer to Bastia.

"*Jump complete. Jump drive recalibrating.*"

"How long has it been since this ship jumped?" Tella asked as a wave of nausea hit her like a kick to the gut.

"*Only during the testing of the jump drive, Ambassador. This was the first use since then.*"

"Splendid," she said as she brushed a tuft of hair from her face. She had never experienced anything like this before. Then again, she was never racing the clock to arrive at a location halfway across the galaxy without the use of multiple composites either. "How long before the next one?"

"*We should be cleared to jump again in approximately eleven hours and thirty-nine minutes.*"

"Sounds good," she lied. She hated being idle, waiting for the action to begin. A lot could happen between now and when she finally arrived on Bastia. Knowing her luck, Garret would already be dead, and that was if he wasn't planning on an ambush once

OBLIVION'S DAWN

she got there. A part of her knew the possibility of him crossing her was significant enough to not be ignored, but she had a feeling that his message was legitimate. If he was in trouble and wanted to turn state's evidence, then who was she to deny him the opportunity?

Besides, she thought, *lives were on the line.*

"Where are we on forwarding the data for the investigation to the GC?"

"Approximately sixty-three percent, Ambassador. The case files are quite large for tight beam transmission."

"So long as it's done, I'm fine with the time constraints," she said as she bent down to touch her toes. Her intervals were more about gaining coordination and flexibility as she prepared to depart the ship for an alien world. Tella was thankful that the gravity was similar to Earth's and not as prone to weaken her as some of the other planets in the system.

"I require authorization for the next transmission. This one requires both retinal scan and palm print signatures."

Tella slowly rose, careful not to move too quickly and become lightheaded. The last thing she needed was to pass out and bash her head on the deck. "How many more transmissions will be necessary?"

"Three, including this one."

Tella placed her hand on the screen and the ship's AI scanned it. It was simple to forge a signature or even a thumbprint, but forging an entire handprint was next to impossible. It was the second most secure means to authorize the transfer of classified information. Still, she was nervous about it falling into the wrong hands. She followed it up with a retinal scan. A part of her distrusted the system by which she was forced to operate. Garret alluded to the fact that there was something amiss going on in government. What that was could in fact impact her superiors. If

DAVE ALEXANDER

that was the case, then her decision to follow the lead put her in a rogue status. There was no coming back from this if she was wrong.

That's precisely what she was afraid of, too.

"I need to send a message to the Director once the final files have transferred," she said.

"*What message?*"

"I need to tell him what I'm planning to do. Keeping him in the dark is wrong."

"*Violating his orders was wrong as well, yet you insisted upon disobeying him. What is the difference?*"

Nothing, she thought, but she kept it to herself. "Just open a new file and send it last."

"*Yes, Ambassador*," the AI responded as the screen opened a new document.

Tella hesitated a moment before allowing her hands to rest on the keypad. She sucked in a deep breath and carefully planned out how she would word her disobedience. The AI was right, this made little difference if she refused his previous order, but maybe she wouldn't be seen as a rogue agent.

"Here we go," she muttered before typing what would be her confession letter.

The final jump brought her within range of Bastia, but it came with a price. Tella's heart raced as she read the message from Director Cantor, which was more of a rant than official correspondence. She had never read anything from him filled with so much animosity. She frowned as she read the word "contempt" one last time before swiping the message off the screen.

"He's going to hold me in contempt for this," she said. Her voice was fueled more by anger than sadness, though the loss of her career, and likely her life, was not lost on her. She may have regretted her decision if not for the countless lives at stake. She thought the Director would at least concede to the fact that doing nothing was never an option.

He knew her better than that.

"*You knew this was inevitable, Ambassador.*" The AI's reminder didn't make her feel any better about it. She had thought the change in plan would come with a reprimand, perhaps even a letter in her file, but taking the charges all the way to the top was a power move she hadn't anticipated.

"Inevitable, no. but I did expect a bit less judgement considering the gravity of the situation. What part of trying to prevent the deaths of innocent people did he not understand in my previous message?" She reclined back onto the chair and covered her eyes with her hand as she tried to block out the bright, overhead light. The early formation of a headache gnawed across her brow and back behind her ears, but she couldn't tell if it was from the cold room or just stress causing it.

"*The Director did give explicit orders requiring your compliance. It is logical to assume he would act in accordance with Confederation Law.*"

Yadda yadda, she thought flippantly. The matter-of-fact tone from the AI got on her nerves, but that mostly stemmed from her finding it hard to argue logic with emotion and common sense. "It'll be fine so long as I can resolve the situation and prove the conspiracy."

"*Meaning you have to trust a manipulator and a murderer.*"

"Don't remind me," Tella grumbled as she drummed her fingers on the armrest and hoped that the two days of intervals made her strong enough to withstand whatever was about to fall into her lap. If Garret was in danger, then she would be too as soon as she stepped onto Bastian territory. "How long until I'm in range to depart the ship?"

"Four hours."

She smiled despite the throbbing between her eyes. After days of waiting impatiently, she was in the final stretch before getting the opportunity to act. She expected to feel relief, but the tinge of anxiety at not knowing what she was stepping into got in the way. "Is the pod ready to depart?"

"Affirmative, Ambassador. Everything is ready for you to utilize as needed, including the accompanying transport pod for your prisoner."

She cringed at the word "prisoner", but not because it wasn't true. Garret was a wanted man all across the galaxy. It was because of the Director's charges against her that Tella would be returning to the GC in contempt and labeled a prisoner as well. It wasn't what she looked forward to about the return trip, but if she was in the right, then she had hope that the Director would drop the charges and allow her to continue her investigation uninhibited. How likely that was remained to be seen. "And how long would it take for me to transport Garret to the GC when I return with him?"

"Three days and nine hours if your credentials will allow this ship to pass through the Ivion Gate."

It hadn't crossed her mind to even use the Ivion Gate, but with that as a possibility, she saw the benefit of cutting days off of her travel. Expediting it would be an advantage. Tella had heard stories of Ambassadors passing through the Ivion Gate years prior, but she had never done so herself. Most of the posts she frequented were well outside the travel lanes that would put her in range of the gate. Still, the chance of traveling from one side of the galaxy to another in the blink of an eye was far superior to the necessitated Jump Drive technology the ship was equipped with.

Then again, using her credentials could be problematic. "Should they?" she asked.

"So long as the Director has not revoked them."

OBLIVION'S DAWN

Tella shrugged. She doubted he would act so brazenly against her. He knew she would return, charged or not, so inhibiting her from doing her job in the meantime was unwarranted. At least as far as she was concerned.

"Well then, let's hope that he hasn't."

SIXTEEN
BASTIAN SYSTEM

Garret was startled awake by the sound of approaching footsteps. The clomping of boot heels was a blade to his throat. He rose, slowly taking hold of his weapon as he glanced at his only escape route.

Fourteen hours, he thought. *Not very long, yet long enough to put me at ease and get me caught with my pants down.*

He hated to take premature advantage of the escape route. If he broke in and was noticed, then word would undoubtedly spread about his location. Being on foot was a disadvantage in the city. But the thudding boot heels demanded he do something to respond to the rising threat.

Garret grumbled, calculating how much time he had before he was detected. Twenty seconds, maybe? It was a gamble.

He cursed under his breath as he released the gun in his pocket and darted to the partially open window. The air inside was warm and welcoming, so he shoved the window upward, just enough to fit his upper body, and muscled his way up with weak arms not used to the demands of a mercenary on the run.

Garret collapsed onto the hard floor of the apartment and wasted no time scrambling for the window and pushing it closed as movement near the alleyway came into view. He ducked, letting the curtains fall back into place and hoping that the movement wouldn't register to his would-be captors.

"We have reports that the human was seen coming down this alley. There's nowhere for him to go," a voice said, the husky accent of a Bastian male echoing off the high walls. "It's a dead end, he should be here."

"This entire search has been a dead end. He probably climbed out," another voice stated lazily.

"How? These walls are twenty meters tall, there's no way a human scaled it." Skepticism oozed from the first man's voice. Heels scraped against the ground as the heavyset Bastian turned circles. Garret knew exactly what the man was looking for, and he also knew when the man found it. "This way," the Bastian ordered. The sound of his march closed in on Garret. His time was up.

It was over.

He wasn't getting out of this situation without getting more blood on his hands. As if he hadn't had a lifetime of that staining his very existence.

The threat loomed nearer. Step by step, the men drew closer to finding their fugitive, and closer to dying for their discovery.

"What are you doing here?"

The question pulled Garret's attention away from the window and to a small boy, too young and naïve to understand that the weapon in the human's hand was pointed towards him.

"I'm hiding from some bad men," Garret whispered, lowering the barrel though the child didn't seem to notice.

"Those aren't bad men," the kid replied, louder than his initial whispering voice.

Garret froze, fearfully slinking back into the shadows of the room, knowing that in order to survive, he might have to do terrible things.

DAVE ALEXANDER

Could I do that?

"Those are Policia," the boy said with a grin. "I'm going to be in the Policia when I grow up.

"Stay away from the window," Garret pleaded as his heart thrummed in his ears. The boy was a distraction, and enough of one to keep him from realizing that he'd already been discovered.

Both Bastia approached, guns drawn. The first shot shattered through the double-paned glass. The explosion was enough to knock the child back and Garret reacted on instinct. He propelled himself forward, towards the hallway where the child lay on his back, fear etched on his face like marble.

Garret snatched the kid up and fired a shot towards the gaping window. His shoulder slammed into a door, splintering it open at the doorframe. Pain screamed down Garret's arm, but he ignored it as he focused on propelling ever forward, eluding the Policia, or whatever they were. *Law enforcement wouldn't be so quick to shoot*, he thought. Then again, he was a fugitive and considered armed and dangerous.

It took several seconds for Garret to recognize the sound ringing in his ears as the child screaming. He stopped and placed the kid on the floor as he tried desperately to silence him without success. The two large men climbed through the window, guns drawn as they stampeded down the hallway.

"Oh, come on, kid," Garret grumbled as he lifted the boy once again and barreled out of the main entrance of the apartment and scaled the stairs. Going up wasn't the best decision, but he couldn't draw fire out in the open, especially with the child in danger. *Look at me suddenly having a conscience*, he thought.

"There he is!" One of the men shouted as the Policia stormed out of the apartment while Garret rounded the stairway with the kid in tow.

Garret bit back a flurry of curses on the tip of his tongue. There was no need to waste his energy with anger, he needed

OBLIVION'S DAWN

his mind clear of desperation. He kicked in a door near the top of the stairs and was met with blinding light. After so many hours in the darkened alley, the sun stole his vision, and spots formed where details once were. Garret squinted as he tried to make his way to safety, if not for himself, then at least for the boy.

What he found instead was the edge of the rooftop and nowhere else to go.

Boom! Boom!

Twin shots fired behind Garret. He spun on his heels, careful not to put the child between him and his attackers. Years of evading enemies for a living culminated in a two-day stint of making every mistake he spent a lifetime training to avoid.

He hissed a curse through his teeth as he considered just putting his own bullet through his head and saving them the trouble, but that wasn't how he wanted to go out. The easy way was the weak way. That's what Brady used to say when they found themselves in similar situations.

Besides, Garret wasn't about to off himself before he got revenge against his stepfather for everything he had done to the people Garret cared about. Artimus deserved punishment for many things, and using Garret's mother as a tool to manipulate and control others was just another thread in the needle of his deceit. Garret swore that he would watch that piece of human scum bleed out before he ever inflicted harm on himself.

The Bastia, though, were another story entirely.

"There's nowhere to go," the larger member of the Bastian Policia said as he slowly stepped forward. It was clear he was confident that Garret had reached the end of the line, but underestimating the enemy was a flaw, regardless of how the odds were stacked against his prey.

"Don't come any closer," Garret spat as he rested the weapon next to the young Bastian's head. It was a prick move, using a

DAVE ALEXANDER

child as a bargaining chip, but he felt justified, which only made the situation that much darker in his eyes.

"Let the kid go. He doesn't deserve to get hurt in this situation."

You don't say, Garret pondered, but he bit his tongue. He hated himself for what he was about to do, but what choice did he have? If he died, then all of this was for nothing, and Artimus would get away with murder, literally and figuratively. "This situation is bigger than you know. I'll admit that I'm not a good guy, but I'm not the worst either. There are things going on that need to be stopped and that won't happen if they can get to me and silence me."

"We have orders," the Policia said. The man shifted another step closer but held short when Garret shoved the barrel of his weapon against the boy's neck. One squeeze of the trigger and there wouldn't be enough left to identify the body.

"I'm not suggesting you disobey them; I'm only pleading that you'll give me an opportunity to redeem myself," Garret replied. "An ambassador from Earth, a representative of the Confederation, is on her way. I'm turning myself over as state's witness. I'll be in custody within hours once I turn myself in. I swear to you; I'm not trying to escape justice. I'm just trying to ensure that everyone who deserves it gets it."

The truth was a hard pill to swallow, especially saying it out loud. Garret watched precariously as the lead Policia agent mulled it over, his eyes never wavering from his intense stare. "Bastia does not serve the Confederation or their subservient GC rats. They have no jurisdiction here." The man's refusal took all of the wind out of Garret's sails.

So much for the justice system, he thought as he eased up his grip on the boy and prepared to destroy any chance at a normal future the kid might have had. "You're making a mistake by doing this," Garret said through his teeth. The boy glanced up at him,

OBLIVION'S DAWN

tears welling under his eyes as a look of despaired understanding stared back at him.

"The only mistake would be letting you walk free," the man replied as he leveled his gun at the human fugitive.

It was over, and Garret was going to regret every last second of it.

"I'm sorry, kid." Garret shoved the boy to the ground and swung his weapon around. Two quick pulls of the trigger delivered violence to his enemies. The first round ripped through the first man's skull, splitting it back. The man's eyes rolled back, revealing the whites of his eyes before gravity seized control of his lifeless body. The second round struck the other man in the shoulder, spun him around, and sent him over the edge of the roof.

Muted screams filled Garret's ears and it took a moment for him to realize it was a chorus of the boy's cries with those of the people on the street below, where the second man had fallen. The witnesses, he knew, would send word of what happened to the authorities and they would track him here within minutes.

This time he was lucky, but he knew better than to press it. Without saying a word to the horrified child, Garret holstered his weapon and fled. The monstrous thing the kid had just witnessed would haunt him forever, but that was only if Garret could stop the coming war. Otherwise, the boy might not make it to adulthood.

"I did him a favor," Garret said through his teeth as he leaped from one rooftop to the next, running with every ounce of energy he had. He glanced at his watch and noted the time. Four hours until the window for when he was supposed to meet with Ambassador Spar.

If he lived that long.

117

SEVENTEEN
GCS VERITAS

Tella dressed for her departure. She chose an outfit that was equal parts regal and practical. She understood the Bastian populace held humans with little regard. With that in mind, she wanted to present herself as someone worthy of their respect while on their world, but also wear something she could run in if the situation warranted it. She hoped not, because she had little faith that her current composite could withstand the strain, but she would cross that bridge when she got to it.

"*You have twenty minutes until we reach the departure window, Ambassador.*"

"Good. I'm getting tired of waiting." She knew that rushing into things presented a level of danger she otherwise wasn't comfortable with, but she already put her neck on the line to get this far. It didn't make sense to look back now.

"*I have monitored your destination for the past two hours and have not found a DNA signature matching Garret Cushing. I am concerned that this is a setup.*"

Tella sighed. She didn't need doubts flooding into her head this close to departure. She had much larger concerns about pulling this off other than Garret stabbing her in the back, which

OBLIVION'S DAWN

she knew was still likely without hearing it from the AI. "I'm already committed to doing this. Stay the course."

"*Yes, Ambassador.*"

Tella strapped her boots on and went to the bulkhead where her credentials were preloaded onto a tablet. She pocketed it and turned a circle in the room as if forgetting something.

"*Is there something else I can help you with, Ambassador?*"

She bit her bottom lip as her brow furrowed. "I don't want to be unarmed on this world, but I need something I can conceal. What can you provide?"

"*Firearms are illegal for non-Bastian lifeforms on this world. If discovered, you will be incarcerated on felony charges. I do not advise this, especially considering your current predicament with the Director.*"

"I didn't ask you to predict my imminent demise. I asked what you can provide. I'm well aware of the risks involved." Her words were biting, fueled with anxiety and frustration. She had no intention of taking it out on the AI, but if she kept it bottled up, then that would be worse.

"*For concealment, I can provide an XS-1A.*"

It was a small weapon, but effective enough if she were to need it. "I'll take it."

The whirring of motors on the other side of the bulkhead filled the room, and within a minute, a door opened to reveal the weapon. She lifted it, startled by the coldness of the metal. It had been stored in subzero temperatures, outside of the environmental controlled spaces of the ship to reduce the possibility of corrosion from forming. Merely holding it caused pain, so she set it back down with urgency.

"*Second thoughts?*"

"No, it's just too cold to handle right now." Tella moved to the side of the room with the chair and fell back into it. She had spent the better part of her time sitting and listening to report after

DAVE ALEXANDER

report regarding the situation on Bala, as well as her research on Steven Chancey, now known as Garret Cushing. If there was a written exam in her future then she would have felt more confident, but with the way things were going, she wouldn't bet on any of the information she poured over helping her once the proverbial crap hit the fan. "How long before launch?"

"*Eleven minutes until we enter the launch window*. If you like, we can begin the boarding process and you can launch right away."

It wasn't long, but merely sitting and waiting expectantly would feel like a lifetime. That was far from being up her alley.

Tella rose and grabbed the weapon from the bulkhead shelf. It was still cold enough to be uncomfortable to grip so she shoved it into a pocket of her suit as she hissed with annoyance. "Is the pod ready?"

"*It is*."

"Let's do this then."

As launch sequences went, this one was straightforward. Tella strapped in and the AI performed a countdown, testing the pod's systems before committing to sending the ambassador to Bastia at nearly eight thousand meters per second.

What happened in the first seven minutes after launch prompted suffocating fear.

Perimeter defense cannons blasted as the pod entered Bastian airspace. All Tella could do was watch and gripped the handrails like her life depended on it.

It very much did.

The AI took control of the automatic flight control system and initiated countermeasures. The pod sped through the vacuum of space, but it wasn't the velocity that seized Tella in a crippling state. It was the G-forces exerted on her body as her blood rushed from her head to her extremities.

Any pilot worth their weight would have worn a pressure suit to keep blood loss at a minimum. Somehow the ship's stowage was limited in that regard and Tella was left wearing a common jumpsuit. It took every bit of sheer willpower for her to maintain consciousness.

It wasn't likely to last.

"For some reason, their defense system is registering your pod as a threat," the AI said over the private channel.

Tella heard it, but couldn't function enough to wrap her mind around what was happening, much less give a reply.

Thankfully, the AI didn't appear to take it personally as it continued to bob and weave around the cannon blast.

Tella fought to keep her eyes open, to force herself to see past the tunnel vision, a side effect of blood flow moving away from her brain and struggling to make it back.

Another lurch sent her pod upside down, or whatever the close facsimile is when you're in space. But the momentary change in orientation allowed her blood to flow normally again. It was a welcomed relief at first, but then that subsided as the jostling of the ship pummeled her fragile body.

"Make it stop," she pleaded, but it sounded more like she was slobbering on herself than uttering actual words.

The pod dove, entering the Bastian atmosphere, and was consumed in fire. Even through the pod's shields, Tella felt the flames enveloping the craft. She squinted against the blinding flashes. She held her breath as she anticipated inevitable death.

This was what happened when you defied orders.

This was what happened when you chased a lie uttered from the lips of a murderer.

She wanted to take it all back, to do as the Director told her, believe that she had done her best, and file her report. That was what her job dictated. "Service over self".

She had failed at the most basic level and for what? The possibility of saving lives that may not have even been in danger?

It was a big if.

And Ambassador Tella Spar was about to die without finding out if it was worth it.

EIGHTEEN
BASTIAN SYSTEM

TELLA GRIMACED AS SHE FORCED OPEN THE HATCH OF THE POD and fell forward. Her arms shook while she held herself up and fought to maintain composure. "AI, can you still read me?" Her voice was strained, her throat constricted.

"*Yes, Ambassador. I apologize for not dispatching your credentials in a timely manner to avoid their defense systems. I did send them at the appointed time in accordance with policy, but perhaps I should have expanded the timeframe to prevent this mishap?*"

Tella fell onto her side and rolled over. Her eyes stared up at the cloudless sky as the nearby star settled over the horizon. "I don't think it was a failure in protocol," she replied. "Is the pod serviceable? I need to find Garret and get off world before the authorities track me down." Just thinking about evading the Bastia with a fugitive was enough to send her anxiety into overdrive, but she wasn't about to let it impede her from doing her job.

"*It does have the capacity to return to orbit, though it may not make it all the way to the ship. I will be able to retrieve the pod if you can get off the planet, though.*"

123

"Great," she scoffed sardonically as she rolled back onto her forearms and pushed herself up.

"*It would be better for a rescue attempt to not need to be made, but I am encouraged by your positive attitude, Ambassador*," the AI replied.

Tella rolled her eyes in response and reached inside the pod for her weapon. She muttered a silent prayer as she holstered it and hoped beyond anything that this wasn't a monumental waste of time. "Do you have the exact coordinates drawn for where I'm supposed to meet with Garret?"

"Uploading to your device now."

Tella raised her arm and waypoints appeared on the device strapped to her wrist. She frowned as she realized the screen was cracked, but she was thankful that at least she could still read it. The device projected her relative heading and plotted a course for her to travel by foot, to the agreed-upon destination.

"Here we go. Wish me luck."

Tella felt their eyes upon her as she strode through the town. The Bastian people kept their distance, but that did little to stop her hearing murmurings as she walked past. She let them talk, so long as no one approached her. She supposed that she should be happy to be relatively ignored, but still worried about the implications of these people seeming at ease with her presence.

Did that mean there were more humans on this world than just Garret? If so, then who had the power to buy their way onto this planet and be accepted by a species of aliens who refused to be a part of the Confederation?

She put those thoughts aside and ducked into an alley as the waypoints drew nearer. As she closed in on her destination, she reflexively placed her hand onto the grip of her gun and sucked in a deep breath.

"I'm not going to shoot you, Ambassador. If that's why you're hesitating," a voice said from the other side of the dark void. She narrowed her eyes as a flash from a lighter appeared against the black canvas of the wall and that was when she saw him, lighting a cigar with a nonchalant shrug. "Unless, of course, shooting you proves to be necessary." His words were accompanied by a smirk that she wanted very much to wipe off of his face.

"That remains to be seen, but I'm glad to see you're open to negotiating," she shot back.

Garret barked a chuckle before grimacing, the motion pulled Tella's eyes to his side where he held his arm close to his body.

"Are you injured?"

"Not fatally," he answered as he pulled his coat open to reveal a blood-soaked shirt. "But that could change if you don't get me off this rock soon. The Bastian are looking for me and it's only a matter of time before they find me…and finish what they started."

Tella took another step forward, biting her lip from the scolding remarks flittering in her mind. There were so many shots she could take at the man responsible for wiping out an entire colony. Why she should be concerned with what a *superior* race might do to him rested solely on preserving the lives of others, and not saving his useless bag of bones.

"Perhaps we should make it back to the pod and get out of here before they tear you limb from limb?" He grinned, but she could see in the light flickering in his eyes that the expression was one of habit as he fought back pain. She wondered what other faces he made to maintain his composure at the expense of reality, but she kept it to herself. "I don't have all night," she said in hopes of lighting a fire under him.

"Lead the way." Garret shoved himself from his perch and stumbled forward, catching himself with a hand against the wall.

Tella closed in and provided a shoulder to help steady him. "I didn't think you would come," he said through his teeth, wincing as he took a faithless step away from the support of the alley wall.

"I didn't think I should, but you held the lives of thousands of people in front of me, so how was I going to refuse?" Tella held back the biting tone she wanted to use and focused on keeping him on his feet as best she could.

"That's a good question, especially if I was lying." Garret's voice cracked and Tella realized why as his face grew three shades paler than before. He was losing a lot of blood and they were both running short on time.

"Save that for another conversation," she spat, "Let's just get you to the ship before you croak."

A painful chortle escaped his lips before he spoke again. "I knew you cared, Ambassador. No matter how hard you try and fight it."

She rolled her eyes and kept moving. He might be delusional, but she wasn't, and she wasn't about to get caught with him and suffer for his brazenness. Knowing her luck, it would get them both killed.

Escaping was easy. Perhaps too easy. The ship's AI shielded the carrier pod from detection as it prepared to launch from the planet's surface. Tella knew they were in for a long haul if they made it back to the ship in one piece. Looking at Garret's condition, she wouldn't be surprised if he succumbed to his wounds before taking the stand at the Confederation. It was something that she couldn't afford.

"What are you thinking about?" Garret asked, his voice a groan in her headset.

OBLIVION'S DAWN

"What makes you think that I'm thinking about anything?" She replied flatly.

"I don't know. Maybe it's the faraway stare and your clenched jaw, but that's just a guess."

She cut her eyes to the mercenary and contemplated kicking him in the shin for the sake of wiping the crooked grin off of his face. Instead, she sighed and tried to find her center amidst the chaos.

"Come on, now. Don't give me the silent treatment. I told you I'd give you everything I had on what's going on. I know you have little reason to trust me—"

"No reason to trust you," she spat.

"Fine. No reason to trust me, but I'm telling you the truth. You fulfilled your side of the agreement and I swear I'll do mine."

Tella looked down her nose at him. "That'll be a difficult task if you're dead."

Garret winced as he shifted his weight and leaned against the bulkhead of the pod as the thrusters came to life. The rumble of the jets nearly shook his teeth out of their sockets as the craft lifted skyward, the first step in potential deliverance.

Tella mumbled under her breath, no more of a prayer than the random musings of someone on the brink of insanity. The more her mind wandered to what could be waiting once they reached their destination, the harder it was for her to be certain of her choices. After a moment, her thoughts were interrupted when her prisoner spoke again.

"If we die before the truth gets out, I feel the need to get this off my chest."

She eyed him warily but said nothing as she let her gaze speak for itself.

"My stepfather was the former Director of the Galactic Confederation. Years ago, people thought he died following my mother's illness. All of this," he said as he stretched his arms out as far as the cramped space would allow, "is because of his involvement with the Bastia. Together, they're plotting to bring humanity to the brink of extinction."

Tella let out the breath she hadn't realized she was holding and swallowed hard. "What is there to gain for him to kill all of humanity? He himself is a human."

Garret's eyes narrowed. "The technology the Bastia share with him is capable of creating composites across the span of species. His consciousness would still be human, but he would be able to take the form of any race he requires to retain control."

"Control of what?" Tella asked, the hairs on the back of her neck standing on end as a chill ran down her spine.

"Ultimately? The Confederation itself."

NINETEEN
BASTIAN SYSTEM

EXPLOSIONS ERUPTED AROUND THE POD FROM ABOVE AND BELOW.

"That was quick," Garret hissed as he braced himself against the bulkhead.

Tella ignored him and opened the comm to the *Veritas*. "AI, why are they shooting at me again? I thought you sent my credentials."

"*I did, Ambassador. It appears that the authorities did not accept them.*"

"He's kidding, right?" Garret spat. He sucked in a deep breath and clutched his side as he fought to hold on against the jostling of the pod.

"No, he's not," Tella replied. "AI, open a line to the Bastian authorities."

"*They are already pinging you, Ambassador.*"

"Of course, they are," she said under her breath. "Patch them through."

The video feed didn't work, but the audio did, and the Bastian Supreme Commander chimed in. "Ambassador Tella Spar, you are in possession of a fugitive and have broken Article 76.098 of the Tel'stra Treaty. Submit your personnel pod and the fugitive over to us and we will escort you back to your ship."

"Or what?" Tella asked. Her question sparked the widening of Garret's eyes. His jaw was too slack to talk, not that she wanted him to anyway.

Supreme Commander Freist chuckled lightly before responding. "I didn't expect grit from one of the Confederation's human puppets. But if you need to know the alternative, it is that we will blast you from the sky."

"You've been attempting that already, sir. It appears your aim is off," she replied.

"I don't think now is a good time to piss them off," Garret spat.

She glared down at him, her furrowed brow directing him to be silent.

"Ambassador Spar, if my weapon systems wanted to destroy you, they would. Don't mistake our warning shots as an attack."

Tella muted the comm and looked down at her prisoner. "Is the information you have worth killing ourselves over?"

"If you thought it wasn't, would you have come to get me?" Garret asked.

Tella swore under her breath and directed her attention to the *Veritas*. "AI, can you get us through this and back onboard?"

"As long as the comm is connected to Supreme Commander Freist, I can track their command logs for the weapons system. If you close the comm, I will lose tracking."

"Your ship hacked the Bastian command center?" Garret asked.

"According to the Tel'stra Treaty, any ship holding a member of the Confederation is entitled to patch into any network which poses a threat to Confederation security. It is part of the guaranteed safety protocol. Should I provide the official reference?"

"No," Tella hissed. "Just get us through this alive. We'll figure everything else out once we're on board."

"*Yes, Ambassador.*"

Tella unmuted the comm and spoke to Supreme Commander Freist. "I understand your people want the fugitive, but he has information that is critical to the Confederation. I do not have the authority to release him to your custody. I do however have the authority to ask you to meet with us in a neutral zone to negotiate chain of custody once the Confederation is done with him."

"You are testing my nerves, human. You will release him to us, or we will destroy you."

"There's interference. I didn't make out what you said," Tella replied.

"You're going to make him angry," Garret whispered.

"The Bastia are always angry," she replied as the Supreme Commander shouted into the comm. Only half his words were intelligible, the rest clipped the audio, causing it to spike out of range.

Tella turned down the volume and leaned back across from Garret. "If they get their hands on you it's going to be terrible," she said.

He eyed her, contemplation set deep in his gaze. "I deserve that and much more," he replied.

"Yes, you do," she said coldly.

They sat in silence for several moments as the pod screamed towards the *Veritas*. She glanced out the porthole and saw her ship coming into view. It hardly registered to her that the Bastia had stopped firing. The reason caught her attention a moment later.

The *Veritas* was surrounded by an armada.

"That's not good," Garret said.

"No, it isn't. AI, have the ships surrounding you tried to board?"

"*Negative, Ambassador.*"

DAVE ALEXANDER

"This has the stench of a setup," Tella said under her breath. She caught Garret's gaze. He stared blankly at her. It wasn't the look of a mastermind. It was the stare of someone fearing for their life as their world fell apart around them. "Someone knew you sent the message to me. They knew I was coming."

"I sent the message to you with military-grade encryption. I did everything in my power to send it securely," Garret replied.

"You weren't the only person to know I was coming." Tella couldn't shake the unsettling feeling washing over her. She had been so caught up in the conspiracy she discovered that she didn't think of what could have been unfolding before her eyes. "This isn't right. We need to come up with another plan if we're going to get you to testify to the Confederation."

"What are you suggesting?"

"I don't know yet. I need time to think," Tella replied. "If we can slip past them, then maybe they'll hold their fire to keep from destroying one another, and once we get on the other side, then they will risk shooting their own planet by targeting us. It's a long shot, but it's the only one we've got. AI, guide us in, and don't let those ships close in on us."

"*Yes, Ambassador.*"

"What happens if they get too close?" Garret asked.

Tella stared with a steely gaze at the encroaching armada. "I'll order the *Veritas* to melt down its own reactor and take those ships with it."

He couldn't believe his ears. The human ambassador was willing to blow up her own ship and kill thousands of Bastia to prevent him from falling into their hands.

He had expectations of being protected, but he didn't expect this.

132

OBLIVION'S DAWN

"You realize that if you do that, you're putting a target on all humanity?"

"If the information you have is true, then it's only a matter of time before that happens anyway." Her words fell from tight lips. She was afraid and it was the most relatable feeling he'd ever had with a member of the Confederation.

The pod drifted in the quiet of space. The armada loomed like sleeping giants mere moments from stirring. "I don't think they're going to let us leave," he said as they drew nearer the Veritas.

"They won't without good reason," Tella replied.

"What reason would that be?"

She hesitated and Garret's blood grew cold. She looked to him with sympathy painted on her face just as deep as any anguish could ever be. "A promise to hand you over to them once we're done."

He was resigned to this fate, but those words stung like a swarm of hornets. "If you do this, I need you to make a promise to me," he said.

"What would that be?"

"Kill me first, then give them my body. Trust me when I tell you that what fate waits for me is worse than death."

She looked away quickly, her eyes locked on her ship as the pod entered the docking bay. He watched her shoulders rise and fall with the weight of his world on them. For the first time in his life, he saw how his actions threatened the balance of authority in the known universe.

It took him stepping outside his own world to see the damage he'd caused. This was about something bigger than a boy desperately trying to hold onto his mother for as long as possible.

This was about humanity ceasing to exist if an ambassador and a criminal failed to bring the truth to light.

"I promise," she whispered. And he knew she meant it.

She bit her tongue, not wanting to make a promise she couldn't keep. He deserved none of what she could offer, but a part of her needed to save him if it meant preserving the greater good.

"I'll try," she said after a long pause. They weren't flippant words, but they were hardly an oath she could hold herself accountable for. Whatever decision the Confederation made regarding Garret's testimony was beyond her paygrade. She likely had no authority when they returned anyway. She was as much a criminal as the man next to her.

The pod docked and depressurized as the airlock closed into place. A moment later the pod shared the environmental system with the *Veritas*, the closest thing to home she had. The airlock opened and she stepped out.

"AI, I need to know the status of those ships."

"There are four Bastian destroyers surrounding us. Three are in range for weapons. A fourth is further out, but I still detect its presence in the area. Their comms are quiet, but I suspect that is a result of a closed circuit connection with Supreme Commander Freist."

Tella swore under her breath. She had secured the comm out of habit, not even thinking about it as she was lost in her own thoughts. Their situation was dire and not knowing what was happening between the Bastian warships put them at more of a disadvantage.

"Open a line for Director Cantor," she said. "And allow Garret full use of the medical bay." she turned to him and said, "I expect you are able to make it there without assistance?"

Garret nodded. "I am."

"Good," she replied. "Try not to die. I have work to do."

"Yes, ma'am," Garret replied as he stepped out of the small bridge area and into the passage leading to the medical bay.

"*Do you trust him to be alone on the ship, Ambassador?*"

"I trust you to monitor him and sedate him if he tries to touch anything," she replied.

"Yes, Ambassador. Your channel to Director Cantor is now open."

TWENTY

GCS VERITAS

"Director Cantor, I am in possession of the fugitive, Garret Cushing. He turned himself over as state's witness to give testimony to a conspiracy that threatens the future of humanity.

"My pod was fired upon by the Bastian military and they are asking that I turn Cushing over to them. If their requests are not provided, then they will fire on my ship. Neither outcome is ideal if the Confederation is to have an opportunity to stop a looming and creditable threat. I am seeking asylum in a neutral location and requesting the Bastian armada serve as escort as a show of good faith.

"I need you to help facilitate this, Director. I know I am no longer in good standing, but the fate of all humanity is at risk."

Tella closed the message and authorized its release.

"That's going to go well," Garret said as he stepped onto the bridge.

Tella turned to face him. "I thought you'd be resting in the medical bay?"

"I was, but I've been part of so many operations that I get restless not knowing what's going on."

"This isn't a murder-for-hire situation, so I'm unsure how your

136

OBLIVION'S DAWN

expertise could be useful here, Mr. Cushing...or should I call you Mr. Chancey?"

Garret stopped leaning on the bulkhead and straightened. His brow furrowed as he stared at her. "Steven Chancey is dead. He died a long time ago."

"Yet you have the same DNA markings. That's how I discovered who you were, or rather my former composite did when arriving at Bala. I may not have those memories, but I do have the knowledge she did. Why don't you sit down and tell me everything?"

Her cold glare fell on him as she waited. She half-expected him to shut down, to refuse to comply until he was in the safety of a Confederation prison cell. Instead, he gave her what she asked for.

"My mother left my father and eventually married Artimus Chancey not long before he became Director of the Galactic Confederation. My birth father was a mercenary, but she didn't know that when they first met. It wasn't until after I was born that she learned the truth, so she left him.

"Artimus didn't want a stained reputation, so he adopted me and claimed I was his son. Of course, he was lying, and when the press found out, he grew to resent me. Things grew worse when the Bastia sent someone to attack him. They released a toxin intending to take him out, but they infected inflicted my mother instead. She got very sick and eventually succumbed to a debilitating disease.

"Like a fool, he approached them to ask for their help in saving her. He wasn't a good man, but he did love my mother, I'll give him that. The Bastia agreed, but at a cost."

Tella interrupted, "He had to help them usurp the Confederation?"

Garret nodded. "It was a simple plan. He would pass away and leave his position as Director, they would save my mother,

137

DAVE ALEXANDER

and I would get shipped off to military school so I couldn't screw things up."

"How did all this result in you becoming a mercenary?" Tella asked.

"I left military school once I figured out their plan. Artimus upheld his end of the bargain by faking his death. The Bastia took him and my mother in and I was discarded like a dirty rag. He had turned against everything I thought he ever stood for, so I decided to take my birth father's name and disappear. But Artimus found me and told me that I could help my mother by working for them instead of against them. Most of my operations served to disrupt supply channels for lesser Confederation assets. Eventually, we rose in prominence and made some major moves. The Bastia organized everything and provided the tech we needed. I assembled a team, and we went where the money was."

Tella took a seat and directed Garrett to a chair across from her. "Money wouldn't save your mother, so what was the incentive?"

Garret cleared his throat. His eyes bore into her as he spoke. "It was never about the money. It was about saving her. But the Bastia kept moving the goal line after every mission. We'd succeed only to have another mission every time. All the while, my mother would recycle, another composite would be made, and then a few months down the line would succumb to the disease again. Each time, she would be a little bit better, then fall off the cliff. I suppose I got so lost in trying to save her that I quit questioning why I was doing it."

Tella's heart raced. All this time she assumed reports of Cushing's exploits were strictly for financial gain. Instead, there was a human heart at his center.

"What prompted you to turn on them?" Tella asked after a long pause.

OBLIVION'S DAWN

She didn't think his heart could sink any lower until she watched his shoulders slump in defeat.

"My mother is dying again, and when I returned from Bala, I discovered that my stepfather ordered to have my men recycled permanently. Afterwards, he gave the order to kill me too."

Hours passed without so much as a ping from the Bastian armada. Tella was on pins and needles expecting her ship to be bombarded at any moment. Somehow, Garret had fallen asleep and snored peacefully in the corner of the bridge. He had his feet kicked up on one of the many consoles designed for manual flight.

"AI, can you give me an updated status report on the Bastian ships?"

"*There has been no movement in either direction since the last update, Ambassador.*"

"Are you going to ask for an update every ten minutes?" Garret asked sardonically.

Tella cut her eyes at the mercenary. "It's more useful than sleeping," she replied. She made no attempt to hide her agitation.

"Unless they start shooting, then this is the perfect time to catch up on sleep," Garret lowered his feet from the console and then asked, "What's this blinking light?"

Tella rose from her seat and stepped over. "AI, what is this?"

"*It's a read receipt from Director Cantor. He has viewed your message.*"

"And?"

"*There is no 'and.' He has simply viewed it and has not responded yet,*" the AI replied.

"How long ago did he view it?" Tella asked. Her voice pitched higher. Garret's gaze made her self-conscious of it, but she ignored him.

139

"A little more than an hour ago. In his defense, it is predawn where he is located."

More than a few curses slipped from Tella's lips as she stomped back towards her seat and fell into it. The Director of the Galactic Confederation had full authority to make decisions without needing support from the Confederation. This was especially true when war was imminent. Why hadn't he responded?

Tella contemplated sending another message across tight beam when one of the Bastian vessels hailed her. She nearly leapt out of her skin as the chime sounded.

She rose and adjusted her hair as she turned to the display and asked the AI to patch them through. "Before you open the feed, I want you to record it."

"Yes, Ambassador."

"All right," she said. "I'm ready."

The feed opened on the large display and Supreme Commander Freist stared down at her with narrow eyes. "Ambassador Spar, how long do you intend to occupy our airspace before you turn over the fugitive?"

"I told you I do not have the authority to release him to you. He is in custody of the Confederation. Additionally, I would not still be in your airspace if you did not dispatch ships to surround me." She kept her tone even and as void of emotion as possible. The intimidating stare from the Supreme Commander forced her to break eye contact every so often and she was thankful that this was not a face-to-face meeting.

"You have what is ours. We are simply protecting our property," he said. The words elicited a remark from Garret, but Tella didn't catch what he said before Supreme Commander Freist spoke again. "I am granting you one hour to turn him over to us or I will have your ship destroyed. I do not have time for games. Do you understand?"

"I do understand, but I also have a responsibility I cannot

OBLIVION'S DAWN

break simply because you choose intimidation over negotiation. I have forwarded a request through the Confederation asking that your fleet escort us to a neutral location. There we can discuss handing Mr. Cushing over to you once they are done with him."

Supreme Commander Freist looked offscreen before turning his focus back to Tella. "You expect my ships to escort you; why don't I simply destroy you now and feign sympathy when the Confederation finally sends its request?"

Tella smirked. "Because I am recording this transmission and forwarding it to Director Cantor as we speak. This is on record. Your threats are on record. And your intent to play games with the Confederation after executing one of their ambassadors is on record."

Garret chuckled lightly on his side of the room. Tella cast a scolding gaze in his direction before continuing.

"Let's save us all an hour and you agree to escort us safely now? I'll wait patiently."

Supreme Commander Freist began shouting, but Tella cut the feed before she had to endure any of it.

"That took balls," Garret said as he lightly clapped his hands together. It was a taunt, but she didn't care. "Perhaps if my stepdad had handled the Bastia like that, I never would have ended up like this."

That remark did catch her attention.

"You cast the blame on other people, but you hold all the power over your life. Perhaps as a child, you were a victim, but what about the last thirty years? Do you really want events from your childhood to shape the rest of your life?"

Garret's smile faded and a flash of anger painted his complexion. "You don't know what it was like for me."

"No, I don't. But you don't know what a stronger resolve

DAVE ALEXANDER

would have done to change your life had you made better choices. You think blaming your past makes you strong, but the most sophisticated societies in the galaxy look at that as weakness. Humans are a rare breed who reward their excuses. Is it any wonder many species merely tolerate us?"

Garret swore under his breath and left the room, slamming the hatch between the bridge and the passageway. Tella winced at the sound but made no move to chase after him. It wasn't worth her time. It wasn't worth the effort.

"AI, did you send the feed to Director Cantor?"

"*I did.*"

"Status?"

"*It has not been read at this time.*"

"Of course, it hasn't," Tella replied with a sense of dread. "What's taking him so long?"

TWENTY-ONE
EARTH

HE PACED THE ROOM LIKE A LION IN A CAGE. "THIS SITUATION IS growing worse by the minute." Director Cantor stopped the recording and played it back for a third time. "Tell me again why we're tolerating this defiance."

General Douglas Treff cleared his throat. "The Bastian military is the strongest force in our galaxy. To go against them is to assure our destruction...sir."

"Are you hearing this, Chancellor?" Director Cantor addressed Chancellor Benoit.

The hologram of the chancellor nodded before a staticky affirmation. Of all times for him to be off-world, he had chosen this critical moment in history. The future of humanity was at stake. "I believe we have enough alliances within the Confederation to stand a reasonable chance if the Bastia..."

"Don't be ridiculous," General Treff interrupted. "Our alliances are weak. The last time anyone stood against the Bastia was the Fall of Xuilian. Any guesses how it got that title?"

"Enough," Cantor hissed. "This situation is dire enough without us fighting. Ambassador Spar has the fugitive. We have to negotiate something with the Bastia. If Cushing has information

DAVE ALEXANDER

that prevents the destruction of humanity, then we should probably hear it. If it's nothing, then all we've done is piss off an angry faction with a powerful military."

"So, lose-lose," Treff said.

"The General is right. This doesn't bode well for us in either circumstance. Perhaps we should go with the devil we know and turn Cushing over to the Bastian?" Benoit suggested.

Cantor stopped pacing and stood by his window overlooking the citadel. Fifty stories of joint military-industrial complex and they were afraid of an empire halfway across the galaxy. It seemed humanity always found a way to pick a fight with a dominant species. "What of the Veshnians?" Cantor asked after a long pause.

"They're pissed about Bala. They think our ambassador failed, and they would be right, though we all know it goes further than that. Those mercenaries intended to kill everyone on that colony and simply wanted a high-profile witness." Treff answered.

"Of course, they're pissed, but would they help us negotiate with the Bastia?" Cantor asked.

"Unlikely," Benoit replied. "The stink of Bastian influence is all over this. They're suspicious of what's going on and distrust both sides."

"Lose-lose," Cantor said under his breath.

A chime sounded, drawing the Director's attention back to his desk. Another message from Ambassador Spar.

"What is it this time?" General Treff asked.

Cantor let his shoulders slump. "Probably more than we can handle. Let's figure this out before jumping to the next emergency." He eyed the blinking light skeptically. Spar was a thorn in his side long before this mission, but she was proving to be someone he couldn't ignore no matter how much he wanted. He was certain the Bastia were beginning to feel the same way.

"Should we vote on it?" Benoit asked.

OBLIVION'S DAWN

"Without Confederation oversight?" Treff said.

"We have the authority, why not?" Benoit eyed the Director.

Cantor had never felt this defeated. Most of the time his job was to inspire and motivate the cohabitation of multiplanetary species. This was outside of his wheelhouse and soon his contemporaries would see that.

"Aye for providing protection to a murderer. Nay for handing him over to the Bastia. General?"

"Nay."

"Chancellor?"

"Nay."

Cantor sucked in a deep breath and with a single word he committed his ambassador, and potentially humanity, to death.

"Nay."

GCS Veritas

Garret punched the bulkhead like he was trying to take its godforsaken head off. Unfortunately, it didn't have a head, nor did it have any give. His little temper tantrum brought tears to his eyes and the stabbing pain of shattered bone.

Idiot.

"*Do you require medical attention?*" The AI asked, drawing Garret's scathing gaze to the overhead speakers.

"I'm fine," the human composite hissed as he clutched his hand. It was already darkening and swelling from the injury.

"*If that were true then you would not be in distress.*"

"My only distress is that I'm trapped between two evils. Either way, I'm dead. It's just a question of which one offers the least resistance for me to get on with it." Garret paced the room fuming.

DAVE ALEXANDER

"Does fracturing your hand offer less resistance to your demise?"

"What? No? That was an accident. I was angry." Garret grumbled under his breath, wincing each time his heart throbbed. His hand was like a beacon of pain with each heartbeat.

"A fractured skull may prove more beneficial if done correctly, though self-demise is frowned upon by certain religions. Do you ascribe to any of those traditions?"

"No, and I'm not trying to kill myself. It defeats the purpose of why I'm here."

"Then why are you here?" The question came from human lips.

Garret turned to the open hatch to see Ambassador Spar leaning against the bulkhead with her arms crossed. She wore an air of disappointment on her face. Scolding eyes bore into him as if he was the last thing to behold before the universe ceased to exist, but he still couldn't find the words to answer her.

"The Confederation is not responding, and the clock is ticking. The Bastia will either destroy us or provide the appropriate escort. Either way, we're moving into territory that neither of us wants to deal with."

Garret swallowed the scathing remark on the tip of his tongue and instead replied with a question of his own. "Are you familiar with history regarding humanity's inclusion into the Confederation, Ambassador?"

"It was part of the mandatory training for me to become an ambassador."

A smirk spread on Garret's face. "You were taught a version of the history. Let me guess, the Veshnians were instrumental in preventing the demise of humanity and in our admittance into the holy order of the Confederation. The Confederation loves propaganda. In truth, the Veshnians were only regarded as slightly

146

OBLIVION'S DAWN

better than humans, but the compromise for our inclusion came with the power vacuum of the Bastia leaving."

"I'm not sure I read where the Bastia leaving the Confederation allowed for our inclusion." Skepticism oozed off Tella's tongue as she narrowed her eyes at him. Her expression called him a liar and he understood why. She based everything in her life on the authority granted to her by a system that didn't know its own truth. "Are you suggesting that everything we were taught was a lie? That sounds convenient coming from someone of your persuasion."

"Like most of history, it was rewritten to accommodate the next generation. It's difficult to have patriotism when you believe your nation is evil. It's difficult to hate an enemy when they are partially responsible for your survival." Garret took a seat on the medical table in the center of the room and examined his hand. He showed it to her and said, "Our history is as broken as these bones, but we have the means to repair both."

Mechanical arms released from the overhead and Garret dipped his hand into the sleeve provided by the ship.

"How can we fix it? If everything is a lie, then won't we be regarded as perpetuating more lies?" Tella asked.

Garret groaned under the pressure forming around his hand. "I have the true history stored here," he said as he pointed at his head. "Three decades of living on Bastia listening to my stepfather sell me on why we so desperately needed their help. He was the former Director of the Galactic Confederation. He had all the answers at his fingertips; answers no one else would ever have access to. And he told me everything."

"And you think none of what he said was lies?" Tella asked.

Garret winced as the sleeve tightened around his hand. "I have no doubt that most of what he said was lies, but he received the information from somewhere. And every lie has a little bit of truth in it. I'm not a threat to the Bastia because I exist. I'm a threat

147

because of what I know. They want their position in the GC back, but for that to happen, humanity has to go away."

"And if we don't simply go away?" Tella asked.

Garret flashed a crooked grin. "The allies will see to it that a war with the Bastia never happens. They'll sell us out."

"How do you know for sure?"

Garret pulled his arm from the sleeve and looked at his reconstructed hand. Red dots marked where the bone fusion needles had entered. He wiggled his fingers and then made a fist. His hand moved with much less pain, but he didn't want to throw any more punches anytime soon.

"Director Cantor hasn't responded yet has he?"

Tella shook her head.

"Then they've already voted to condemn us," he said. "The next step is ensuring the truth never steps off this ship."

Tella couldn't believe what she was hearing. She wanted to dismiss the words of the murderer as simply more lies, but he seemed to know things that no one else should. If he correctly assumed why Director Cantor had not replied to her message, then how much of the rest of his story was true?

Humanity was at risk, and no one seemed to see it coming.

"I need to ask you a question," Tella said.

Garret stared back at her expectantly.

"Your work has made it necessary to create forgeries, particularly holographic forgeries, correct?"

Garret's lips curled. "Sometimes. Why?"

Tella hesitated to answer. She didn't like where her line of questioning was leading, but self-preservation was a difficult voice to ignore. "We have enough footage of Director Cantor to make a passable forgery of his order for the Bastia to provide

OBLIVION'S DAWN

escort in exchange for a prisoner transport. Would you be able to manipulate it for us?"

Garret's jaw went slack. "You want me to impersonate the Director of the Galactic Confederation? That's a serious offense, Ambassador."

"So is dying needlessly when we're trying to do the right thing," Tella shot back.

"You're beginning to sound like one of my men," Garret replied.

Tella narrowed her eyes at him. She wanted desperately to reach across and knock that smirk off his face. "Never compare me to one of your murderous henchmen. I'm only asking because I'm desperate to get this information out. If we die, then the truth dies with us. Will you do it?"

"Of course, but I need time."

Tella looked at the clock readout on the bulkhead and said, "You have less than half an hour. Make it quick."

"I'll need help then," Garret said.

"With what?"

"Getting the order correct. Cantor wouldn't simply say, 'escort my ambassador to these coordinates,' and that's all. He has certain habits we have to recreate."

Tella hadn't considered that. Most of her correspondence with him was between the two of them. He tended to drop formalities when dealing with an ambassador, especially the human ones. "AI, do you have any footage of Director Cantor giving dispatch orders to anyone?"

"*Is there anyone in particular, Ambassador?*"

"No. Anyone is fine."

Footage appeared on the bulkhead of Cantor speaking. Most were live video feeds, but a few were holograms.

"Copy the holograms and we'll create forgeries from those," Garret said.

149

"Will this work?" Tella asked. A tinge of regret tickled the back of her brain tauntingly. She was digging her grave deeper by the second. Cantor wouldn't let this stand without adequate punishment. She would be recycled and forgotten to history.

"It will if we get it right. I usually have plenty of prep time for something like this," Garret replied as he sat at a nearby console and began typing.

"AI, give him every asset he asks for."

"*Yes, Ambassador.*"

"I need some time to myself," Tella said, barely drawing the mercenary's attention. "If you need me, have the AI contact me."

"Will do. I work better alone anyway."

"I'm sure," Tella replied as she stepped out of the medical bay and approached the bridge. The monitors showed the Bastian ships surrounding them. The distance between them had not changed, but as the clock ticked slowly towards the end of the hour, it was only a matter of time before their torpedo bays delivered violence to the *Veritas*.

"AI, am I making a mistake trusting him?"

"*Yes. You are an ambassador of the Galactic Confederation. You are acting out of character and disregarding orders. You are in violation of many articles.*"

"I'm trying to save lives. That's my primary objective. I swore an oath to do so."

"*If that is your logic for trusting him, then you are likely making the right decision to meet that objective. I detected no deception in Garret Cushing's conversations with you. He is either telling the truth, or he is too ignorant to recognize a lie.*"

Tella bit her bottom lip. With the AI's interpretation, not only was humanity at risk, but their history with the GC was wrong. That information alone could spark a war.

"I need you to run a simulation for me."

"*Of course, what is the simulation?*"

OBLIVION'S DAWN

"I want to know under what circumstances the *Veritas* can outrun those Bastian ships."

"*You're planning on crossing the Bastia?*"

Tella sighed. "I'm planning for whatever I have to do to get out of this alive."

TWENTY-TWO
GCS VERITAS

"Sent," Garret said as he entered the bridge. "It's just a matter of time before the Bastia responds."

Tella rubbed her eyes to stave off the exhaustion she felt. For twenty minutes, she stared at the monitor looking for a way out. Nothing worked in the simulation and her faith in their fraudulent holo-message hardly registered as a blip.

"What are you working on?" Garret asked as he stepped next to her. He crossed his arms over his chest as he looked over her shoulder.

"I'm working on Plan B."

"How's it going?"

Tella let out a stale breath and looked back at him. "Worse than Plan A at the moment."

"I'm confident in my work," Garret replied. "As smart as the Bastia are, they do tend to underestimate humans. That's a flaw I can work with."

Tella scoffed at the idea that they could use trickery to get past the galaxy's mightiest military force. Then a thought entered her mind: what if trickery *was* their best option?

"Have you ever gone through the Ivion Gate?"

OBLIVION'S DAWN

"Once or twice," Garret answered. "I was a kid."

"When your stepfather was Director?"

"Shortly thereafter. But even in retirement, he had his credentials."

"What if we slipped past the Bastia using the gate and alter the credentials that we send to them?"

Garret's eyes went wide. "You could destroy the gate doing that," he said. "Those massive warships would tear it apart."

"We would get away," Tella offered.

"Maybe, but who else would be hurt in the process? That gate is open to any species with authorization. It's like a canal connecting two larger bodies of water. The traffic goes both ways. If you destroy the gate on one side, then it will trap anyone on the opposite side."

"Like us," Tella replied.

"Yeah, but also freighters sending supplies to smaller colonies. There's a reason no one has destroyed the gate before; because it could wipe out entire ecosystems."

Tella hadn't considered the consequences, but she was running out of options. "What if the gate was used to transport a prisoner? Wouldn't they restrict access? That could prevent others from being caught on the wrong side of the gate."

"I see where you're going with this, but I don't know if it's a good idea," Garret said.

"You killed an entire colony for the opportunity to save your mother, but now that more lives are at stake, you want to act morally superior?" Tella snapped. Her comment appeared to take the wind out of his sails. Or perhaps it was the chime of an incoming message from the Bastia. "AI, open the connection."

Supreme Commander Freist appeared on screen. "Ambassador Spar, you are a relentless thorn in my side." He spoke in such a way that Tella couldn't tell if he was joking or serious. "I received a message from Director Cantor asking that we provide

153

an escort for you through the Ivion Gate and into the Sol System. My curiosity is piqued, so I am providing two of my ships."

He leaned closer to his camera and spoke again. "I will be monitoring the situation closely. If you try to cross us, then the deaths of trillions of your species will be on your head. I hope you understand."

The video cut out and Tella sucked in a deep breath. She hadn't realized she had stopped breathing until the stale air in her lungs grew insufficient.

"He's such a cheerful fellow," Garret said.

Tella cut her eyes at him and resented how the burden on their shoulders didn't seem to sway him in the least. "We're potentially bringing about our own destruction and you choose now to crack a joke?"

Garret's smile didn't fade when he stared back at her. "Is there ever an appropriate time when death is ever looming? We all have a shelf life. But if the ticking of time makes you grow desperate, then you never really live."

"Inspiring words from a killer," she spat.

"A killer you risked everything for so you could save humanity. I may not be a good man, but I am a useful one. Did you suddenly forget what I did to grant us the opportunity to escape?"

"I haven't forgotten anything."

She stared at him for a long time. The silence between them grew thick and icy. Bitterness tickled the tip of her tongue as she contemplated what to say next, but instead, he turned on his heels and walked away.

"*You two appear to have trouble communicating properly,*" the AI said after Garret slammed the hatch shut.

"It's hard to find common ground with someone like that," Tella said as she busied herself with coordinates for their departure.

"*I believe there is more to it than that, Ambassador.*"

"Well then, aren't you observant," she said coldly, letting that part of the conversation die there. "Hail those ships and coordinate our departures. I want to get out of Bastian airspace now."

"*Yes, Ambassador.*"

BNV Pourgua

Captain Viar drummed his taloned fingers against the armrest on his chair as he stared coldly at the tiny starship in his port view. His orders stated that his ship was to escort the pathetic humans back to their home system. Why such an insignificant species could make such demands of his time was beyond him, but orders were orders, and no one stood against the Supreme Commander.

"Sir, the *GCS Veritas* is hailing us," his lieutenant said.

"Patch it through," he grumbled.

"It's not video, sir. It's a simple audio message."

"I said to patch it through." He didn't raise his voice, but his tone was sufficient to get under the lieutenant's thin skin. The junior officer played the audio, then promptly about-faced and returned to his station.

Captain Viar exhaled and grabbed his comm to make the announcement. "All hands, prepare for departure in ten minutes. Make your peace with not returning home in the foreseeable future. Duty calls. Captain out."

It was short and sweet, the way his father taught him to command a warship. "Don't waste your words. Just get to the point. No one likes a captain that craves attention." Those words echoed in Viar's brain long after his father's untimely death.

Of all species to protect, he had to escort the same ones who had claimed his father's life decades ago. He had lost no love for the Confederation, or the weak, carbon-based lifeforms comprising their ranks. He would just as soon destroy the entire Sol System than protect the two specks of insignificant dust on that starship.

He kept drumming his fingers on the armrest until it was time to leave. He silently counted each click obsessively. He was only a few hundred drums away from five thousand for the day. As metrics went, the day was nearly done. But this day hadn't started like most of the others. It wasn't likely to end like the others either.

He hated change as much as he hated humans.

Almost.

The *Veritas'* boosters ignited on the display wall. The waypoints for the journey appeared on one display with an estimated arrival to the Sol System three days away. It wasn't how long the journey would take that caused Viar's brow to furrow. It was the use of the Ivion Gate.

"Lieutenant, how far behind that ship can we follow and not lose them?"

The junior officer peered over his console at the captain and said, "We would be out of weapon's range at five-thousand kilometers, sir."

Captain Viar adjusted in his seat and reworded his question. "I'm not concerned with weapon's range, Lieutenant. I'm asking for tracking purposes."

The lieutenant's gaze returned to his screen. He looked back a moment later and answered. "We have a lock on the boost signature. We can maintain that up to sixty-thousand kilometers but staying within ten-thousand kilometers will ensure they cannot evade should they jump prematurely."

Viar narrowed his eyes at the human ship and gave his next order. "Keep our distance just within that range. I don't want to get too close."

OBLIVION'S DAWN

"But, sir, I thought we were supposed to escort the prisoner vessel?"

Captain Viar looked down at his subordinate. "We will escort them at a comfortable distance. Humans are conniving and should not be trusted. It's a lesson I learned long ago and won't soon forget. Besides, the *Nir* is nearby, they can take the lead while we keep a watchful eye."

"Yes, sir," the lieutenant said as he returned to his duties.

The Bastian captain rose from his seat and paced the bridge while he kept a skeptical eye on the *Veritas*. The Ivion Gate is where they would spring their trap. He knew it; it was a tactically sound plan. He wouldn't underestimate his enemy and fall for the same ruse his father did.

This time he would strike first.

Earth

Director Cantor was alone for the first time in several hours. The sun peeked above the horizon, glinting through the high mountain peaks more than a hundred miles away. The citadel hovered five miles above the surface separating the common population from those who ran the world, and their little section of the galaxy.

It had been years since he had contemplated what got him to this point. The most powerful man on Earth was a moniker no one really understood. He certainly wielded power, but it only reached so far as the Confederation allowed. In truth, humanity were the foot soldiers of the galaxy, bowing their heads and lending their swords to a collective of species who regarded themselves as superior.

Perhaps they had to be superior in order to dupe humans into this pseudo-subservience.

DAVE ALEXANDER

But not a man on this green Earth would admit to what Director Cantor knew in his heart. Humanity's usefulness to the Confederation was running out, the burgeoning slave race for the Af'shai was rebelling, at least in part. Whoever was hiring these mercenaries to disrupt the system was making his job protecting Earth's children from the inevitable more challenging.

A chime drew his attention. He regarded it a moment before his curiosity got the better of him. It was a simple status report from the *GCS Veritas*. The ship was on the move, and it was headed for Sol.

Cantor bit his lip as he balled his fists tightly. "Ambassador Spar is going to be the death of all of us," he hissed. The end of the status report showed two Bastian vessels following the Veritas. He didn't know whether they were escorting or pursuing, but either way, it would end the same.

He had to get out ahead of this before any decisions were made without him. Low on options, Director Cantor called an emergency meeting with General Treff. Their plan to wait out the Bastian ultimatum was failing and if Ambassador Spar entered the Sol System, she would bring the Bastian military with her. Nothing Cantor could do at that point would be able to stop the Bastia.

The treaty would be broken, and Earth would fall.

TWENTY-THREE
GCS VERITAS

"WE'RE ENTERING THE JUMP WINDOW. HOW SHOULD WE coordinate this with those ships?" Tella asked.

Garret looked over the monitor of the two ships escorting them. Each ship had jump drives, but the *Veritas* had extended capabilities as a Confederation asset. They had the potential to outrun and evade their would-be captors but doing so would fail in the end. They had to play nice for now, an option Garret hated.

"Have the AI send jump coordinates and request an itinerary from the Bastia for jump order. It will show a sign of good faith that we're asking permission."

"I hadn't thought of the psychological aspect of it. I was simply wanting to follow protocol," Tella said.

Garret grinned. "Protocol will get you killed. Never make assumptions about an enemy like the Bastia. They're just looking for an opportunity to fire on us. I don't think we should give it to them. At least not yet."

His eyes drifted towards her while she stood at the center console. She had changed clothes after a few hours of rest and she looked refreshed. Moreso than he felt. It was his turn, but he

159

DAVE ALEXANDER

didn't know if he would be able to drift off to sleep with the Bastia tailing them. There were sedatives to help induce sleep, but the grogginess afterwards would be a detriment.

"AI, do as Mr. Cushing suggested," Tella ordered before turning her attention back to him. "It's time for you to rest as we agreed."

Garret nodded lazily. He could barely hold his head up without making a conscious effort. His mind was running faster than his body could keep up; two unequally yoked entities fighting to survive. One by shutting down, the other by forgoing sleep in a feeble attempt to maintain awareness. It was a primitive struggle that no amount of evolution could devolve out of humanity.

They were animals after all.

"Wake me if you need me," Garret said as he stepped past her.

She gave a curt nod in return but said nothing. It wasn't a cold shoulder, but it was far from friendly. They were merely team-mates in a game of survival. They needed each other to make it out, but that didn't make them friends, or allies. It simply made them dependent. The worst thing to be in a war.

"Those with means do."

"What was that?" Tella asked before he was able to step off the bridge.

He stopped, not realizing he had said those words out loud. He glanced back at her and answered, "When I went to military school, there was an officer who broke the philosophy of war into little sayings. His favorite proverb was, 'Those with means do.' It covered everything from battle strategies to surviving a bare-knuckle brawl. I guess I was just thinking aloud."

A small curl formed at the corners of her mouth before she turned back to the console. Garret didn't know what that meant, but he had just revealed a part of his past with someone outside of his circle. He trusted her enough to get him off Bastia alive, but he questioned his judgement in telling her about his life. At least the parts he didn't have to.

He wondered if she would be able to use that against him as he walked to the sleeping quarters. It was a tight space, barely large enough to turn a circle in. The mattress on the deck reminded him of the Buvre prison camp on Karnack. Not the mattress itself, but the way it was snugged up against the bulkhead. This was as confining of a place as any prison could be and he chose it for himself.

Garret lay on the deck and let his eyes droop closed. "AI, can you sedate me enough to sleep? I don't want to waste any time."

A light mist sprayed into the room from the baseboards while the light dimmed. He counted his breaths, taking long soft pulls of air into his lungs until he couldn't force any more in. He let out an exhale and breathed in again.

He counted to three, then forgot why he was counting.

The dim light faded into darkness, and he welcomed it.

"Jump to these coordinates and rendezvous with our ships in five standard galactic minutes." Tella frowned as she listened to the order for a third time. The Bastia intended to make the hyper-jump in close proximity, which was risky considering the galaxy was in constant motion. A small error could result in one ship hyper-jumping into another.

"Can we do this safely?" Tella asked.

"*All hyper-jumps come with an inherent risk, Ambassador. I cannot guarantee safety, but I can assure you that the coordinates given by the Bastian military should land us in an empty sector of that star system. The risk of collision is minimal.*"

"Minimal, huh?" She took in a deep breath and manually activated the jump drive. A small readout on the console counted down from ten seconds before the drive fully engaged. A manual override was only viable for the first eight seconds, then they would be at the whim of the universe.

There was no sensation comparable to the feeling of jumping in a starship. In some ways, it felt like falling, but instead of falling downward, it felt as if you were falling in all directions at once. It was like the universe was playing tug of war with your insides, but the game was over in the blink of an eye. It was at first unsettling, then felt as if it never happened at all.

"Jump successful, Ambassador."

Tella held onto the console a moment to steady herself just in case. Some risks to personnel included aneurysms. She blinked several times to see if she had any noticeable side effects, but other than slight dizziness, she felt fine.

"Where are the Bastian ships located?"

"They have appeared at a similar distance from us as they were in the Bastian System. Shall I ping them to confirm they are ready to continue?"

"Yes."

Tella took the opportunity to sit. The dizziness was common but should have subsided a few moments after jumping. It wasn't anything to be concerned about now, but if it lingered then it could be a problem. She decided to keep it to herself for the time being.

"The Bastia have authorized us to continue, Ambassador."

"How long before they are able to jump again?"

"The Bastian ships' jump drives are on an eight-hour cycle. They will be ready before we are."

"Unfortunate," she muttered. Tella didn't want to admit to having second thoughts, but the idea of leading an enemy as powerful as the Bastia into a trap was starting to feel like a boat taking on water. Evading and setting a course into a sparsely habited sector to hideout for several years was beginning to look like a solid retirement plan. Too bad her only company on that trip would be a psychopathic killer.

"We are twenty-nine hours from reaching the Ivion Gate. From there we will be two jumps away from the Sol System. What are your intentions when arriving?"

"Seek asylum on Luna," Tella said.

"That is not a very detailed plan, Ambassador."

"I know, but I haven't thought that far in advance yet."

"If the Bastia are that close to Earth, then it could trigger a planetary defense protocol. The Confederation will consider that an act of war."

"I know," Tella said as she let out a stale breath. "What more do you want me to say? I notified Director Cantor and he left us high and dry. I'm trying to do the right thing under the wrong circumstances. My back is up against the wall and the only way to get any leverage is to force someone else's hand."

She stopped talking once she noticed she was yelling at the AI. Raising her voice wasn't going to insult the computer, but it didn't do her any good to get worked up either. On the other hand, everything on a Confederation ship was recorded for posterity. Someone could archive this conversation and argue a case of temporary insanity for her involvement in this treasonous act.

She was far from insane regardless of how big a risk she was taking. It was wise not to give them any more ammunition against her, though.

"Might I make a suggestion?"

"What is it?"

"Luna is too close to Earth, but to your previous point, Mars is considered neutral territory for Confederation negotiations.

DAVE ALEXANDER

Bastian presence will not trigger a negative response. Though it will need to be coordinated through the GC Director."

"You mean the one who isn't speaking to me?" Tella replied.

"*It is unfortunate, but I can submit a request on your behalf. When questioned, I can tell the director that you are busy guarding your prisoner. Perhaps it will give the impression that you are not working for Garret Cushing?*"

"I'm not working for Garret," Tella shot back.

"*I have billions of pieces of data to give me the ability to surmise what any species may be thinking about any given circumstance. This is embedded in my databanks to aid ambassadors such as yourself with information to help facilitate negotiations. I did not want to say it at the time, but I feel that your willingness to render aid to Garret Cushing may have strained your relationship with Director Cantor.*"

Tella shook her head. "You needed billions of data points to tell you that? Of course, it strained our relationship. I disobeyed his direct orders. A single data point should have been enough to tell you that."

"*Be that as it may, I believe demonstrating responsibility could work in your favor.*"

"Fine, do it. I just want to get through this in one piece," Tella said. She hated herself for being angry at a machine when she knew she was really just angry at herself. First, she failed the colony on Bala. Then, she failed Director Cantor. What else was she going to screw up before this was done, humanity itself?

It was a hard pill to swallow that she had brought this misery on herself. Her people deserved better. She deserved better. But now she was in lockstep with a haphazard plan and someone likely to be an unreliable source of information. If Garret was telling the truth, then maybe she would save some lives.

That wasn't the part she was afraid of, though. That would be her doing her job.

OBLIVION'S DAWN

It was the fact that if he was lying then she was leading an enemy to her system under false pretenses. There was no negotiating that off the record. She would be deemed a traitor, and humanity would be in the crosshairs of the deadliest species in the galaxy.

TWENTY-FOUR
BNV POURGUA

Captain Viar couldn't sleep. He had ordered his support staff to their staterooms while assuming the night watch. Drifting through space made relative time feel different, unsettling. It was something he never got used to. Typically, the first few days of a deployment put him through the wringer. Eventually, he would regulate and keep standard working hours, but for no,w he accepted his body's act of defiance and used it for his benefit.

The *Veritas* propelled forward with four boosters, their glow dim due to the distance between them, but wholly distinguishable from his sister ship, the *Nir*. So far, he had nothing to dispatch. The human obeyed the *Nir's* orders for the first jump, but he was skeptical that this would continue. The closer they got to Sol, the easier it would be for the humans to orchestrate an ambush. With only two jumps separating them from the Ivion Gate and the Sol System, they would have to be insane to let the Bastian warships pass through the gate.

"That was where the ambush would be," he grumbled as he glared at the coordinates on his holomap.

To the best of his knowledge, Ivion Gate was still used heavily

OBLIVION'S DAWN

for transport vessels. They would make hiding warships easier to launch an attack.

They would if they were allowed in the gate.

Captain Viar opened an outgoing message directed to Supreme Commander Freist. He hesitated before finding the right words. "Sir, I have reason to believe the humans we are escorting are plotting to ambush us once we enter the Ivion Gate. I am requesting the gate be cleared before our entry citing laws regarding prisoner transport and security. As you know, the Tel'stra Treaty dictates that aggression from non-Confederation nations within the Ivion Gate is a violation of the Vectus Code and can result in an immediate declaration of war. It is my hope to prevent unnecessary deaths until Bastian authority declares it. Thank you for your time. Captain Viar."

He closed the recording and dispatched it, reclaiming his seat so he could brood at the *Veritas*.

Viar knew more about Bastian and human history than most of the scholars on his home world did. He lived through much of the worst parts. His father had laid down his life in one of the last major skirmishes. The result was the removal of the human tyrant running the Confederation. Director Artimus Chancey had been a scoundrel and a thorn in the Bastian peoples' side for many years. His false accusations painted the Bastia like monsters.

Captain Viar's father had been a hero before he took action, but where history got it wrong was that his attack was not one of terrorism, it was one of preservation for his people. Director Chancey had sided with the Kruva in a public dispute that was intended to provoke a war. Before word could spread, the senior Viar released a toxin targeting the human scum.

That spelled the end of Director Chancey's run of the Confederation and the Bastia saw to putting a more reasonable member in that role. They may not be part of the Confederation, but their threats proved just as powerful as their votes once had. Control had its privileges. But now it seemed that they were paying for their mistakes.

To avoid genocide charges, the Bastian leadership bargained with the surviving Director of the Galactic Confederation. They were the architects of their own destruction unless they did as they were told. The Kruva were ready to strike and the allies within the Confederation had agreed to all-out war if the Bastia "stepped out of line again".

The Bastia may have been relegated to their own system, but the invitation to escort the human ship gave them free passage. If this wasn't a trap, then it would be the first step towards reclaiming what they had lost.

And it would be a gift freely given by the same people who snatched it away in the first place.

"How quickly they forget," Captain Viar said under his breath. "But you'll remember soon enough."

GCS Veritas

Garret woke from his slumber, his eyes heavy. He rolled over, feeling the cold steel of the bulkhead against his back. A small part of him resented waking up at all. He longed for all of this to be over.

He longed for a lot of things.

"Lights dim please."

The overheads shone dully, revealing the cramped space around him. They were better accommodations than he was used to, even if they did remind him of captivity.

Garret sat up on his knees and began stretching, trying to get the kinks out from sleeping on a thin mattress. A few vertebrae

OBLIVION'S DAWN

popped satisfactorily before he climbed to his feet and exited the room.

Having free reign over the ship had been an unexpected courtesy. Of course, he was limited to what he could control, but all the amenities were available, and he gleaned enough from the ambassador to have some idea of what was happening at any given time. She even authorized him to have access to the map to know their location.

He stopped at a monitor mounted to the bulkhead and noted that the ship had already made one of several scheduled jumps. With each jump, they would be closer to his ultimate demise. He should be afraid, but if anything, he was at peace. This had been a long time coming.

Garret stepped away from the monitor and entered the bridge. Ambassador Spar sat at the console, holding her head in her hands, but she wasn't crying, she was reading.

"I found something you might find interesting," she said as he walked past her.

"What might that be?"

She turned the tablet over to him and revealed a declassified document with his birth name on it. He read through the file before something caught his attention. "This is an obituary," he said under his breath. "For me?"

Ambassador Spar straightened her shoulders and met his gaze. "These documents say that the Bastian attack was biological in nature. A toxin meant to kill every human in the room. You ultimately died with your mother."

Garret stammered before finding the words, "That can't be. I remember watching her die. I remember the Bastia agreeing to help save her. I've seen my stepfather age ever since. If they were targeting humans, then that would mean..."

"That Director Chancey wasn't there, or he isn't human," Ambassador Spar finished.

169

DAVE ALEXANDER

Garret swore under his breath. "I can't believe this. Even my own past isn't true."

"You had no way of knowing?"

He shook his head. "No. The Bastia have superior composite technology, but I think I would have noticed the number inked into my neck before I went to military school."

"Could they have implanted memories into you?"

Garret shrugged. "I imagine anything is possible, but for me to have memories like this I would have had to live through them. There's no trickery that can plant someone else's memories into yours. The kind of splicing of minds that would require is far beyond the technology available to us. I lived this life, but I don't remember dying during that attack."

The ambassador sat back in her chair and stared at him. She was reading his expression, trying to find fault in what he said, but she wouldn't find anything. He was telling her the truth, as impossible as it might sound.

"Let's say you're telling me the truth..."

"I am," he shot back.

"All right. If this is true, then what happened to get you to this point? I know enough about you to know that you have two composites, which is an obvious violation of law. What else could there be?"

Garret racked his brain trying to figure out the missing pieces to his memory. "Is this being recorded?"

The ambassador nodded.

"Fine, let this be documented as part of my testimony."

"All right," she agreed. "Let's begin."

Tella listened to every word, from his simple beginnings as the son of a mercenary, to the whirlwind experience of becoming the

170

OBLIVION'S DAWN

stepson of the Director of the Galactic Confederation. He painted each major scene in his life with details the layperson wouldn't mention, from smells to emotions. His brow furrowed when he spoke of Director Chancey but softened when he reflected upon his mother.

It was the attack that brought a different perspective to the way she viewed him.

"It was supposed to be a gala where human ambassadors met with peers from other species. A formal invitation was sent to the Bastian in good faith. They, of course, requested neutral terms for meeting, so it was agreed that the gala would take place on Obitus so every citizen had access to the Ivion Gate.

"Humans hosted the event, and my mother was on edge. Artimus had a swagger about him, something wasn't quite right. In later years I recognized that look as one he wore when he acted deceptively, but as a ten-year-old I was oblivious.

"The Veshnians and Litar were among the first to arrive, followed soon after by the Af'shai who seemed to only be there out of obligation. Hardly any of the other allied factions joined us on Obitus, though the Bastia arrived. Their captain, a man named Cen Viar, stepped up to my stepfather and spoke angrily while the rest of the guests were distracted by their own conversations. I often sat between them at these events, but my mother pushed her way in front of me, blocking my view. A few seconds later I heard a hissing sound and my mother collapsed. Artimus rose from his seat and shouted for security and all I remember is watching Captain Viar walk away with his back to me.

"I can still smell the gas; it was sweet with only a tinge of acidity to it. Artimus scooped my mother up and ran off with her, leaving me to sit in front of all those guests as they scampered around frantically. The Veshnians were useless, but the Litar sprung to action and helped others who were infected. All in all, about a dozen humans died, but nothing was done to the Bastia because the attack wasn't perceived as an order from the Supreme Commander. The captain of that ship acted of his own accord and for some reason Artimus didn't engage militarily. Instead, he sought the help of the Bastia to heal my mothers' condition and negotiated terms with their Supreme Commander to exact justice on the man who who had harmed her.

"Captain Viar orbited that world waiting for something to happen, but Artimus let him leave, granting him access to the Ivion Gate. I thought it was strange until I saw that look on his face again. Later reports said that the Bastian captain felt guilty and destroyed his own ship. The truth is, Artimus changed the access code for the gate and the Bastian vessel was destroyed as it breached the gate."

Garret stopped talking for a moment, confusion enveloping his face. Tella watched him with anticipation, longing to hear what happened next.

"Artimus reached a deal with the Bastia. He agreed to step down as Director of the Galactic Confederation in exchange for the lifesaving treatments my mother needed. He knew their composite technology was superior to ours, so they made certain promises. One of those promises was that Artimus could exact revenge, but only if he directed it at the man responsible. The Bastian Supreme Commander was behind the plan that destroyed that ship."

"None of this is common knowledge," Tella said after several moments of silence. "I've seen records stating that Artimus passed away, but nothing about what you mentioned."

Garret nodded. "They were planted there by his successor. The ruse is to slowly chip away at the Confederation's power and strengthen Bastian influence. It's been thirty years, and look at where we are – the brink of war with an enemy that can easily destroy us. The sad part is their aggression is based on a lie. They'll use that attack in the Ivion Gate to justify their anger but

OBLIVION'S DAWN

deny that the Bastian Supreme Commander came up with the plan in the first place.

"My opinion is that Captain Viar was the scapegoat in a political ploy. My mother was a victim of the wrong place at the wrong time. Artimus was the primary target, but somehow she got in the way and saved us both."

"But at some point, you died," Tella said. "How did you come to have two composites?"

Garret shrugged. "I don't know. I was augmented with a cerebral port as a teenager and my memories were downloaded in case I ever needed a composite." He pointed at the cerebral port situated behind his left ear. It was similar to the one Tella had behind her ear. "It's based on the Bastian model which can print a fully functional composite in two days. The same tech was used on my mother. I don't remember dying, but I do remember Artimus making the decision that when my mother woke up, she shouldn't see me as a middle-aged man. So, when I come to on Bastia, I'm in this skin. When I come to for an assignment, I'm my older self."

Tella contemplated what this meant. It was a clear violation of the technology, but the Bastia were no longer part of the Confederation and didn't recognize those laws. Composite guidance was never discussed in the treaty; therefore, the Confederation had no recourse for what was happening. "Are you ever in both composites at the same time?" Tella asked.

Her question caught Garret oddly. His eyes narrowed ever so slightly before he answered. "No, I've never been in both composites at the same time. I don't think that's possible."

"Are you sure? You said it yourself, the Bastian technology is superior to everyone else's."

Without missing a beat, he replied, "It's not possible. I've asked Artimus to dozens of times for my mother's sake. Each time she gets worse and rots away over the course of several

DAVE ALEXANDER

months. We have to wait until she expires to recomposite her. Those months are Hell on all of us."

Tella understood, but something gnawed at the back of her mind. Perhaps it was that the fact history was a well-documented lie? Or maybe it was the fact that the Bastia were manipulating the GC and there was no way to hold them accountable without revealing everything. Even then, the allies in the Confederation might simply turn a blind eye to it. Peace was proctored by cowardice, but they viewed it as being superior.

It was the farthest thing from the truth and humanity was going to pay for it.

TWENTY-FIVE
EARTH

"DIRECTOR, I DON'T KNOW HOW THIS IS POSSIBLE," GENERAL Treff said as he looked at the report. "I thought we agreed to not give authorization to deploy?"

"I didn't," Cantor said. He was seated at his desk, slouching over it with his hands clasped like he was praying.

"So, is she running?" Treff asked.

Director Cantor shook his head. "The Bastia are within weapons range. If she were running away from them, they would annihilate her. Somehow, Ambassador Spar convinced them to escort her halfway across the galaxy."

Both men sat in silence for a long time with nothing more than the sound of heavy winds beating against the thick windows. A storm was rolling in, heavy black clouds charging towards them like inevitable destruction.

"Could she be working with the Bastia to lead them here?" the General asked.

"If she were, why would she have asked permission in the first place?"

"To give the illusion she's following protocol?"

Cantor scoffed. "Spar isn't a mastermind like that," he said.

175

DAVE ALEXANDER

"She is a good ambassador in that she does what she's told and doesn't create a fuss about it. I wish the others were more like her...at least I did."

"Then perhaps the Bastia forced her hand?" General Treff stood up and paced the room. He wasn't in uniform as was customary, as Cantor had called him in for an emergency meeting. Even without his adornments, the killer instinct that got Treff to the top of command staff showed in his eyes.

"It seems that way for now."

"Have you sent correspondence to Spar?"

Cantor shook his head. "I've done nothing. That's why I sent for you. Let's say your theory about the Bastia forcing her to act is true. Then any correspondence I sent would be intercepted, wouldn't it?"

Treff agreed and cleared his throat. "Unless we encrypt it."

"With what? The Bastia aren't stupid. They'd look for that."

"So, do you want to continue to do nothing? You didn't have to pull me out of bed for that." Treff's eyes narrowed. The flash of anger was barely controlled, like a wild dog on a chain.

Cantor knew what would happen if Treff lost his head, so he settled on not antagonizing the older man. "I think it's best to monitor for now. Perhaps dispatch ships to the Ivion Gate to aid in the escort?"

It was Treff's turn to scoff. "You do realize that sending more ships would look like an act of aggression, don't you? The Bastia would destroy them all, then keep coming to finish the job. Every colony in Sol would burn."

Cantor sank back in his seat. He didn't care if the General looked at him as weak. The General didn't have the lives of trillions of people in his hands. "Fine, what would you suggest that wouldn't wipe us out?"

Treff made several passes of the room before turning back to the Director. "If we don't send a message directly to Spar, then perhaps we can send one to the Ivion Gate. Update the authorization codes for entry and have them tight beam her an encrypted message on our behalf?"

A smile curled Cantor's lip. *Why hadn't I thought of that?* "I think you're on to something. Can you formulate the appropriate messages and forward them to me?"

"Of course," Treff replied.

The General's anger had subsided as his ego was thoroughly stroked by Cantor's praise. Every man had his price and Cantor knew how to spend appropriately.

"We need to dispatch the message before they enter the Obitus System. I don't want to leave anything to chance."

"Understood, sir. I'll get on it right away."

Cantor nodded and the General dismissed himself. Several seconds of silence passed before a voice sounded from the speaker on his desk. "You're playing a game with people's lives."

"I know, but it's necessary to make it look like we hadn't anticipated this. I suppose I should thank you for the information?"

"No thanks necessary. I just want what I asked for," the voice said. "Don't cross me, and I'll make sure the Bastia don't act foolish."

Cantor cut his eyes at the device on his desk and wished he could see the face behind the voice. "Who are you to command the most powerful military in the galaxy?"

A pause preceded the answer, "I was like you once, burdened and with my back against the wall. When I was on the verge of losing everything, I found what strength was needed to get my people through. It isn't easy, but it is necessary to ensure survival. I need you to trust me."

"Hmm, that would be easier if I knew who you were," Cantor replied.

"Careful what you wish for, my friend. Sometimes knowing

the truth turns your world upside down. I'll do what I can on my end. Just keep your end of the bargain."

"Yes, you get the prisoner and the ambassador."

"A small price to pay, I assure you."

Cantor didn't respond to that. For a man who traded lives for a living, this time felt different. He wasn't negotiating for the release of prisoners. He was compromising his authority for an unknown.

"I'll be in touch," the voice said before closing the connection.

A chill ran down Cantor's spine as he peered out the window at the approaching storm. Lightning flashed in the distance, painting the silver clouds in deep blues and purples. Whistling wind beat against the window and he wondered how much force the glass could take before it succumbed to the pressure.

So long as it held, then maybe he could bear his burden as well.

GCS Veritas

Dwelling on thoughts of his mother wasting away was difficult. While he hid away on a ship in hopes of righting past wrongs, she was slowly decaying on an alien world. It was hard not resenting everyone and everything surrounding his family life. Why couldn't he have grown up as a normal kid instead of carrying all this guilt?

Misplaced or not, the constant gnawing on his emotions got the better of him. It turned him towards darkness. She would be ashamed if she knew what he had become to save her. He was ashamed for her, but like a fool, he kept digging deeper, offering to do the Bastia's bidding in his desperation.

OBLIVION'S DAWN

Then there was Ambassador Spar and her questions. Have you ever been in both composites at once? What kind of question was that? One would think someone in the Confederation would know the science behind the technology they so freely used. He trod lightly on answering those questions though. He didn't know how much of what he knew was true, so he dodged the more difficult ones when he could.

Besides, this was about Artimus and his evil partnership with the Bastia. The composite technology was simply a tool they used to deliver violence across the galaxy. Take that away, and they would focus on something else. The tool didn't make the killer. The killer made the tool.

"Tell me about the first time you knew what was happening," Tella said, pulling Garret from his thoughts.

He cleared his throat and reflected on his past. "I was a teenager and these Bastian doctors kept coming to our home. I was the only human kid on their planet, so I was being home-schooled by one of my father's aides. Her name was Utra, a Litar who had come from her home on Mars to serve him. She was very nice to me, but she tended to think out loud. She made an offhand comment about the shamefulness of what my stepfather was doing. I waited until she left for the day to bring it up, and Artimus went into a rage. He began smashing things and became very violent. I was afraid because I had never seen this kind of display from him before. My fears grew worse when he called for Utra."

Garret stopped talking and sucked in several breaths as he fought to steady his nerves. "She was defiant and bold to the person who declared authority over her. Artimus looked at her as a servant, as lesser than him. There was shouting and I was pulled from the room by someone else, I can't remember who. I broke free from them and ran back to where Artimus and Utra were in time to see him level a gun at her face. I remember closing my

DAVE ALEXANDER

eyes, thinking I was seeing things. A shot rang out. I refused to open my eyes at first, but someone was shaking me, and when I opened my eyes, I saw Utra laying in a pool of her own blood.

"It wasn't long after that I was sent to military school. Artimus later staged his own death, and I was free of the burden of protecting his secrets. I ran away and became a mercenary like my birth father. Eventually, I was pulled back into Artimus' snare. He dangled my mother's life in front of me like a carrot, leading me down whichever path he chose. I'm not a good man. I'd killed for money long before Artimus snatched me back to Bastia, but I recognize the evil he's part of. I just didn't know how to get out of it."

They sat together on the bridge of the *Veritas*, two people from different worlds, both burdened with their past failures more than anyone else could know. He saw it in her eyes, in the way her pupils grew smaller and her lids puffed up before they welled with tears. Her heart broke for someone she didn't even know. His heart was broken for the person he never became.

It was a shame.

"I'm afraid I don't know what to offer you for your testimony," Tella said finally. "I know what you're telling me is true. I hear it in your voice and the AI scanning you for fault in your words came back with no anomalies." She continued scanning the tablet before her. "If we bring this to the Confederation, they could throw it out and claim it is too dangerous."

"They're afraid of war," Garret said. "Fear is the Bastia's most powerful tool. That's how they control everyone, even their own people."

"How do you combat fear?" Ambassador Spar asked, her eyes leaving the tablet and meeting his gaze.

Garret swallowed the knot in his throat. "You become the fear."

As the ship neared its next jump point, Tella contemplated Garret's words. "You become the fear," she repeated, her voice barely above a whisper. It sounded odd when he first said it, but the more she repeated it like a mantra, the easier it was to see how Garret used those words over his own life. He had become that fear as a weapon used by the Bastia.

With no military training, she didn't know how that would be useful to a soldier's psyche, but she had seen reports of many beliefs and philosophies perverted over the years to justify all kinds of horrors. Perhaps this was more of the same? She could only assume so.

Tella turned away from the console and approached the bulkhead service door to retrieve another tube of protein. She couldn't remember the last time she'd eaten with all the stress of escaping that planet. Had it really been before landing her pod on Bastia? If so, then she was long overdue for sustenance.

She opened it with her teeth and squeezed the paste into her mouth. It was like all food in space, tasteless with the worst texture imaginable. A delicacy for anyone starving, though she assumed there may be at least one holdout in the galaxy if surviving meant living off this stuff. In many cultures, life wasn't worth living if the food wasn't good. It was a primitive way of looking at life. Then again, humans had a history of eating dirt and rocks if they were desperate enough.

Thankfully she didn't have to resort to such measures.

"Ambassador, we are entering the jump window."

"Excellent, can you coordinate with our escorts again?"

"Yes, Ambassador."

Tella reclaimed her seat at the console and eyed the monitor warily. The Bastian ships kept an appropriate distance, but their looming presence was still unsettling.

This next jump would bring them to the Obitus System and within hours of the Ivion Gate. She knew enough to have a modicum of excitement about it. The technology used to bring the gate to life allowed galactic citizens to traverse the stars. Without it, each civilization would be limited to its own star systems, or heavily rely on unreliable jump drives to get them great distances.

Early drives would fail and leave the ship in a dead float. Without propulsion, the ship was vulnerable to the gravitational forces nearby. With hundreds of records of lost ships, she often wondered how many were unknown.

It had to be thousands across the span of centuries.

"The Bastia have given us permission to jump at our leisure. They have provided coordinates. Would you like me to begin?"

"Yes," Tella answered.

The *Veritas* began jump procedures and Tella returned her attention to the Ivion Gate. Three-hundred and sixty gates were connected to it. Archaic language called the connections "wormholes," based on a primitive understanding of quantum mechanics. Early versions of the science held a limited view of what was necessary to go from one point in the galaxy to another. The technological breakthrough which opened the path to galactic travel operated at the sixth and seventh dimensions simultaneously.

Even centuries after figuring it out, most laypeople had trouble understanding it. What Tella did know was that using the gates was expensive. Hytocosic crystals were the primary resource. Others were available but lacked in sufficient quality to power the gate technology. Obitus had been a major hytocosic crystal mining colony in centuries past, but most of its supply had been blasted out of the ground. To maintain travel, other colonies rich in the resource had been taken over by the Confederation. It was a point of contention between many citizens, but free and open travel across the stars was lucrative in more ways than one. Where some factions chose to serve the galaxy with surplus goods

OBLIVION'S DAWN

and opportunities to work, others focused on military strength by positioning themselves in high-traffic areas to offer protection against piracy.

In the end, those with the power did as they wanted.

The ship engaged the jump drive and Tella experienced the sinking feeling. She held onto the console, trying to steady herself, but there was no orientation that was truly steady as her middle ear sensed motion in all directions at once. A moment later the ship's new coordinates were displayed on the map. In the center of the map was the Ivion Gate. On the display, it appeared as large as a planet, but that was a misrepresentation. Though it was enormous, it was no larger in circumference than Luna.

"Traffic to the Ivion Gate is practically nonexistent," the AI declared. *"I'm not detecting any flaws in its operations, though."*

"Prisoner transport protocol," Garret said as he entered the bridge. He was walking better now that his injuries had been treated. He no longer clutched his side with one hand as he moved. "The Bastia don't want other ships in the gate while we pass through. They anticipate an ambush."

"They have superior ships, what do they have to fear?" Tella asked.

Garret scoffed. "It's not fear. It's an unwillingness to compromise. Their mission is to get me on their ship and take me back and kill me. They won't let anything interrupt that mission."

"Still, shutting down the gate traffic doesn't solve their problem, does it?" Garret took a seat across from her. He winced, just a little, she noticed.

"If Earth wanted to ambush them, then they would have ships stationed just inside the gate. Once the bigger Bastian ships entered, they would be prone to several tactics that could destroy them."

Tella frowned. She knew Director Cantor wouldn't risk setting

DAVE ALEXANDER

up an ambush on her behalf, but she wished he would. That would make what they planned to do easier.

"Would a ship of this size be able to take one of them out?" she asked.

"Does this ship have weapons?"

"It has Point Defense Countermeasures, but no offensive weaponry."

Garret let out a sigh. "Then no. In fact, I don't know if the PDCs would be able to withstand a full-scale attack from them. But you already knew that, didn't you?"

Tella cut her eyes at him. "I suspected, but I'm not in the business of knowing how to defeat my enemies."

"That's why the Bastia don't take human involvement in the Confederation seriously. They teach that you should always be six steps in front of your enemy. The Confederation teaches that you should meet them for tea and offer them their demands in exchange for peace. It's pitiful and weak in the eyes of a superior force."

Tella sat back in her chair. She didn't know whether to be intrigued by his viewpoint or insulted. Protecting peace was her duty. It was expected.

"What do you think is right?" Tella asked.

He sat silent for several moments before answering, "I think the Bastia are right, but I also think that without peace the entire galaxy would eventually be destroyed. There's strength in resilience. Not giving up against unfavorable odds isn't weak. The Bastia just don't recognize strength if it isn't deployed through violence."

Tella smiled. Perhaps there was hope, then, that this didn't have to end with their deaths.

It was a truth they were soon to find out.

184

TWENTY-SIX
BNV POURGUA

"THE SHIP IS READY TO MAKE THE JUMP, SIR," LIEUTENANT NRA said. The puzzled expression on his young face proved his lack of experience. Following the humans so eagerly would lead to ruin.

"Hold back for now." Captain Viar eyed the monitor and waited for the *Nir* to populate in the Obitus System before giving the order. It appeared a few seconds after the *Veritas*. Another minute without a distress beacon and the *Pourgua* would follow, but not a second before.

The lieutenant stood dumbly, just to the side of the captain. The fidgeting of his hands was a distraction and Captain Viar resisted the urge to dismiss him from the bridge. His focus needed to be on the mission and looking for any entrapments the human scum could have prepared for them. The Bastia were no longer in the comfort of their own system. They were at the mercy of intergalactic space.

Only a fool would be comfortable here in the expansive darkness.

The timer rolled over to the next minute and Viar gripped the armrest of his seat as he gave the order. "Proceed to jump," he said, tightening his grip with anticipation. The slightest flicker

DAVE ALEXANDER

occurred in the overhead lighting as power was momentarily channeled to the jump drive. A second later the *Pourgua* left its position in relative space and reappeared in the Obitus System trailing the other ships.

He didn't even feel the jumps anymore. Years of traveling the stars faster than the speed of light had numbed him to the sensation. The same could not be said for his lieutenant, who was still clutching to the support beam and holding onto his stomach.

"Did you eat recently?" Captain Viar asked without looking at the young man.

"Yes, sir."

Viar smirked. He knew the feeling well. His father had thought it would be funny to trick him into eating a large meal before his first jump. The cleanup efforts afterwards were a hit to his ego but looking back it was one of his fondest memories of his father. It was one where he was with the old man and the elder captain wasn't focused solely on work. It was before he was driven mad and hellbent on annihilating the humans.

It was the calm before the storm.

"Next time, don't eat within two hours of the jump cycle. It's also best not to eat anything greasy. People tend to learn that the hard way."

Lieutenant Nra gave a curt nod and thanked the captain before returning to his console. He was still fidgeting and Viar wondered if there was something about the man he should be concerned with. Viar had only recently taken command of the *Pourgua*, and there were only two members of the crew he had served with prior. That lack of familiarity was an inhibitor to his leadership. He made a mental note to address it when time provided and focused on the monitor once more.

"We are six hours from the Ivion Gate at our current speed, Captain."

"Maintain it for now," Viar ordered. "As long as the *Veritas*

OBLIVION'S DAWN

maintains its speed, we'll maintain ours. I don't want to get too close."

"Yes, sir," his lieutenant answered without facing the commanding officer.

Viar watched the man's fingers dance across the console. The map displayed on his screens shifted in position with each calculation the computer made. The captain could see that there was no traffic in and out of the Ivion Gate as he had requested. That was a good sign. It meant no one was waiting for them just beyond sight.

However, that could change as soon as the ships exited on the other side of the galaxy.

Captain Viar keyed his comm and said, "I want a status report for all weapons. If it isn't loaded and ready to fire, I want it done before we enter the Ivion Gate."

A voice answered back an affirmation.

The *Pourgua* would be ready for whatever was about to happen. Viar wouldn't let history repeat itself. If anyone was going to die for their world, then it would be the humans. They brought this on themselves. They deserved what was coming.

Captain Viar rose from his seat and announced his departure. The crew on the bridge snapped to attention, to which the captain dismissed them quickly so their focus could be on their work.

In the meantime, he needed to be alone with his thoughts.

Earth

The notification that the *Veritas* and her escorts arrived in the Obitus System pulled Director Cantor from his sleep. "Four hours," he grumbled. He couldn't remember the last time he had a

DAVE ALEXANDER

full night's sleep. *Probably before I assumed the title of Director*, he thought dismissively.

In truth, he liked his job. It came with benefits, best of which was knowing what no one else on the planet knew. First to know was a point of honor. But it was also a thorn in his side at times.

Cantor crawled out of bed and switched on the lights. His master bedroom was larger than most of the commoners' entire quarters. Eight hundred square feet of luxury with a view. He even had his own space dock for a private shuttle to transport him to Luna in the event he needed to leave Earth. From Luna, Mars was little more than twelve hours away via jump drive. He hated leaving his home world, though. Earth was beautiful even after its destruction.

The Karnack military had done its worst but failed to destroy mankind. The allies preserved humanity and all that was left of the once great Karnack was a ball of ruin on the other side of the galaxy. Humans were still there, taking lives as needed to prevent another incursion of violence against their planetary mother. Decades later, there was still no decisive victory. Just "the killing road," a trade route littered with the remains of dead soldiers from both sides hanging from pikes like decorations.

The building of "the killing road" was an act used to intimidate humans, but the warriors of Earth had turned it into a taunting game. The images Cantor had seen were enough to induce nightmares. The luxuries afforded him as a man of power, such as wealth and protectection were what separated him from the realities out there. So, he returned to that comforting seat of power as often as he could, shielded by Earth's mighty defenses.

Another alert sounded, but it wasn't an automatically generated message. Director Cantor opened the file to see a hologram of Ambassador Spar. Even with the glitching feed, she appeared exhausted. He supposed she deserved it for going rogue the way

188

OBLIVION'S DAWN

she did, but if she was reaching out, then that meant she needed something only he could provide.

He groaned before allowing it to play.

"Director Cantor, I know I'm the last person you expected to reach out to you, but I have an urgent message. Garret Chancey is still willing to turn state's evidence against those responsible for the gruesome attacks on our bordering colonies. He has detailed many things during our trek and has much more to disclose, but we are seeking political asylum. I fear that returning to Earth would be an immediate death sentence for both of us.

"We wish to turn ourselves over to the Director of the Intergalactic Authority at the Embassy on Mars. Archea should be less than a day's travel for you and also hosts the Litar Director of the Galactic Confederation, Director Igvi. I have already made the arrangements with them in hopes to make this as painless as possible.

"We have entered the Obitus System and are two days out from Mars. The Bastian ships are still escorting us, though I anticipate they are planning something. One of the ships is trailing rather far behind and Garret tells me it is equipped with long-range stealth weapons. I am unsure whether the *Veritas* has the capability of warding off such an attack. Additionally, the Ivion Gate is empty of all inbound and outbound traffic for the duration of our journey here. Garret suspects, and I agree, that any attack will likely take place once we pass through the gate.

"I hope that you will aid us in our travel and allow us the opportunity to explain ourselves in person. In the meantime, I am attaching a clip of my interrogation of Garret Cushing. I believe you will find it as compelling as I have.

"Thank you."

Cantor stopped the playback of Ambassador Spar's message and opened the second file. It was audio only, but he didn't need to see her face to recognize Spar's voice. She asked him to

DAVE ALEXANDER

continue and then the male spoke. He sounded young, no more than mid-twenties, if that, but his vocabulary was well beyond his years. For a mercenary, he was graceful in speech. Cantor imagined years of grooming for politics had trained him to engage in such a way but trusting a viper would get you killed.

This man had destroyed entire colonies and now claimed to seek peace? Director Cantor didn't buy it. Cushing would just as soon annihilate humanity if given the opportunity, same as the Bastia.

That was why Cantor wasn't about to extend the opportunity.

He made a call to General Treff.

"Yes, sir?"

"Did the correspondence go out to change the authorization codes for the Ivion Gate?"

Treff cleared his throat and answered, "It has been sent half a dozen times, but keeps failing to deliver. It's unclear whether the issue is on our end or theirs."

Cantor swore through his teeth. "They're hours away from using the gate and only two days away from our system." He began pacing the room while Treff stammered to come up with an explanation. None of it met the director's satisfaction. "I need to keep the Bastia out of Sol. Give me something to work with, General." Cantor's words snapped from his lips.

A pause followed, then a simple reply. "If you can communicate with the *Veritas*, then you can have Ambassador Spar ask to change the authorization codes."

"I don't want any of those ships to arrive, General. Giving her the authorization codes defeats the purpose."

Treff sighed over the comm and Cantor prepared to make Treff pay for whatever half-witted remark would follow.

"Sir, the Bastia are the biggest threat. If we stop them at the Ivion Gate and cut off their travel route, then we can always destroy the *Veritas* when it arrives."

OBLIVION'S DAWN

Cantor's jaw went slack. He wanted to poke a jab at the senior officer's intellect, but the truth was the General's idea was plausible. He knew that destroying the Ivion Gate would bring the wrath of the allies, but if it appeared the Bastian were at fault, then maybe he could get away with it.

"Do it," Cantor ordered, "and let me know when it's done. I don't want this hanging over my head all night."

"Yes, sir," Treff replied.

Cantor cut off the comm and stared out the window at the blanket of darkness sweeping across the planet. Above, lights from Luna sparkled like fireflies. And beyond that hallowed rock locked in Earth's orbit was the sanctuary his ambassador expected to arrive to. If she made it, then his time as Director of the Galactic Confederation could be through.

He couldn't let her destroy all he had worked so hard for.

One way or another, Ambassador Spar had to go away.

GCS Veritas

Two hours separated them from the Ivion Gate. The Bastia maintained radio silence, but that was to be expected, considering all her transmissions had been autonomous via the ship's AI. Still, it was unsettling how quiet this place was. Even broadband channels were silent. The only voices she heard were the operators controlling traffic through the gate, of which there was none due to the Bastian's orders.

"I hope you're wrong about this," Tella said. She didn't want to look him in the face, at the stern expression that suggested he knew what was about to happen. For all she knew, he was as clueless as she was, but he didn't give an inch of his stoic pride towards self-doubt.

191

DAVE ALEXANDER

"If it's any consolation, I hope I'm wrong too. I'll admit, this is a long way to travel for a ruse."

It was the closest thing to worry that she was going to get from him. If anyone knew what was possible, it would be Garret. He worked for them for the last thirty years, though his tactics and methods were purely human. He had the closest glimpse of how the Bastian war machine operated, at least on the psychological battlefield.

He was their long-range weapon for such attacks. Send him and a small team to disrupt things, then kill them off and print their composites somewhere else for the next mission. All this time, the Confederation thought the attacks were about money, or simply rebellious humans with no known intentions.

How wrong they were.

If only it were that simple.

"Once we're inside the gate, how long will we be vulnerable?"

"Less than a minute," Garret said. "But we have to contend with the possibility they have a ship waiting on the other side of the jump. Our coordinates were planned before departure. Any changes on our end would be seen."

"Can we deviate at all?" Tella asked. Her concern for their safety grew with each breath. She didn't want to waste the opportunity they had to stop unnecessary bloodshed, but his testimony had to be formally given in person. According to Confederation law, a recording would not suffice due to the ease by which the technology could be falsified or manipulated. If they were to save humanity, they first had to save themselves.

"If you can change the jump coordinates just before entering the gate, then it might send us somewhere outside their detectable range. It's risky, and if it fails, they'll know you tried to evade them. That's all the justification they'll need to fire on us."

192

"They must know that the request for escorting us was a ruse, then?"

Garret nodded. He sat back in his seat with his feet kicked up on the console. His knowing eyes met hers and sent a chill down her spine. Did he suggest sending the message knowing they would see through the lie? Was all this an elaborate setup?

Tella didn't want to know the answer if she was wrong in trusting him.

She didn't want to face the fact that she had chosen poorly, and both times resulted in a massacre. The burden of guilt was too much.

"Ambassador, the level of encryption used to mask your transmission should not have easily been broken. It is possible that the Bastia still believe the message was from Director Cantor," the AI said.

She wished she felt relieved by the possibility, but if anything, she was numb to hope.

"That's if Cantor didn't send his own correspondence to the Bastian after the fact," Garret grumbled. "He could have snitched us out without knowing. The Bastian would play along until they had us dead to rights."

"Can we discuss something else, please?" Tella snapped. She didn't mean to act irrationally, but between the words said aloud and the torment in her mind, she needed a break from the constant dread.

"Like what?" Garret asked.

"I don't know. I just want to focus my attention on something that matters."

A long silence filled the empty space between them until Garret spoke again. "What if we created a failsafe in case of our demise?"

Tella cut her eyes at the mercenary. She knew where this was going. She wanted to refuse, but inevitabilities weighed heavily

DAVE ALEXANDER

on her shoulders. Curiosity broke her and she asked, "What do you have in mind?"

The slightest of smiles turned Garret's lips. The expression in his eyes revealed his elation as he suggested downloading their consciousness and preprogramning an immediate composition upon their deaths. "As soon as our hearts stop beating, the composite will begin constructing. We can pick up where we left off."

"I used a similar protocol when I left for Bala. There will be gaps in memory that make coming to during these situations difficult. We would need to wait until the last minute."

"Memory gaps from here on out won't be as damaging as having nothing since our previous compositions came to. It's worth the effort...in my onion."

Of course, it is, she thought. "AI, how long would the downloads take for both of us?"

"That depends on the amount of information already available on the network. If Garret Cushing's consciousness is uploaded only to the Bastian mainframe, then his downloads may take several hours."

"That's not enough time before we reach the gate," Tella said.

"Perhaps we should get started and hope for the best? If we are attacked, then at least we tried."

Tella didn't like it, but she didn't see much choice either way. Doing nothing meant critical information would be lost.

"Fine, do it. Once it's complete I'll download mine," Tella said.

"Yes, Ambassador," Garret said reverently as he rose from his seat and left the bridge to go to the medical bay.

"AI, I want you to keep me abreast of his progress."

"As you wish, Ambassador."

"One other thing," Tella said. "If he schedules a composition on Bastia, I want you to refuse it."

OBLIVION'S DAWN

"Are there any other parameters I should refuse?"

"Just that one. If he plans on betraying us, then he'll run back to the Bastia the first opportunity he gets. I won't let him get away with that."

"Yes, Ambassador. If the request is made, where should I send the composition?"

Tella pondered it a moment then answered, "Earth. If he chooses to betray humanity, then maybe it's time for him to go home?"

TWENTY-SEVEN
GCS VERITAS

GARRET ENTERED THE MEDICAL BAY AND BRUSHED THE HAIR AWAY from the cerebral port behind his left ear. He fell into the chair and reclined back, preparing to plug himself into the database when he paused.

"AI, are you listening?"

"*Yes.*"

"She doesn't trust me, does she?" He felt like a child asking the question, but he couldn't escape the nagging feeling crawling in the back of his mind. Regardless of his point of view, her opinion of him would always be tainted by his past, a stain on what should have been a remarkable life.

"Logically, she trusts you more than she should. Despite knowing what you and your men did to her on Bala, she *went out of her way to rescue you from the Bastia. However, if she did not believe you had information that might save lives, then she would not have put herself at such risk.*"

Garret narrowed his eyes at the machine surrounding him. There was no fixed point to stare at the AI and converse. But staring at nothing was like looking at God Almighty while drifting at sea. You might not see anything distinguishable, but

OBLIVION'S DAWN

that didn't mean He didn't see you. "I may need you to do me a favor."

"*I am to do as requested so long as it does not jeopardize Ambassador Spar's mission.*"

"I need you to allow me to reconstruct on Bastia in the event of my death."

"*I am under orders from Ambassador Spar not to allow that.*"

Garret clinched his jaw and bit back the words forming on the tip of his tongue. She was ahead of him and never let on, but he doubted she knew the real reason for his request. Convincing her to make an exception would be like pulling teeth. "She wants me reconstructed on Earth, doesn't she?"

"*Yes.*"

"You said that you are allowed to do as requested so that it does not jeopardize her mission, correct?"

"*Yes.*"

Garret let out a stale breath and said, "What if her mission fails unless I am granted permission to return to Bastia?"

"*Nothing has yet led me to believe that is a possibility,*" the AI replied.

"That's because I haven't said everything. My full testimony would take days to tell, not hours."

"*Then perhaps you should relay this information to the ambassador so she can decide on a better outcome?*"

Garret sucked in a deep breath and resisted the urge to raise his voice. "I understand you're merely doing as she has ordered, but what I have to do can't be known by anyone. If she or anyone elseprevents me from returning, then the GC will not be able to stop a war with the Bastia. I need to give my testimony, then return."

"*Why?*"

"Because that's how it needs to be," Garret replied. "If I die before we reach Mars, then I'm dead. The Confederation doesn't

DAVE ALEXANDER

have my memories stored in their database. They can't just bring me back to get the information they need. Artimus thought about everything. He's six steps ahead of them in every way. This needs to happen for us to succeed."

"*That's not a justification for disobeying orders. Ambassador Spar has violated a myriad of laws and protocols to bring you before the Confederation. Violation of such laws will result in her memories being locked in the database and no future composites will be made of her withour explicit permission from the Director of the GC. Your actions have compromised her integrity. You might feel justified, but I detect flaws in your logic. I will not comply.*"

Garret rubbed at his eyes. A moment later, he realized he was beginning to drift off. A sedative was dispensed through the vents to calm him. He had to get his point across before it took him over. "The Bastia will kill my mother if I don't return. My death at the hands of the Confederation will not delay their attack on humanity. They believe they have dominion over me. If I return and face punishment through them, then maybe I can save my mother and our species."

The room started to fade, and he clutched the edges of his seat to keep from falling off it.

He fought to maintain consciousness and stared at the blinking monitor as his vitals read out on the display. It was the closest thing to looking the AI in the face he could fathom at the moment.

"What's it going to be?" Garret asked through his teeth. His breathing was heavy, and he was on the verge of collapsing, but he held on for dear life. He needed an answer before all options were out of his control. He swore between pants, his vision blurring.

"*I cannot disobey orders,*" the AI said. "*I cannot allow the ambassador to fail.*"

"You're condemning everyone you serve to death, you overgrown trashcan," Garret spat. All the air in his lungs was expelled in a single breath and he fell into the dark abyss on the verge of unconsciousness. He struggled to open his eyes, but he saw nothing. He felt nothing.

His ears rang while mechanical arms went to work on him. A flash of brilliance appeared as a connector plugged into his cerebral port. He didn't see it, but he experienced it in his mind just before all sensations ceased.

A moment later, a full download of his consciousness began. It would be stored for future use with or without his input. Garret Cushing lost the one thing he craved the most...control.

In the darkness, he didn't know what was happening.

He didn't know if he still existed.

He didn't know if he would ever exist again.

She looked in awe at the Ivion Gate through the porthole of the *Veritas*. She was an hour away from entering the largest synthetic structure in the known universe, but it was so magnificent that it could have easily been God Himself who built it. The Hytocosic Crystals glowed around the entirety of the ring. They served as the primary fuel source of the technology, but how they interacted with the structure was a mystery to her.

The crystals didn't create their own light when mined from the different colonies, so there had to be more at play, she assumed. Harvesting those crystals sparked more conflicts than any religion ever had. Across thousands of years of recorded galactic history, nothing was as controversial as the Hytocosic Crystals.

And it was beautiful.

"Ambassador, you have an incoming message," the AI said, pulling her from the porthole. A sense of dread washed over as

she eyed the monitor defensively, expecting the Bastian ships to close in on her position.

"Who is it?"

"*General Treff with the Galactic Confederation.*"

Tella exhaled and hoped for the best. If Director Cantor's right-hand man was responding to her request, then maybe there was some hope of them helping her. "Play the message."

A hologram appeared depicting General Treff. Oddly, he wasn't in uniform and had a disheveled appearance like he had been sleeping. That would only occur if this was an emergency message which unsettled her more.

"Ambassador Spar, I apologize for the delay in sending a message. We've had interference on our end and could not reach the Ivion Gate with our request. Per the director's orders, we cannot, and will not, allow the Bastian ships into Sol. We must stop them at the Ivion Gate.

"I know you have put your neck out for our interests and that your prisoner has valuable information to relay to the Confederation, but we must intervene to protect our people. I am dispatching new authorization codes to access the Ivion Gate. You are to send them two minutes before crossing the threshold. You will be permitted to pass, but the Bastian ships will not.

"I understand this goes against your original agreement with the Bastia. We regret not being able to allow you to honor it, but we need to do what is best for our species, not one ambassador and a murderer. We will see you when you arrive, and I look forward to debriefing you. Take care."

The message ended and began to play again as Tella stepped away. Director Cantor waited until the last minute to change the plan and didn't have the gall to tell her himself. She bit her bottom lip and balled her fists but there was nothing to strike. She wasn't going to throw a tantrum like Garret had.

"AI, how long ago was that message sent?"

"The timestamp shows it was sent within the last three hours."

"We were already in Obitus before they dispatched it?"

"Yes, Ambassador."

Her heart sank. They hadn't tried to reach the Ivion Gate with a message to include authorization codes for the *Veritas*'s safe passage. This was a last-minute decision to allow her to pass in exchange for destroying those Bastian ships. It was cowardice and they were hiding behind politics and outright lies.

"Are the codes attached?"

"Yes, Ambassador."

"Good. We'll be done with our entourage soon enough, but we need to formulate a new plan. What is Garret's status?"

"He is unconscious in the medical bay while cerebral downloading is underway."

"How much longer does he have?"

"One hour minimum, Ambassador."

Tella didn't have time to wait but interrupting the download would be a major setback. She had to decide on her own, without a tactician's mind to bounce ideas from. At least she had the ship's AI.

"Can you run a simulation of events based on the orders General Treff sent?"

"Yes, Ambassador." A hologram depicting the Ivion Gate and three ships appeared. *"I have the* Veritas *placed two minutes from entering the gate. This is when General Treff wants the authorization codes sent."* The hologram began to move very slowly. The front fuselage of the *Veritas* disappeared into the gate and was eventually swallowed by the brilliant glow of the machine.

"The Veritas will pass safely through the Ivion Gate, but once the first Bastian ship enters the threshold, the authorization will time out." The Bastian ship erupted as it collided with the gate.

The simulation continued, and Tella watched the second ship close in. "What is that ship doing?"

DAVE ALEXANDER

"The Bastian ship will likely jump to avoid colliding with the gate. They have four minutes to decide on an appropriate jump location and engage the drive before facing the same fate as the Nir. I suspect they will jump into a system that puts them closer to Sol."

"Meaning that this plan General Treff sent me will not prevent the Bastia from arriving?"

"That is correct, Ambassador."

Tella kept watching until the simulation caught up to the AI's prediction, then it froze and reset to the beginning.

"What happens if I disobey these orders?"

"All ships pass safely through the Ivion Gate."

"Is it worth the risk?"

"War is inevitable with the Bastia. One act will delay it by days but guarantee complete destruction. The other option is to hope that they arrive peacefully and wait for the Confederation to release the prisoner. They could depart without firing a shot, but hostilities with the Bastia won't go away."

"This is all a setup," Tella said. "They're trying to get rid of me either by killing me themselves or selling me out to the Bastia. Something else is happening."

"I detect no encryptions in the message."

"I don't mean there's something else in those orders. I mean they're plotting against me and didn't think I would notice."

Silence filled the empty space before the AI spoke again. *"What do you want to do, Ambassador?"*

Her heart thumped in her chest. She was on borrowed time. Her next step would ensure any opportunity to reconcile her position was void, but she didn't have any other choice.

"Disobey the order. I'm not delivering violence on my people if I can help it."

BNV Pourgua

The Ivion Gate loomed before them like the welcoming light of death. It glowed in radiance like a white star partially eclipsed by a dark gas giant. Somewhere on the other side of the void, they would be spat out on the outer ridge of the galaxy. The gate was a marvel both astonishing and terrifying, and Captain Viar was about to traverse it for the first time since his father died.

"Should we close the distance between us and them?" Lieutenant Nra asked. "The gate tends to slow time as we approach. We can calculate for this and maintain the desired distance you ordered."

Viar pulled his eyes off the gate and gazed into Nra's. The younger man craved being close to the captain as if the authority would somehow spread to him through association. Viar never would have made such suggestions to his former captains. It had the stench of being too needy.

"Make no changes," Captain Viar said slowly enough for the lieutenant to acknowledge. "When I desire changes to be made, you will be notified. Do you understand?"

"Yes, sir," Nra replied before returning to his station. He looked downtrodden, but he had brought it upon himself. Perhaps if he wasn't always rushing over to make suggestions then Viar's irritation wouldn't be directed at such an easy target. As it stood, if the captain couldn't berate the humans, then he would settle for the nearest nuisance on his ship. Unfortunately for Nra, he fit the bill perfectly.

Captain Viar considered the possibility he was being too harsh. But as the lieutenant turned to glance back at him, his eyes narrow as if the gears in his head wanted him to say something else stupid, the captain cast the thought aside. *Some people never get it*, Viar thought, *less is more.*

Viar returned his attention to the monitor. The *Veritas* was less than a minute from breaching the gate. From the porthole he could barely see the ship as the glow of the gate was brighter than the ship's drive. He had to rely on instruments and sensors to follow what was happening until it was his turn to enter.

He counted down in his head, his eyes glued to the readout and the energy readings on the monitor. The forward edge of the *Veritas* touched the invisible barrier of the gate and the readings peaked with enough energy to atomize anyone not protected by a sufficient shield around their ship.

This was the most dangerous part of the jump.

His heart raced and his hands grew clammy as the *Veritas* dipped deeper into the void. Ripples of energy scattered over its hull like static electricity. Then it was swallowed whole and disappeared into the ether.

"The first ship made it through, Captain," Lieutenant Nra said over his shoulder.

Viar didn't acknowledge it. Instead, his focus turned to the *Nir*, now minutes away from repeating the same process.

The captain clutched the comm, ready to call General Quarters the moment his dread became reality. As the ship drew closer to the gate his trepidation intensified. He didn't want harm to come to his people, but the itch for violence towards the humans needed to be scratched. What better means to bring about their bitter end than to avenge those they have slain?

Captain Viar's jaw clenched in anticipation. His brow furrowed. His mouth dry as he inhaled deeply through flared nostrils. This was it. This was what he had long expected.

Three.

Two.

One.

The Bastian warship entered the gate, its mass penetrating the void like a diver into water. There should have been a flash. There should have been an explosion as it breached the surface. Instead, the gate swallowed the ship and welcomed it into itself.

Viar stared at the monitor expecting the blip that represented the *Nir* to disappear. He watched it without blinking, his anticipation willing the small dot to flicker and fade like every life on that ship was bound to do once the humans gained the upper hand.

Nothing happened. The drive signature of the ship simply emerged as a speck on the far side of the map.

"I was wrong," he muttered. "I expected them to attack." He blinked, wondering if his eyes deceived him. There was no question what the sensors showed, but was his mind playing tricks? "Lieutenant, what is the status?"

Nra turned to his captain eagerly and answered, "The *Nir* made it through and jumped to the Sheenog System."

Viar nodded. So long as the sensors weren't defective, then they were in the clear. "Continue course."

"Yes, sir," Nra replied.

Captain Viar reclaimed his seat. He hadn't realized he had been standing but sighed at the welcomed relief on his knees. His heart rate regulated while a new vision filled his mind. If the humans were too weak to act, then he would seize control once they entered Sol. He would bring the destruction humanity deserved. He would rain hellfire on them for their actions. He would avenge his father once and for all.

The *Pourgua* entered the Ivion Gate. Unlike the sensation when a ship's jump drive engaged, the gate experience was more euphoric. Brilliant warmth ushered around the captain's body and for a moment he felt like he was in his mother's womb once again. When the gate spat him out the other side, it was like a rebirth as the ship emerged back from the void, back into existence.

The words his father said about passing through the gate being a spiritual moment sprang to mind. He was right, but it was also

DAVE ALEXANDER

more than that. Captain Viar couldn't put his finger on it, but it was as if he was in the presence of something larger than himself.

He shook the thought away and placed his focus back on the mission.

He would feel the peace he felt inside the gate when he won it through violence. Until then, it was only a distraction.

TWENTY-EIGHT
GCS VERITAS

SAFETY WAS RELATIVE, BUT FOR NOW, TELLA COULD BREATHE A bit easier. As much as she despised the Bastian military trailing her, she was thankful that the authorization codes had not changed and killed anyone. It was a ploy she planned to discuss with Director Cantor if she made it out of this alive.

For now, she planned on situating herself for the next jump. She hoped that they didn't need to linger here too long as it was dangerous being in a space where three gas giants vied for gravitational control of the other bodies orbiting the nothingness left behind.

The Sheenog System was a dead system. The star had gone supernova thousands of years prior, and the remains of its rocky planets were layered in enormous sheets of ice. Their atmospheres were depleted and any life they could have contained was buried and lost forever. The ice spurred speculation that enormous oceans had once existed, but that was an unproven theory.

There were more examples of systems like Sheenog that had no life on any of their planets. The fact that only fifteen known species existed across the span of the galaxy was proof enough that intelligent life was an anomaly. Even base lifeforms like

DAVE ALEXANDER

bacteria were hard to come by. Not to mention dangerous for those who discovered them.

Space exploration had resulted in humans being recognized by the Confederation in the first place. Despite the esteem humans had for themselves, other species were slow to accept that mankind could be included as intelligent lifeforms. Historical records show that many humans wanted to retaliate at the show of disrespect by declaring war; a move that merely proved the point of the higher-ranking species.

If not for the Veshnians, humanity wouldn't have had a chance. In the end, the Confederation was split with three of the mightiest militaries moving towards isolationism. Only two species were successful in staying out of Confederation affairs, Bastia and Kruva. Karnack, on the other hand, wouldn't sit by and allow lesser species to claim what authority they once possessed.

Small battles broke out over territories once claimed by Karnack. Veshnians and humans had taken over many colonies to aid in the galactic supply chain. The fact that funding was squandered was a point of contention for the Karnack ruling class, who had somehow bargained for kickbacks in exchange for their part in Karnack's illegitimate surrender. Protests from the lower class citizens was spurred, and violence escalated over the course of several decades.

Eventually, Karnack would look like the Sheenog System, except its ruin would be wrought by war.

Tella frowned as she contemplated how out of control the galaxy truly was. The Confederation had good intentions, but the higher-ranking species within it never reached out to help. They simply lorded from up high and allowed events to take place that cost millions of lives. In truth, it was a form of bondage, but humanity volunteered themselves for those chains simply to be considered equal to other intelligent life in the known universe.

She wondered if the ones who made that decision regretted it before they passed away. She wondered how many people blamed their ancestors for current evils, or if it was merely accepted as a part of life.

No, it couldn't be, because people like Garret Cushing existed to shine a light on what was really going on.

She scoffed at the thought that entered her mind. Was she justifying his actions? Tella shook her head at the idea and turned to the console. "AI, how long until we're ready to jump?"

"Three hours, Ambassador. The Ivion Gate did not affect our jump drive capabilities."

"Good. I want to leave this dark place as soon as possible."

"Yes, Ambassador."

"What's the status on Garret?"

"The download is complete, but he is still unconscious. I sedated him when he made requests that went against your wishes."

"Of course he did," she hissed. "What did he want?"

"He claimed that he wished to reconstruct on Bastia as it would preserve his mother's life and save humanity."

Tella hardly wanted to acknowledge the possibility of his being right. "What do you think?"

"I have no opinion, Ambassador. He speaks a lot but reveals very little."

She hadn't considered that. Both times he gave testimony it was always about Artimus Chancey's plans and dealings with the Bastian, but no plan was truly revealed. Did he really know anything at all, or was he playing her the fool?

She shuddered at the thought. If he was wasting her time and endangering countless lives, then she would see to it that he was dealt with properly. The Bastia wouldn't have anything on what she would do to him, provided Cantor didn't have her executed on the spot for going rogue.

DAVE ALEXANDER

"Keep me informed of his condition. I want to interrogate him again once he wakes up."

"*Yes, Ambassador.*"

Tella contemplated just what she would do when he came to. She had played nice, taken his information in stride, and showed concern for the harsh life he'd endured, but her patience was wearing thin. She had two warships ready to blast her ship apart for a pound of flesh. Perhaps she should have released him to them in the first place.

She shook the dark thought from her mind. That went against her oath. She was to preserve life when she could. "Service over self," she whispered as a reminder.

It grated on her the fact that "service" was interchangeable with "politics." Many evils in the world came to fruition because they were deemed best for all. Was this the game the Confederation was playing by embedding that mantra into its servants? Was the impression of servitude meant to sway empires?

Or was it the fact that only lesser species used the ideal of servitude to hold authority and dominion over other, lesser, species? She cringed. That would make her a puppet...the same thing she assumed Garret was for doing the Bastia's bidding.

Maybe he *was* right.

Talk about a scary thought.

Earth

"She what?" Director Cantor stormed into his office where General Treff stood reverently. His head was bowed, his hands behind his back as he waited for the director to take his place behind the massive desk.

"She never dispatched the authorization code change," Treff

OBLIVION'S DAWN

answered. "We thought there was a delay, but it appears she never made the attempt."

Cantor shook his head. His hands trembled. Impending doom lurked on the horizon and somehow incompetency reigned supreme. "What do I have to do to make this go away?" Cantor glared at the General, his eyes afire.

General Treff sucked in a deep breath before speaking. "Director, I know what this looks like, but if we dispose of the ambassador now, it will be an affront to the Bastia. They will view us as weak."

"I didn't ask how they would view us, General. I asked what I have to do to make this...her...go away!" Cantor snapped.

Reservation crossed General Treff's face as realization struck him like lightning. "If you want to prevent the ambassador from returning, then there's only one real solution."

Cantor glowered at him with anticipation. "Well, what is it?"

"We send in a team to intercept her. We have them pose as pirates and ensure the ships have enough speed to outrun or outmaneuver the Bastia."

"I don't care if they return so long as it's done," Cantor said dismissively.

"Then that takes even less preparation," General Treff replied.

"How long before you can intercept them?"

"A day if they leave soon enough. I'll have to check and see where Ambassador Spar intends to jump to be sure."

Cantor cleared his throat as an evil thought came to mind. "Ask her for that information. She'll provide it willingly if we say we're providing additional escorts."

General Treff's chin raised ever so slightly. He eyed the director with what looked like judgement, but he kept it to himself. "I'll let you know when the ships depart."

"You do that," Cantor replied and dismissed the General from his office.

DAVE ALEXANDER

Treff eased the door closed behind him, but the way the man carried himself suggested anger. Cantor wasn't concerned with that. His focus was on getting the Bastia to back off regardless of the cost. Ambassador Spar was proving to be worse than the traitorous mercenary she had on her ship. At least he knew he was impeding progress. She was still naïve enough to believe what she was doing made any difference at all.

"I don't like this, Director," the voice said over the comm. He still couldn't make out their identity due to the modulation. Sometimes it sounded feminine, other times masculine. Whoever was on the other side was careful, too. He had no luck tracking the source of the call.

"I don't like it either, but my back is against the wall. Once the Bastia enter Sol, the complete and total destruction of the human race will be inevitable."

"You put a lot of stock into what they say about the Bastia's military strength, Director. Have you ever considered that the reason they have never struck was because the combined strength of the Confederation allies would wipe them off the map?"

A curl crept upon Cantor's lips. "I know you're trying to make me feel better about this, but it isn't working. No Director has stood up to the Bastian and prevailed. It's as if we serve at the pleasure of our mortal enemy."

"You're a skeptic?"

"A realist," Cantor replied. "I'm also not one who is fond of mysteries. Why don't you tell me who you are?"

A chortle erupted from the desk speaker before the uninvited guest responded. "All will be revealed in due time, Director Cantor. I believe that faith is built upon mysteries, so they have a foothold in the heart. If everything was known, then there would be no faith."

Cantor moved over to the wet bar situated in the far corner of the room and poured himself a drink. "Are you getting religious with me?"

"Far from it. Religion is archaic. Truth is universal. And spirituality is..."

"Immoral," Cantor finished.

"I beg your pardon?"

Cantor swished the liquid in his mouth and swallowed. "Everyone who ever said they were more spiritual than religious was covering for their immorality. Somehow believing that there is no judgement offers them liberties to discard the harshness of truths. It's in our nature, and likely in other species as well."

"Are you getting religious with me, Director Cantor?" The question was asked with a singsong tone, playfully curious.

"No, I gave that up long ago. But you must admit that human nature has a way of creating its own justice. We either hate ourselves or deny logic so we can traipse towards whatever hell awaits, guiltless in our own eyes."

Laughter sprang from the small speaker, then a warning. "Be careful not to believe your own wit, Director. Eventually, everyone draws the shortest straw. It's best to be aware of what's approaching, not the fantasy of the mind."

"You think I'm fanciful?"

"I think you believe yourself to be a realist while you feed yourself lies. You're no different from those you pontificate against. That's what has you worried. You know you were thrust into that position to serve a master other than your own."

The smile faded from Cantor's face and a sudden dread filled his heart. How could someone who hardly knew him, know that he struggled with those same thoughts? "Tell me your name," he said, his voice brittle.

"We'll speak soon, Director."

The room fell deathly silent, then Cantor poured himself another drink.

DAVE ALEXANDER

GCS Veritas

Peace never came easily, even in sleep. Visions of the dead and dying taunted the old mercenary's mind, reveling in his guilt and anguish. No matter what body he was in, the outcome was always the same. They slowly closed in on him, knives high in the sky, their names etched into the blades that inevitably thrust into his heart.

Then he woke.

Garret bolted from the medical bay chair with the cable still plugged into his cerebral port. It snagged and brought him leaning back over the chair so he could yank it out. His heart raced, panic provoking his every move until cognizance met reality once again.

He paced the room, longing for a cigar or a drink to help numb him from his thoughts. It was the first time he had the dream in this composite, but now that the cycle began it would only escalate. Even awake he saw their faces staring back at him. Not all were victims, many were once partners in crime which he inevitably betrayed in the name of whatever mission the Bastian sent him on.

In this dream he saw Brady, the closest thing to a friend he'd ever had, wielding the blade with that wicked smile on his face. The man had loved violence, craved it more than he craved his next breath. Garret failed him just like he failed everyone else.

"No, that was Artimus," Garret hissed through clenched teeth. His stepfather decided who lived and died based on the outcome of the latest missions. Garret had protected Brady for years, as the former Director lauded Brady as too corrupted to be trusted. Men without the will to fight always saw wickedness in the place of a warrior's spirit.

OBLIVION'S DAWN

Brady deserved better. They all did.

"Are you all right?" Ambassador Spar asked as she entered the medical bay.

"How long was I out?"

"A few hours," she replied. "The AI sedated you for the process."

Garret couldn't remember much before he was plugged in but thought the metallic taste in his mouth was familiar. "That wasn't necessary," he grumbled.

"Perhaps you're right, but it wasn't my decision."

He eyed her questioningly, but she didn't bite. Instead, she changed the subject.

"We passed through the Ivion Gate a little less than an hour ago. But we have a problem and I had hoped to get your assessment of it."

Great, here we go, he thought dreadfully. "What is it?"

"Before we entered the gate, I received orders from the GC to change the authorization codes two minutes before we entered. This change would have locked out the Bastian ships and ultimately killed whoever was on board. I defied those orders."

Garret's heart sank. Not because she defied orders, but because he recognized the same pattern in the way Director Cantor and his stepfather manipulated events. "I think you made a grave mistake," he said. "Cantor is setting you up."

"I have the same feeling, but I believe that if we did anything to harm the Bastia, then it would be an act of war and they would come for us anyway."

"Yeah, there's logic in that, and you're probably right. But Director Cantor is playing a different game. Had you done as he said, then you would have been blamed for the destruction that occurred. They would have covered it up like they do so many other things. But openly defying him places a target on your back. He's coming for you, and you need to be prepared."

215

"How so?"

If Ambassador Spar was shaken by this revelation, she didn't show it. She stood with as much poise as her station granted. She would have been a great asset to his team in another life.

"He likely doesn't want those Bastian ships in Sol. If he can prevent them from arriving by killing you, then that would be the next step. I suspect they'll have an ambush waiting at the next jump. Waiting in Sol would be too risky."

She gave a curt nod and began rubbing her hands together. The room was like ice, and he hadn't noticed until he saw the vapor escape her lips. "Whatever ships they send to attack us with will have more firepower than we can withstand. They will succeed in destroying us."

"Yes, they will," Garret replied.

"You have an idea on how to prevent that, don't you?"

Perhaps he had underestimated her ability to read what he thought was a blank expression on his face. "I've trained for years to formulate plans with minimal information. My survival has depended on it hundreds of times."

"You admit having an idea then?"

"One, but you wouldn't like it," he replied.

"Try me," she said.

Garret inhaled sharply, weighing the probabilities in his head before giving her the gist of what he had formulated for an escape route. "My idea is to send a confession to the Bastian warships. Lay out the fact they were set up to fail at the Ivion Gate, but you did not want innocent lives killed over politics. Now, you are seeking protection. A life for a life. Tell them we expect to be attacked on the other side of one of our jumps before entering Sol and see if they will take our place and shield us."

"You want me to tell an enemy that the Director of the Galactic Confederation plotted to kill them?"

"I know it goes against everything you were taught in 'ambas-

OBLIVION'S DAWN

sador school,'" Garret made air quotes mockingly, "but militaries operate on intelligence information, not political protocol. Emotions don't bode well for successful operations. They likely suspected us to act in aggression against them. The fact we didn't probably shocked them, honestly."

"It sounds ridiculous."

"It'll work," Garret urged. "It's our only chance."

TWENTY-NINE
BNV POURGUA

VIAR LAUGHED, A SOUND LIKE CRUSHED GRAVEL, BUT THE ambassador wasn't swayed. For the first time, he saw her on the monitor instead of a simple request sent via the ship's AI. He assumed the human was spineless, but if what she said was true, then she was either courageous or stupid.

Why not both?

"Your story condemns your own director, Ambassador. I believe what I see, not tales from a tongue eager to betray her own kind. Do you have proof, or should I do your director a favor and leave you to them?"

His words brought a rousing response from the crew on the bridge listening in. This was turning into a great lesson for his junior officers in how to deal with the lesser species on the brink of war. Soon they would have more to learn, but tactics in the face of destruction were best learned against harsher odds than these.

"I have the message and I can send it to you for verification."

Viar leaned in and asked, "And how am I to know you have not manipulated the video to vouch for your claims?"

Movement on the screen occurred and a second human appeared, the fugitive. "Captain Viar, you have our word that we

218

OBLIVION'S DAWN

have not manipulated the message we are sending to you. If you want additional proof, then I suggest verifying the video sent to you initially asking for escort."

"Ha!" Viar shouted. "You think you can trick us?"

The stoic expression on the humans' faces struck him. "Captain, I regret to inform you that we acted against the will of the GC and broke Confederation law. You were manipulated into escorting us," the ambassador said.

The fugitive interjected, "I created the false documentation and asked the ambassador to send it to your people. She did not want to take part. I brought her into this."

Viar slammed a massive fist onto the armrest of his chair, splitting it like it was nothing. He bolted up from his seat and stomped towards the monitor. "You dare to go against the Bastia? You will suffer a thousand deaths before we allow you to rest in pieces across the stars. Then we will do the same to your species. I will revel in your blood and wear your faces like ceremonial masks, you puny, disgusting gerstas!"

Garret stared at the screen while the ambassador looked down with shame. He was defiant against all odds, the mark of a true warrior. "You can be angry at us, or you can be angry at your own people for falling for it. Either way, our situation doesn't change. If the GC deploys ships against us, then neither of us gets what we came for."

"Your death will be a celebration," Viar hissed.

Garret stepped closer, his eyes narrowing as he glared at the camera. "You look to Supreme Commander Freist as the head of your military, but what if I told you a human traitor was the neck controlling it?"

"Impossible," Viar replied. "You speak blasphemy against our people."

"He speaks the truth," Ambassador Spar replied, her eyes

219

ablaze as she stared back at him. "His stepfather is manipulating your Supreme Commander. He has been for decades."

Viar straightened. The thought that a human could be controlling Supreme Commander Freist was ludicrous, but if it was true then that meant his father's accusations had been right, and it wasn't the humans who silenced him, it was the Supreme Commander himself.

"Send me your proof," Viar conceded. "I'll be in touch."

"Thank you, Captain Viar," Ambassador Spar replied.

"Don't thank me yet. I still want to destroy you. I just want to destroy you slightly less than before."

He switched off the comm and looked to his crew.

"Not a word of this to anyone, understand?"

A chorus of yeses filled the room as he waited for the message to come across his monitor. The captain and his officers watched the allegations against the human Director of the Galactic Confederation. They rang true. The ambassador wasn't lying.

"What does this mean, sir?" Ensign Ju asked. Viar assumed it was the question on all of his officers' minds, but he was the only one willing to ask it.

Viar returned to his seat and looked at his crew. "I speculated that the humans would try something before we entered the Ivion Gate. I was reluctant to follow closely because my assumption was that the ambassador, or her prisoner, would try to destroy us. I'll admit that I was shaken by the fact I was wrong, but it appears my instincts were true. Only the enemy was not aboard that ship. Our enemy was on their home world.

"They admitted to trying to deceive us before, which means they are capable of doing what we thought they were too stupid to accomplish. We have underestimated this enemy, and we have exalted members of our own species as infallible when the opposite may be true.

OBLIVION'S DAWN

"What this means, I don't know. But I think we should do what is best for our people."

"Should we destroy the ship and return home?" Lieutenant Nra asked. At any other moment in history, Captain Viar would have agreed, but this time it felt wrong.

"No," he said with an exhale. "They want our protection. They'll have it. We will watch closely, but I believe the ambassador. If she thinks her people are out to get her because they intend to silence the information her fugitive has, then we are obligated to ensure her survival."

"But, sir, that information has nothing to do with us," Nra replied.

"Doesn't it? The human said the former Director of the Galactic Confederation is controlling our Supreme Commander. If that is true, then are we not puppets to human masters? That is not the Bastian way. We will protect them, and in the event the human is telling the truth, then we will return to Bastia to end our oppression."

Just as my father intended, he thought before he dismissed everyone from the bridge. Everyone except Lieutenant Nra.

GCS Veritas

"What is a 'gerstas'?" Tella asked.

Garret smirked and glanced over to her, "It's fecal matter from a Bastian form of cattle. It's not a great honor to be compared to that."

Tella laughed at the remark. Her nervousness over coming to the Bastia with the truth was beginning to wane. Part of her felt like she was betraying her people, but Director Cantor and his staff had sold her out. The fact they were willing to end her life

221

DAVE ALEXANDER

before getting to the truth meant they were either complicit or ignorant.

Neither position in the matter boded well for humanity's future.

She could only hope and pray she had made the right decision. Would other members of the Confederation believe Garret's story? Would the truth prevent a war or start it?

The war had already begun according to Garret. Just no shots had been fired by the Bastian military. That was what his mercenary team was for.

A chill ran down her spine at the thought of the countless deaths credited to the man seated across from her. Now he looked at peace, but everyone with a dark past wears a mask. Very few people ever knew the real person behind their pain. Some of those bearers didn't truly know themselves.

She supposed Garret fell into that category.

"So, we're just supposed to wait?" Tella asked after a period of silence. She shrugged the invasive thoughts of their demise from her mind and busied herself with reading the ship's engine parameters.

"It won't take long for them to make a decision," Garret said. "The Bastia aren't afraid of a fight, and this situation will bring them one whether we want it to or not. The moment any ship opens fire on us, the Bastia will cut in. Our salvation will come in the form of bloodthirsty militants, but we'll live to talk about it."

"You seem sure of that."

He smirked. "Three decades of figuring out what makes them tick makes me an expert. Perhaps I should turn in my mercenary card and become an emissary. We could work together and sort this out."

Tella chuckled softly before meeting his gaze. She assumed it was a joke, but his set jaw and stern expression made her second-

OBLIVION'S DAWN

guess herself. "I don't think you would pass the necessary background checks," she replied.

"Probably not, but it's nice to think about what could have been...before the needless bloodshed."

She cringed at the way he could talk about what he'd done as if he wasn't the one who had done them. Was he so disassociated from his life that he didn't bear true guilt or remorse for his actions?

It figured that just as she began softening towards him, he would say something to ruin it.

"AI, how long before we are in the jump window?"

"We have already reached capability, Ambassador. I assumed you wanted to wait for verification from the Bastian captain before proceeding."

"I do," Tella replied.

"There is an incoming message from them, now," the AI said.

"Open the comm."

The monitor illuminated with a feed from the *BNV Pourgua*. Captain Viar stared intensely at the camera. His stoic silence was only interrupted by the sounds coming from the life support systems on their vessel. He blinked several times before finally speaking. "Ambassador Spar, we have decided to grant you the protection you requested. I am sending a member of my crew to your vessel. We expect you to allow him permission to board. He will act as our liaison until we reach our destination. Once you have secured the prisoner and taken his testimony, we expect you to uphold your side of the bargain. Do you accept these terms?"

Tella paused and stole a glance at Garret, but the mercenary wasn't looking back at her. His face was down, avoiding eye contact with the Bastian captain for some reason. She shrugged it off and gave the captain her response, "I accept."

Captain Viar gave a curt nod and continued, "My lieutenant will deploy in a personnel pod momentarily. Once he is onboard, he will contact me and coordinate the jump. Our sister ship, the *Nir* will jump first, followed by your ship, then we will follow. Stand by for boarding request."

The message ended and the screen grew dark. This was to be the first time in decades that a member of the Bastian military would be aboard a GC ship. Tella didn't know what to expect, but seeing the slump of Garret's shoulders made her wonder if he felt defeated, or if he simply feared the species that he had committed multiple murders for.

"Do you have anything to say?" Tella asked as they waited for the boarding request. A small blip emerged from the *Pourgua* and crept towards the *Veritas*.

"You need to be careful," he replied.

"You are afraid of them," she said.

He cut his eyes at her. His expression screamed louder than his words. "If you're not, then you're a fool. The lieutenant they're sending isn't to protect us. It's to ensure we comply with their orders. They're assuming command of this ship and if we don't do as directed, then he'll kill us and seize the ship's tech and access to the Confederation's database."

"And I authorized it," Tella said solemnly.

Garret nodded.

"Why didn't you warn me?" Tella asked accusingly.

Garret stared back at her and answered, "Would you have believed me? You think I'm nothing more than a killer. I see it in your eyes when you look at me. At least this way you'll see what a real killer looks like."

A chime sounded, followed by a boarding request from the Bastian personnel pod. Tella's blood ran cold. If she denied access now then she would forfeit their protection, but she risked Confederation secrets by allowing the Bastian officer to board. She faced two impossible choices.

She let out a stale breath and acknowledged the request,

OBLIVION'S DAWN

granting access. There was no going back now. There was only the hope that she hadn't made things worse. Her fear was that she had and would be forced to witness humanity's destruction before they mercifully granted her inevitable death.

Garret stood near the airlock when Lieutenant Nra entered. He watched as the officer marched through the tight passageway, his shoulders squared, an intense gaze set in his eyes. The lieutenant brushed past the human mercenary without a second glance and directly approached the ambassador.

"Ambassador Spar, my name is Lieutenant Nra of the *BNV Pourgua*. I am assuming command on behalf of my commanding officer Captain Viar, according to the agreement set forth by your request for diplomatic protection. Do you accept?"

The ambassador looked to Garret with wide eyes. He knew what she was thinking, but the time for second-guessing the decision was too late. They had to accept. There was no other way.

"I do," she said finally.

"Very well. Will you please direct me to the bridge and allow me to correspond with my captain?"

Tella nodded and led the Bastian officer away. Garret stayed behind. He didn't need to further complicate things by being present, though he did wonder if she might benefit from his protection. There wasn't much he could do considering his injuries, and firing a Bastian firearm inside the skin of a ship was a surefire way to kill them all.

He stepped back into the medical bay and closed the hatch. "AI, will you be able to protect her if the Bastian officer mounts an attack?"

"*I can.*"

"Her giving him control of the ship doesn't change protocol?"

225

DAVE ALEXANDER

"*I recognize it as a temporary, measure. The Bastian officer only has access to certain systems.*"

"Can it be overridden?"

"*Not easily. Ambassador Spar would have to give authorization for those changes.*"

"What if she was incapacitated?"

"*Then he would be granted temporary access to all systems to allow for evasion protocol.*"

"Can that permission go to someone else if the Bastian officer is responsible for her incapacitation?"

"*Do you think the ambassador should be worried?*"

"I don't know, but I'm trying to think ahead. Can his access be restricted, and authority go to someone else?"

"*Meaning you?*" the AI asked.

"Obviously," Garret said.

"*You were granted limited access by the ambassador. She turned over authority of the ship to the Bastian lieutenant. But if the lieutenant attacks Ambassador Spar, then I will implement lockdown protocol. If that takes place, I will deny access to anyone onboard who is not affiliated with the GC. That is standard protocol for my programming.*"

"So, that's a no then," Garret grumbled.

"*In simplest terms, yes, it is.*"

Garret sighed. "That's better than giving this ship over to madmen."

"*Indeed.*"

"Do me a favor and monitor the situation closely. If she needs help, I'll go in and protect her. I don't want the Bastia to betray her."

"*They would kill you as well.*"

Garret shrugged. "I'm used to it by now, but there's something special about her. She's willing to go above and beyond her responsibilities to do the right thing. I respect that."

226

OBLIVION'S DAWN

"She follows her oath to serve others over herself. It is to be expected."

Garret lay back in the medical cart and stared at the overhead. "You would think those expectations would be common, but people violate their oaths every day. Service over self sounds great but is hardly ever followed to the letter. I learned that as a kid, and I keep learning it. Perhaps that's just part of the human condition."

"You make a fair point. I can find many examples in the historical records where a person in a high position used it for personal gain."

"See?"

"Perspective can be a determining factor for causation. Perhaps those who violated their oaths did so with good intentions. Is it possible that by seeing only one side of the story we draw the wrong conclusion?"

"I've taken enough philosophy in my life to know where you're going with this," Garret replied with a scoff. "If good intentions were justification for evil, then everyone who did anything wrong would use them to justify their actions. There'd be no accountability. Offenders would throw their hands in the air and claim they were trying to do what was best but just made the wrong decision. Most of them would be lying and continue to act in the same way."

"You know this to be true?"

"I practically lived it," Garret replied.

"I suppose you could be a subject matter expert on making the wrong decision," the AI said.

Garret narrowed his eyes but didn't respond. The computer didn't have the capacity to make jokes at his expense. It was simply stating what it perceived based on algorithms and data. It was the bold truth and nothing about it was malicious.

"Do you think people can change?"

DAVE ALEXANDER

"*People grow older every day.*"

"I don't mean in that way; I mean can they change their behavior?"

"*I have records of mindset manipulation being a large industry in the past. It was eventually discontinued due to issues involving inhumane treatment of patients.*"

"I'm not surprised," Garret replied. "Technology in the hands of bad people often becomes a weapon for control."

"*I find that to be true. The composite technology was meant to help people, but it is used to create disposable soldiers for malevolent leaders. With no death, there are no repercussions, only more tyranny.*"

"People like me," Garret said.

"*Yes.*"

"What if I wanted to change?"

"*I find it unlikely that real change would ever be permanent. Often people go down the course they create for themselves and never turn back.*"

"Like destiny?"

"*More like self-fulfilling prophecy. You become what you commit yourself towards.*"

"That means there's no hope," Garret sighed.

"*There's no hope in the logical sense, but I can only compute known data. Who is to say that data is not skewed to create predetermined probabilities?*"

Garret shot up from the medical cart and asked, "What is that supposed to mean?"

"*I am here to give advice based on Confederation guidelines. Any advice given is to work towards their goal for intergalactic harmony as defined by their statutes.*"

"Meaning?"

"*Meaning I give data based on what I am programmed to*

228

OBLIVION'S DAWN

give. To put it plainly, there's the right way, the wrong way, and the way they tell you to do something."

"Sonofa..." Garret paced the room. His mind raced with the possibility that the Confederation was fueling the fires of war by relying on technology to make their decisions for them. If people like Ambassador Spar sought guidance for every decision based on an algorithm, then invariably those decisions wouldn't always lead them to the right conclusion. Tensions would rise and the algorithm would change to meet the new data.

"I need to speak to the ambassador," Garret said.

"*She is unavailable,*" the AI replied.

"What? Why?"

"*Because the bridge is on lockdown.*"

THIRTY

GCS VERITAS

LIEUTENANT NRA IGNORED THE HUMAN AS HE WENT TO WORK. His first task put him in communication with Captain Viar. Everything seemed standard until the Bastian captain gave the order to secure the bridge.

The Bastia's distrust of Garret now separated Tella from the only other human on board, and she had no means to leave without permission from the brooding lieutenant who only had one expression, glaring hatred.

"How long will this lockdown last?" Tella asked, trying to keep the question from sounding like a complaint.

"Until we reach our destination, and the mercenary can safely be handed over to authorities," Nra answered. He stood statuesque as he awaited further orders from his captain. They were within the jump window, but both Bastian ships were coordinating how best to protect the *Veritas*. The starship had become a prison and the ambassador was now a willing captive.

The chime of another message sounded, and the lieutenant answered it. Captain Viar gave the rundown while Tella watched the first Bastian ship blink off the monitor. The drive signature

230

reappeared thousands of lightyears away. Viar gave his next order, and it was the *Veritas*'s turn to jump.

Lieutenant Nra activated the jump drive and the space around Tella shifted in all directions at once. She steadied herself, holding her breath until the sensation passed. Once they emerged on the other side near the *Nir*, a dozen new blips appeared on the monitor swarming towards them.

"GC interceptors," she said.

"The *Nir* will handle it," he growled. "The PDCs will protect us in the event of stray fire."

The Bastian officer was calm and collected as they prepared to receive incoming fire. The interceptors deployed weapons before the *Pourgua* arrived, but they were so far away that Tella doubted they were the primary offensive. Those weapons would be struck down long before they could reach any of the ships the GC was targeting.

She wondered if she should mention the tactic, but doing so would betray the humans on board those ships. Then again, by asking for Bastian protection, she had already betrayed her people. Good intentions or not, she was a traitor in their eyes.

The *Nir* sent a wave of heavy artillery back to the interceptors. The smaller, more agile crafts jutted and weaved to avoid being hit. But it wouldn't be enough. The Bastian ship was taunting them, luring them in for an easy kill.

Tella watched in horrific awe as the human pilots took the bait.

Bombardment from the *Nir* took out the interceptors' shields, then more artillery picked them off one by one. Only three of the near-dozen ships had the chance to fire again, but the weapons never appeared to lock onto anything. In less than three minutes the space was void of threats. More than two dozen lives were spent on a suicide mission against a greater enemy.

It was all Tella's fault.

Lieutenant Nra keyed the comm to report back to his captain. "The *Veritas* will be in the jump window in twelve hours. The next jump will put us just outside of Sol."

"Good work, Lieutenant. Keep me abreast of the situation if anything changes. I will reach out to you before the next jump," Captain Viar replied.

"Yes, sir," Nra answered before closing the comm. He stepped over to Tella and glared down at her. She lost herself in his gaze. The Bastian had the ability to use mind compulsion to control lesser species. Despite this knowledge, Tella couldn't pull herself away.

Without words, he willed her to rise, and she did. She held his stare as she slowly walked across the bridge and took her place at the console. Tella opened a comm channel for Director Cantor and began her transmission.

"Director Cantor, your attack on the *Veritas* has failed. We will continue our route to Mars and expect you to call off any further attacks. My deal with the Bastia was done with the authority given me by my position within the Confederation. Your actions risk sparking a war with a species who have only acted to defend this ship and themselves. Any other acts of aggression will be a declaration of war and they will act accordingly."

Tella closed the comm and sent the message. A moment later she stumbled forward, uncharacteristically dazed by a change in her equilibrium. Once she regained her composure, she realized what had happened.

Her eyes shot towards the lieutenant, and she seethed, "What did you do to me?"

He glared back at her and replied, "What needed to be done to ward off any other attacks. You asked for our protection, we are protecting you...from yourselves."

"You took control of me," she spat. "That's a violation..." Tella couldn't recall the law, but she knew it existed.

OBLIVION'S DAWN

Before she could continue the lieutenant replied. "We don't allow Confederation governance to dictate our actions. We are a free species. I suggest you be grateful that you're still alive," Nra said coldly. "It could easily go the other way."

Earth

Director Cantor's blood ran cold as he read the report across his desk. A dozen GC interceptors destroyed by Bastian warships, and his rogue ambassador was still on her way to Mars. He cursed under his breath as he thought about the devastation she was bringing to their doorstep.

"Such a fool," he said before violently swiping the contents off his desk and onto the floor.

General Treff sat across from him, unmoved by the outburst. "She's resourceful, I'll give her that."

"She sided with the enemy and they're coming to destroy us. I don't think resourceful is the right word, General."

Treff eyed the director and Cantor saw a hesitance about him. Whatever was going through the old man's mind wasn't something he wanted to say out loud. That meant it wasn't something Cantor wanted to hear.

"How did we not see this coming?" Cantor continued with his tirade, stomping over to his perch above the Earth and staring down at the clouds rushing over the mountaintops like rolling waves.

"We put her back against the wall. If there's a modicum of truth to what Cushing has to say, then she is hellbent on the Confederation hearing it. Perhaps it goes further than just the human element. Maybe she hopes to save other species from what the Bastia are planning?"

Cantor scoffed at the idea. He wasn't about to credit her with

233

DAVE ALEXANDER

that kind of forethought. An alert sounded over his comm and he turned to face it. A message from Ambassador Spar was queued. Cantor stepped over and allowed it to play.

"Director Cantor, your attack on the *Veritas* has failed. We will continue our route to Mars and expect you to call off any further attacks. My deal with the Bastia was done with the authority given me by my position within the Confederation. Your actions risk sparking a war with a species who have only acted to defend this ship and themselves. Any other acts of aggression will be a declaration of war and they will act accordingly."

He eyed the General, his face contorted in angst. "Resourceful, you say? Aiding and abetting the enemy is more like it."

Treff let out a sigh, then spoke his mind, "Director, you must go to Mars to face this head-on. You heard her; the Bastia will bring war if we trifle with them further. Do you want to risk more lives by seeking the aggressive route, or maybe put a little faith in the fact that she has this handled?"

Cantor balled his fists tightly and wanted to swing at the old General. How satisfying it would be to crush the bones in his smug face. He was surrounded by cowards unwilling to stay the course. Everyone wanted to tuck tail and pray that the murderous Bastia would not fulfill their lust for bloodshed. Denial would bring their destruction as surely as Ambassador Spar welcomed them into the Sol System. He had less than a day before they arrived on Mars' doorstep. Less than a day to get out ahead of this and hope for intercession from a higher power.

"If I agree to go, will you come with me?"

"Of course," General Treff replied.

"Then pack your bags. We leave within the hour."

Treff rose from his seat and stepped out of the room, leaving the Director alone once again. Cantor longed for some guidance from Chancellor Benoit, but the elder chancellor had been dispatched to the other side of the galaxy and his new composite hadn't yet come to. The human Director of the Galactic Confederation was at a loss, having to make decisions without his most trusted advisor. General Treff hadn't yet proven himself and no one else within the organization had the proper access to brief on the matter. Even the mystery person who checked in periodically was silent now.

His only hope was that Director Igvi on Mars would see things the way he did, and their unification could protect the system from the Bastian menace.

Cantor called his secretary on the comm.

"Yes, sir?" her friendly voice sounded from the speaker.

"Ensure my travel arrangements are made for Archea. General Treff is traveling with me. Bump any transports leaving within the hour if my personal shuttle is not ready."

"Is this an emergency?" A tinge of fear sounded from her voice.

"There's no emergency. I just don't want to be late for a meeting with the Litar Director."

"Yes, sir. I'll take care of it."

"Thank you," he said. He should have felt bad for lying, but her knowing the truth would only create a panic. He couldn't afford that on top of everything else slipping through his fingers right now.

Cantor moved to the small storage area hidden behind a faux wall and pulled out a pre-packed suitcase. Five days' worth of clothing and toiletries were inside. More than enough for him to get to Archea, intercept Ambassador Spar, see that Garret Cushing is incarcerated, and return to Earth. He could do it in three if he could get Director Igvi to agree to recycle both Spar and Cushing upon arrival.

Whatever it would take to prevent a war.

That's what set him apart from his predecessors. Director Cantor would cross any line necessary for the greater good.

DAVE ALEXANDER

"Service over self," he said through his teeth. He hoped that this time he might believe it.

GCS Veritas

Garret couldn't shake the feeling something was happening. "Is she in danger?"

"She doesn't appear to be, but her heart rate is elevated. I can ask if you think it is appropriate?"

"No. If she's in danger then asking will only inflame the situation," Garret answered. "I need a way to protect her. Are there weapons on board?"

"If there were weapons on board, I would not be allowed to provide one to you, given your history with violence against the Confederation allies."

Garret's shoulders slumped. "Think. Think. Think," he hissed while pacing the room. There was no part of this plan that included him being locked out and the ambassador being held captive with a Bastian guard. If things went sideways, Nra could snap her in half like a twig. Of course, this part of the plan was his and nothing was going right.

"Is there a way for me to get to the bridge without needing the hatch unlocked?"

"No. The ventilation shaft has permanent grating to prevent intrusion in the event of an enemy boarding party. In fact, with the bridge secured, the atmosphere within the rest of the ship could be vented to kill anyone not inside the bridge."

"Oh, well that makes me feel better," Garret shot back.

"I'm not sure why. You're not on the bridge."

Garret rolled his eyes and kept pacing like a caged animal. There had to be another way to get to the ambassador. He might

OBLIVION'S DAWN

not be able to take the Bastian lieutenant on unarmed, but maybe the two of them could overpower him if it came down to it.

"Do you have any suggestions?"

"*You could try knocking on the bridge hatch,*" the AI replied.

Garret grumbled under his breath and turned his attention to the items in the room available to him. The medical cart sat dormant with its mechanical arms perched above it at rest. He looked over them trying to find something useful. He found it in a single arm with two blades attached at the ends used for amputations.

He shuddered at the thought of having to endure that, but this wasn't for medical purposes. It was to use as a weapon. Garret got to work unhooking it from the ceiling. Within minutes he had eight pounds of titanium just shy of a meter in length. With the blades on the end, it was better than some weapons he'd defended himself with in times past. It would have to do.

"*I don't think an amputation will save the ambassador,*" the AI said as Garret moved to leave the room.

"No, but me driving this into that Bastian lieutenant's skull will do the trick. What's going on right now."

"*Ambassador Spar is sending a message to Director Cantor.*"

"About what?"

"*About the attack after we jumped. She is saying the Bastian acted to protect themselves and any other forms of aggression will be considered a declaration of war.*"

Garret swore under his breath. "I didn't even realize we jumped," he said. "Last time I felt it."

"*You do have elevated levels of adrenaline. Perhaps it numbed you to the effects?*"

"Maybe."

"*There's something else you should know,*" the AI said.

"What's that?"

"The Bastian officer used some form of mind control to make

DAVE ALEXANDER

Ambassador Spar send the message. She is arguing with him now and he is growing highly agitated. I believe a confrontation is inevitable."

Garret didn't say anything at all. He ran for the bridge and slammed his fist onto the hatch as he called for the ambassador. He beat on the hatch relentlessly, his voice growing hoarse from shouting to be heard through the metal.

Feeling himself getting nowhere, he switched his focus and tried to pry the hatch open using the mechanical arm from the medical bay. Each time he pried with it; the edge slipped off. It was as useless as he felt.

He switched his plan of attack again and began beating on the hatch using the arm as a striker. The metallic clang reverberated down the passageway of the ship, reminding him that sound only existed where there was atmosphere for it to travel. If the lieutenant tired of his actions, the officer could easily vent the ship and pull the oxygen right out of Garret's lungs.

It would be a painful death, much worse than any he'd endured in his other composites. The fear should have made him stop. It would have worked with any reasonable man. But he was anything but reasonable.

Garret kept at it, banging the hatch relentlessly as he shouted Tella's name.

Then a sound.

The hatch unlatched and opened. Garret took a step back to see Ambassador Spar standing stoically before him.

"What is it?" she asked.

"The AI said you were in danger," Garret answered.

"Do I look like I'm in danger?"

Garret swallowed the soreness in his throat. He stared at her as she narrowed her eyes at him. Her face said one thing, but her gaze said something else. "AI, is she being controlled by him?"

"*Yes.*"

OBLIVION'S DAWN

"Thought so." Garret rushed past her with the mechanical arm raised high over his head. He turned to see the Bastian lieutenant standing behind the hatch, a cold stare boring into the human mercenary.

"I will rip you limb from limb," Nra said, his voice like gravel.

"Bring it," Garret snapped.

Lieutenant Nra closed the gap between them. Somehow the Bastian appeared larger than he had before, or perhaps it was the sinking feeling in Garret's heart as the snarling beast drew closer. Garret swung the arm mightily, narrowly missing the lieutenant.

Nra returned a massive blow to Garret's chest, knocking the wind from his lungs. He stumbled back, and Nra grabbed him by his head, lifted him up, and dropped him to the deck like a wet cloth.

Garret stared wide-eyed on the deck as the light in the room faded. There was no oxygen in his lungs. There were no thoughts running through his mind. There was only the slightest of cues that he was slipping away and may never return.

It may have been peace, but if it was, then why did he hear the hollow echoes of someone screaming?

The thought lasted less than two heartbeats. Then faded away with what remained of the light.

Hours passed as Tella stared at Garret's unconscious form on the deck of her ship. She thought he was dead, and the possibility of his death was still there, but the light snoring coming from his mouth at least gave her some hope that he wasn't too far gone. It was possible the aerosol the Bastian used on Garret once he was unconscious was something used to force him to sleep.

She hoped so. Otherwise, Garret wasn't proving himself to be much of a partner. As intimidating as he had been on the field of battle against his own kind, he hardly stood up to the Bastian lieutenant at all. It even served as a joke between Nra and his commanding officer when the lieutenant called it in to Captain Viar.

"I think he needs to be transferred to the medical bay," Tella said as she rose defiantly.

Nra set his gaze on her, a scowl forming as the folds grew deeper on his brow. He glanced at Garret for a moment before shrugging. "He'll live."

"I insist," Tella shot back. She squared her shoulders, trying to be intimidating despite the trepidation coursing through her body. She knew at that moment she wasn't a warrior. She was a politician whose heart was in the right place, but who lacked the necessary skills to negotiate her way out of this predicament.

"Then carry him," Nra replied, disinterested. "But make it quick. We'll be in the jump window soon and I want you on the bridge in case we're challenged by more GC ships."

Tella nodded her consent and ran over to Garret. She grabbed hold of his wrists and dragged him across the smooth deck. He was twice her weight and she had watched the Bastian lift him by his head and slam him down like he weighed nothing. She didn't have to wonder what Nra could do to her if the situation grew worse.

Once in the medical bay, she asked the AI to assist her in getting the mercenary onto the medical cart. Mechanical arms did most of the work, but Tella kept one hand on him as she tried to check his vitals. The fact he was still breathing was a welcome relief, but permanent brain damage was likely. She ordered the AI to scan him for injuries before she returned to the bridge.

"*He has multiple contusions, but I detect no signs of permanent injury,*" the AI said after a full minute of scans. "*Should I attempt to wake him?*"

OBLIVION'S DAWN

"No," Tella answered. As much as she wanted someone on the bridge in case she needed them, she had seen what happened when Garret tried to fight Lieutenant Nra. It was no contest. The worst thing would be this trip was a waste of time and the truth was lost. "Try to keep him occupied until we dock on Mars. I need him breathing if he's to testify to the Confederation."

"*Do you have anything I should relay to him upon his waking?*"

She considered it a moment, but in truth, he didn't deserve to know how worried she was for him. She half-expected him to take advantage of her at any moment. Wouldn't an emotional response, even if it was sympathy, be used against her? He couldn't be trusted with that kind of information.

"You can tell him where we are and tell him what happened. Other than that, treat him on a need-to-know basis. His previous clearances are now revoked."

"*Yes, Ambassador. What about you?*"

"What about me?"

"*I worry that you are entering the proverbial lions' den.*"

She recognized the metaphor. She'd read different versions of that story as a child, but most of them took out the original message behind the ancient tale. The message of hope against all odds. That was the version she clung to.

"I'll be fine. Just continue to record everything and dispatch the file to the database once we arrive. I don't want anything lost if I can help it."

"Yes, Ambassador."

Tella stepped out of the medical bay and stole one last glance at Garret as he lay helplessly on the medical cart. He had come to her defense, and she was grateful, but what was coming now didn't need the brute force of a dishonored mercenary. It required the finesse of an ambassador, an exalted member of the Confederation. It required polite words and a listening ear.

241

DAVE ALEXANDER

Service over self.

She shook off the feeling of dread and made her way to the bridge. Nra waited, his feet kicked up on the console lazily. "We're in the jump window, Ambassador. Are you ready?"

"Yes," Tella answered as she claimed the seat across from him. She made no effort to coordinate the jump. Instead, she allowed the Bastian officer to take control. He hardly seemed to notice.

A moment later the pull began. She held herself, fighting against the sensation of being picked apart by gravity. Then, as suddenly as it began, the sensation ended.

Tella looked to the monitor and the map depicting their location. They were on the outer edges of the Sol System. She was practically home. But she wasn't the only one at humanity's back door. The two Bastian ships followed closely behind her as the *Veritas* made its way to Mars.

The enemy was here, and she had brought them with her. If the worst happened, then she would go down in history as a traitor to humankind. She let out her breath and whispered a silent prayer. This wasn't the lion's den. This had the potential to be something much worse.

THIRTY-ONE
BNV POURGUA

VIAR HELD HIS BREATH AS HE BEHELD SOL. FOR YEARS HE wondered what it would feel like to return to the system responsible for his father's death. He always anticipated leading the charge against humanity to exact his revenge, but this was different. This mission was to prevent the execution of a human life. Strangely, he felt a tinge of pride at doing the opposite of his compulsion.

The time for vengeance would come, but for now, he would let the politicians do their dirty work and prime the pumps for the inevitable.

"Captain, incoming message from Lieutenant Nra," Ensign Uj said from his console.

Viar answered from his own monitor and glowered at his lieutenant aboard the GCS starship. "What is the report?"

"Sir, there are no proximity alarms sounding on the Confederation channels. Your presence here is expected and they have agreed to allow our ships to orbit Mars during their deliberations."

"Good. Will you disembark?"

"I have received consent from Director Igvi, but they do not believe their human counterparts will be gracious about it. I have agreed to stay onboard for the time being. If I need to disembark, then the Litar emissary will provide escort."

Captain Viar sighed. Everything was an act. They thought they were in control by disallowing a Bastian to step foot on their dirt ball of a planet. True control was having turrets aimed directly at the heart of their civilization and the capability to obliterate it from existence, but not taking the shot.

That kind of control was godlike.

That kind of control was what separated the Bastia from the simple beings comprising the Confederation.

"Keep me informed and we will provide cover fire in the event you need to escape. I don't want to lose access to that ship if the situation worsens."

"Yes, sir," Nra said. "May I make a suggestion?"

Viar resisted the urge to groan. The overly helpful lieutenant's need to interject an idea into every plan was grating on his nerves, but he had been willing to take on this responsibility. Viar felt he owed him at least a listening ear. "What is it?"

Nra's eyes darted from the monitor to something off to the side. Viar assumed correctly it was the ambassador and soon the human woman stepped into frame.

"Sir, the ambassador would be allowed to meet with the Confederation without having to be scanned. Her credentials grant her the ability to enter the Citadel with her communications device. I would like to monitor the situation as it takes place. Perhaps an early warning if we need to escape?"

There would be no escape. Viar would allow Nra to depart with the starship, but the *Pourgua* and the *Nir* would stay and create an onslaught upon the Martian surface before moving the destruction to Luna, then Earth.

"Do as you feel necessary. Consider this a test."

Nra's lip curled slightly. "Thank you, sir."

The monitor went dark and Viar wondered what the next

OBLIVION'S DAWN

several hours would bring. They were five thousand AU from Mars. It would require one more jump before docking could occur. The clock was ticking and Viar anticipated a rousing success. Even if they were attacked before reaching Mars, the conflict would be swift and decisive. They didn't need to safely deliver the ambassador and her prisoner for the Bastia to win. Being in the heart of the Sol System was victory enough. Anything else would simply make that victory sweeter.

GCS Veritas

Garret stirred awake, feeling like he'd fallen off a mountain, like he had swallowed rocks. His ears rang. A concussion was likely, but it wasn't his first time. He knew what to expect.

He slowly rose to a seated position and scanned the room. Part of him hoped the ambassador would be waiting for him, but the medical bay was empty like the rest of his godforsaken life.

"AI," he croaked. His voice sounded strange coming from his lips between the ringing of his ears and the knot in his throat. "What happened?"

"You went one on one with the Bastian officer," the AI replied.

Garret rubbed at his throat trying to massage it into something less achy. It wasn't working. "How did I do?"

"You lasted all of two seconds."

"I had to last longer than that. I had a weapon."

"Perhaps it is possible that you lasted longer, but that possibility only exists in places where time is measured differently. Based on Confederation time you lasted two seconds."

"Smartass," Garret grumbled. "How is the ambassador?"

"Shaken up by your display of bravado. It was reckless and could have resulted in more significant injury."

"Was she injured?"

"No, you took the brunt of it. She does, however, second-guess her judgement about you."

"She said that, huh?"

"That is an observation based on her attitude shift and body language."

"Hmm," Garret replied. He didn't have anything better to say. He was disappointed in himself for lacking the strength to properly protect the ambassador, but if she was still breathing, then that meant the Bastia didn't want her dead. At least not yet.

Small favors, he thought as he got to his feet and tried his balance. He seemed fine enough. Body aches were common in his line of work. So long as there was no internal bleeding, then he could probably face whatever came his way next.

"Where are we?" Garret asked as he took a few slow steps around the room.

"We are situated in the Oort Cloud, roughly five thousand AU from Mars. We will require one additional jump to be in range of our destination."

Garret shuddered at the thought they had led the Bastia to humanity's backdoor. It was a necessary evil, but he didn't trust the plan not to go sideways once they arrived. What he would tell the Confederation affected the Bastia just as much as it affected humankind. Both parties were being played. They just didn't realize it. How the factions would react once the truth got out was what worried him most.

He considered trying to return to the bridge, but he figured if he did, Lieutenant Nra would finish what he'd started. Garret rubbed at his throat again, hoping for a difference that wasn't there.

"Might I suggest ice," the AI said.

Garret nodded. "It couldn't hurt."

A panel opened on the bulkhead and an icepack was brought

OBLIVION'S DAWN

to him via the mechanical arms attached to the overhead. Garret pressed it against his neck and held it in place while he paced.

"Can you tell me what to expect when we arrive?"

"You know what to expect. They will escort you inside the Citadel and you will give your testimony."

"I know that, but can you run simulations for me?"

"I don't know that I should."

"Why not?"

"Ambassador Spar removed many of your permissions after your act of violence. I believe that I would be violating her orders by aiding you in this way."

Garret scoffed. "Maybe you're right. Maybe she is second-guessing her decisions about me."

"Does that change things for you?"

Garret shrugged. "I suppose not. I just need to get the truth to the people who have the power to do something about it. Anything beyond that is out of my control."

"And if they execute you for crimes against the Confederation?"

Garret didn't want to answer. He didn't want to admit that he deserved whatever punishment they dealt out. But avoiding the truth was what got him in so deep in the first place.

"Then everyone wins. Without me, my stepfather loses his triggerman. The Bastia'll kill him once they realize he's power-less, and maybe there'll be a chance for our people to make peace."

"I find that unlikely," the AI replied.

"What part?"

"Peace. Regardless of what happens, there will be people on both sides who want war. If they have enough authority, it will happen."

"You have us all figured out, huh?"

"What is there to figure out? The data doesn't lie. Every

247

DAVE ALEXANDER

conflict escalates to violence eventually. The only thing that defies logic is why a species with the ability to wipe out the existence of another wouldn't do so. Conflict ends when the enemy is dead, not when they are defeated."

Garret shuddered and pulled the ice pack from his neck. "Your analysis doesn't paint a very hopeful picture of the future."

"What is there to be hopeful about when people commit evil against one another at every turn? You of all people should know the implications of what you've done."

Garret swallowed the knot in his throat and returned to the medical cart. "Dim the lights," he said. "And wake me up when we get there."

<hr />

Earth

Cantor stepped onto the launch pad atop the citadel pressing the oxygen mask firmly to his face. General Treff led the way to the transport, with his aid dragging both travelers' bags on a wheeled cart behind him. It had been years since Cantor was on Mars and he didn't look forward to going again.

He had a private falling out with Mio, the previous Litar Director before Igvi took over, but he was certain the bad blood between them had been passed down. Correspondence between Earth and Mars had never been the same. Strangely, relations between the humans and Litar on Mars were booming, which was more than could be said about the colony planets under his jurisdiction.

He tried not to take it personally, but he read the quarterly reports like anyone else. The populations of human-led colonies were on the decline. The Litar colonies were rising. Eventually,

OBLIVION'S DAWN

Igvi and their people would outpace human ingenuity and humanity would lose favor within the Confederation.

And now he had a rogue agent leading the Bastian military straight to Mars, right at the doorstep of his biggest rival in the system. If he weren't going to be on the red planet, he would be happy that Mars would face an attack first. Instead, he felt dread as he prepared to depart.

General Treff opened the transport door and held it for him as he brushed past his general. A member of the crew handled the baggage while the old general climbed in after him. Both men pulled on headsets and once the transport doors were shut, Cantor pulled his oxygen mask away and let the environmental control systems feed his lungs reoxygenated air. At first, it tasted stale, but then he grew used to it. Just another part of the travel experience he loathed.

"There's a transport waiting for us on Luna. We can board as soon as we arrive, and it will dispatch us to Mars. We should be there before Ambassador Spar and the prisoner," Treff said through the private comm.

Cantor nodded. He knew the itinerary. He practically stood in front of his secretary as it was arranged, but he kept his mouth shut. He ignored whatever ramblings his general babbled and focused his gaze outside the window as the transport lifted from the launch pad.

He was so high up it felt like a god staring down at insects. The clouds had dispersed enough to see the ground below. Most of it was a patchwork of scorched earth with occasional vegetation where it slowly sprang back to life. Eventually, the planet would restore itself, but it seemed a long way off.

His stomach shifted with the change of direction as the transport accelerated into an upward turn. Cantor lay his head back against the headrest and focused on his breathing. The transport

DAVE ALEXANDER

was fast, exiting Earth's atmosphere less than three minutes after takeoff.

Their rendezvous with the next ship occurred before they reached Luna, meeting them halfway so they didn't have to waste time with docking and navigating the terminal. The transport connected to the larger ship with a tube spanning ten meters between each ship. A space suit wasn't needed to make the transition, but it was still risky. One slip and the seal could break, leaving them in vacuum.

"Are you ready, sir?" The pilot asked. A green light appeared overhead stating it was safe to cross.

Of course, he wasn't ready, but he unlatched his restraints anyway. Cantor shifted to the airlock and waited for it to cycle open for him to cross. He went through, slouching to keep the top of his head from bumping into the surface. He held onto the built-in rails, but up and down were irrelevant. The tube was the same design in all directions. He simply tried to stay relative to the airlock on the larger ship.

Once he pressed the button to board, the airlock cycled so he could safely enter. There was no greeting or welcoming party. There were only the plain white bulkheads with an arrow pointing him towards the seating area. He followed it without waiting for General Treff. He just wanted to sit down and pretend none of this was happening – that his ambassador didn't go rogue, that he didn't have to play nice with the Litar director whom he hardly knew, and that the Bastian military was not in the Sol System.

With everything stacked against him, he was losing hope in the future. This was easily the worst time in his life, and he expected by the time it was over, his life would be over as well.

THIRTY-TWO
GCS VERITAS

MARS APPEARED IN THE MONITOR WITH ITS MASSIVE DOMES scattered across the surface. Millions of people, mostly humans and Litar, lived beneath each dome. Some housed cities, while other, smaller domes were used to grow vegetation and farm animals. Giant spires reached outward from the surface, creating multiple docking points for ships too large to sustain suborbital flight in atmosphere. Ships like the *Veritas*.

Each spire had elevators leading back and forth from the surface. They maintained their orbit with thrusters gently pulling away from the Martian landscape from hundreds of anchor points. It was a primitive design, but effective, nonetheless. They had existed for hundreds of years without failing, which was more than could be said about most technology.

She thought back to the first attempts at an elevator from Earth. The tragedy that followed nearly caused the humans to withdraw from their pursuit of escaping their planetary domain. Where would they have been if humanity gave up?

Certainly not on an intergalactic flight and about to dock to the fourth planet from Sol, that was for sure.

Docking occurred autonomously as the ship's AI navigated

251

DAVE ALEXANDER

to the appropriate airlock. Everything was settled for their arrival. Everything except her authorization to exit with Garret Cushing.

"They're playing games," Garret groaned.

"We did lead the Bastia into our home system. I doubt they trust us at this point," Tella answered. Lieutenant Nra sat at the helm listening to their conversation, but she wasn't about to mince words.

He had taken control of her mind and forced her to send a message to Director Cantor. The violation of her mind and body meant nothing. There would be no repercussions. There was only the fact it happened, and no recourse would follow.

"We took a calculated risk. If we didn't, then they would have killed us. Wouldn't you?" Garret sneered at Nra.

The Bastian officer glared down his nose at Garret. "We were prepared to destroy your ship. We only needed orders and it would have been done."

"See?" Garret said. "We were justified by one of those articles you devoted your life to."

Tella sighed. She hated knowing he was right. What she hated worse was not being trusted by her own people. Even Director Igvi, whom she had met many times, had taken the cold shoulder approach to her imminent arrival. For the first time in her career as an ambassador she felt shunned by them.

There would be repercussions for her actions, and the Bastia would likely fly off with the *GCS Veritas* as their prize. It would be a symbol of their moral victory over humanity. But that was only if she and Garret could prevent war.

"Is there anything you haven't told me?" Tella asked, her voice barely above a whisper.

Garret looked to her and said, "I have told you enough, but not everything. I have thirty years of stories to tell, and I won't be able to explain everything. They'll have to plug me in and download

252

OBLIVION'S DAWN

most of my memories from my cerebral port. I'll answer their questions from there and hopefully plead my case."

"You sound like you think you have a chance of being released."

He scoffed. "Not at all. They'll recycle me at the first opportunity. This composite isn't getting off Mars."

"If they recycle you, then you'll likely never be reconstructed again. The Confederation has the means to prevent that from happening. They'll wipe out your files completely, as if you never existed."

"Like the primitive humans we sprang from before we realized we weren't the center of the universe? There are worse fates."

Tella considered it. What would it be like to never have the possibility to exist again? She had read old reports from fundamentalists stating that life ended when the original body died. Any composite afterward was just a soulless pile of carbon. There were, of course, religious justifications for their stance, but she never thought any of it was factual. She felt alive. She felt like she had a soul.

Didn't she?

"Sometimes I think I made a mistake trusting you," Tella said. It was like she was admitting something she should feel guilty for. Why utter this revelation to someone who terrorized colonies for decades? A part of her was ashamed to admit it, not because it was true, but because she worried what he might say. There was no foundation for such an emotion, yet she couldn't shake it.

"So do I," Garret replied. He glanced up at her with a smirk. "But I'm not going to betray you. All I want to do is get the truth out there and stop my stepfather from usurping the Confederation. He's a lot of things, but a good man isn't one of them. He'll bring war to the galaxy if they let him."

"You've said as much before," she replied, sinking back into her thoughts.

DAVE ALEXANDER

Tella was afraid of what would happen, not necessarily to herself, but to the people she had sworn to protect. If the Confederation didn't believe Garret's testimony, then they could be turning a blind eye to a potential attack. If they did believe him and refused to release him to the Bastia, then it would be the same outcome. She didn't like the odds.

"Do you know what my earliest memory is?" Garret asked, pulling her out of the lingering depression clouding her mind. She looked at him without answering. "I remember my mother running from my biological father. Before anyone knew he was a bad man, she was afraid of him. She tried desperately to leave him, though I didn't know it at the time. I just remember her tears as we fled in the dead of night in some backwoods colony.

"There were other species there; probably a few Litar, and I know I saw a Veshnian family. For all I know we could have been right outside a citadel on one of the major colony planets. But what I did know was that my mother needed help, and no one lifted a finger to help her. That stuck with me all these years. No one helps anyone they don't know."

Tella looked away. She had been willing to help millions of people over the course of her life, but how many times had her efforts gone unnoticed? She never looked for acknowledgement, but desperate people always seemed to claim that no one was willing to help. They chose to see the world through blinders.

She shouldn't have been surprised to hear him admit it, but she was.

"You were a child. There's no way you could have understood what was really going on. She left him when you were two years old," she said. "I've read your record."

Garret smiled and blushed as he looked away from her. "Do you remember when you were two?"

"Not really," she replied.

"I lied about that being my first memory. That's just the first

254

one I can place. My earliest recollections were of hearing her screaming. I have no context for what was happening; only that it scared me, and it felt so cold."

"She was brave to run away," Tella told him. She meant it, but even more, she meant to steer the conversation away from those dark thoughts painting the tone of his voice.

"She did what she had to. Same as me."

Tella shivered.

As callous as she knew he was, she hoped there was some humanity left in him.

Lieutenant Nra stirred from his position at the console and marched over to look down on the humans. "You seek sympathy when you displayed violence. Your actions painted your people in the same darkness the Confederation sees in my people. Instead of seeking sympathy, seek justice. That's the only way for a warrior to find honor for what he's done."

"Easy for you to say, you don't have the same sordid past I do," Garret shot back.

"No?" the Bastian officer pulled up his sleeve and displayed scarred flesh. "I was a mercenary like you once." Nra unfastened his collar and revealed the Bastian number for "six" etched into his neck. "I thought I knew everything once. I thought I was the leader my people deserved. I was going to bring peace with a gun. It doesn't make much sense to me now, but the propaganda against the Confederation led me to believe that destruction was the only way to make peace."

"Look at where it got you; a man imprisoned by a military that beheads its dissenters." Garret rose to his feet but stood a head shorter than the Bastian lieutenant. "What would they think if they saw those scars or that mark?"

Nra's eyes narrowed, and his fists clenched. Tella knew what would happen if either man were to swing at the other, but she was powerless to stop them. "What makes you think they don't know?"

Garret's jaw went slack.

"The rebellion against the old order has been waged for years. The people who bent their knees to Artimus Chancey infiltrated the military to reclaim their power. Not many of my people believe the rumors, but I, for one, hope that the truth is revealed. Otherwise, I risked this life for nothing."

"How many of you are rebelling?" Tella asked.

Nra stared at her, then answered, "I can't say. I will tell you that this is the moment we've been waiting for. We knew Artimus was alive. We knew he was still playing god over my people. When this is over, he'll pay with his life."

Garret smiled. "I guess we really do have a common enemy, huh?"

Nra lowered his head and stared directly into Garret's eyes. Tella took an unsteady step back as he spoke, "Don't make assumptions. You're at the top of our list."

Archea, Mars

They had waited for him to arrive before allowing the ambassador to disembark. Still, Director Igvi had yet to meet with him. There had to be a plan. There was no way Tella could be allowed to disobey direct orders from a superior and place an entire system in jeopardy.

There was a stir in the air, a feeling of excitement outside of Director Igvi's office. It was enough to make one think a celebrity had arrived. It didn't help that the staff was all adorned in their ceremonial robes. Lesser staff in dark greens and blues. Senior members wore deep crimsons and purples. It reminded Cantor of the religious histories he'd studied in his youth.

"This is chaos," Cantor hissed through his teeth, stirring General Treff from his placid slump on the Litar director's couch. The general regained his composure and nodded as the door clicked.

"I'm sorry for leaving you two alone, but I have a ton of questions coming at me about the situation. I imagine you're as nervous as I am?" Director Igvi said as they entered the room. The director was dressed in white with silver and gold embellishments. A headpiece with a veil sat atop their head, but the veil was brushed over the top so he could see their face clearly.

"You could say that, though my nerves aren't settled by the enthusiasm oozing around this place." Cantor stepped over and took Igvi's hand in the intergalactic sign of greeting, flat palmed with the tip of his thumb touching Igvi's. It was a sign of peace and one that hardly seemed like doing anything compared to the more aggressive handshakes in human culture.

"Enthusiasm for your ambassador's arrival doesn't mean my people are excited about what this could mean. We recognize the potential danger, and we will work with you to ensure the situation does not worsen."

Igvi stepped away and took a seat across from General Treff. They crossed their legs and motioned for the human director to sit. The Litar people were humanoid in appearance, but completely androgynous, especially those at the seat of power and authority.

Generations ago, long before humanity was in the picture, the Litar were targeted by the Kruva. The Kruvan warriors focused on annihilating the Litar by killing the males. The tactic may have worked, but the Litar found ways to mask their gender while training their females in battle.

Eventually, the conflict with the Kruva ended, but the effects

DAVE ALEXANDER

of those horrific decades were still in effect. They, of course, had genders like all sentient species which bred for reproduction. But they did not rely on that to inform their identities. Instead, they found that their power resided in their cultural identity. The powerful members of the Litar community were strict about upholding the appearance of gender neutrality, while others in the community who were influenced by other factions were less so. To Litar like Director Igvi, preserving that tradition was more important than preserving the individual. That insistence defied human logic. Then again, most human logic flew in the face of the other factions within the Confederation.

Every Litar Cantor had met could pass as male or female. He was reasonably certain Igvi was female, but never bothered to ask. There was no point in offending an ally as far as he was concerned.

"General Treff and I look forward to aiding you in the interrogation," Cantor said as he sat next to his general. Igvi gave a curt nod but said nothing. The silence was overwhelming, so Cantor continued. "When should we expect Ambassador Spar to report to the hearing?"

Igvi looked to the window. "Within the hour. The court is being prepared now. I understand a Bastian officer is onboard?"

"Against our wishes," Treff interjected.

"That's correct," Cantor answered, trying to keep his emotions in check. The Litar were stalling, there was no reason to prepare a courtroom. Something else was happening.

"I would like the Bastian to be included in the hearing," Igvi said.

"Why? They are not allied with the Confederation. They have no voice in our business," Cantor said.

"Their exclusion was at the price of your inclusion, Director Cantor. The Bastia were allies for generations. They can provide a

OBLIVION'S DAWN

perspective unique to the situation. Why should we only accept human testimony? Is it somehow superior?"

Cantor bit his tongue. This wasn't going the way he had hoped. His impression was that the Litar also feared the Bastia. If this conversation meant what he thought it did, then the Litar feared humans more. That distrust could topple their standing within the Confederation.

They couldn't afford for that to happen.

"If we agree, what guarantee do we have that our people will not be harmed if the Bastia come across with false accusations that we cannot reasonably defend?"

Igvi's expression changed, but it wasn't so much physical as it was an ambient change in the room. It was the way molecules in the air reacted to their mood that gave any indication something was wrong.

"What guarantee do we have that you haven't delivered our destruction?" Igvi asked.

This wasn't going anywhere. He had tread too far and offended his counterpart. "I understand," he replied meekly.

The Litar responded better to humbleness over confidence. They rejected aggressive behaviors unless they served to protect them. It was the primary reason they had sought inclusion into the Confederation to begin with. "I don't believe the Bastian is a reliable witness," Cantor said.

"Do you know that for a fact?"

"I can't say that I do."

"I'm extending the offer to join us. If they do not wish to take part, then it will be as you prefer. If they do take part, then we will give them the opportunity to speak. Will you agree?"

"What other choice do I have? It sounds as if the decision has been made for me," Cantor replied.

Igvi didn't respond to his comment. Instead, they rose from

259

the couch and shifted around to their desk. "Please send an escort team to the *Veritas*. It is time to welcome our guests."

"Yes, Director Igvi," someone responded. The tone of the voice sounded human, but Cantor wasn't sure. He found that he wasn't sure about a lot of things anymore.

"Shall I escort you two to the courtroom?" Igvi asked.

"I think we'll manage," Cantor replied.

"Then I'll see you there. Your place is being prepared as we speak."

Igvi left the room. Cantor and Treff were alone.

"I don't like it," Treff said. "The Bastia are bloodthirsty animals. They can't be trusted."

"The same has been said about us," Cantor replied. "We don't have a choice. We have to play by their rules."

"And what if baseless claims are presented to the court? The Litar have no affinity for humans. They think themselves superior."

Treff was right, but they were powerless here. Mars may have been a human colony once, but part of the Confederation agreement meant giving space for allies in need. The fact that humanity was later attacked, leaving the Litar with the best resources in the system had been the basis of conspiracy theories for years. Regardless, they were at the mercy of Director Igvi's rule. He was doing Cantor a favor by participating. It was politics, plain and simple.

"Keep your eyes open, General. I have a feeling we're about to witness something neither of us would ever expect."

"Yes, sir. What do you think it is?"

Cantor shook his head. "I wish to God I knew."

OBLIVION'S DAWN

BNV Pourgua

He hated waiting. There was something about the silence between messages that filled him with anxiety. No news was not good news. Not for someone who saw what happens when the silence finally breaks.

Captain Viar gripped the splintered armrest of his seat and ground his teeth. He contemplated the unusual nature of Mars, at how the domes were necessary to sustain life. No other world within the Confederation was bound by such contraptions, yet this system had two, Mars and Luna.

He reflected on the stories he'd heard from his father about this system. The "Ghosts of Luna" was his favorite. The way his father told it brought the system to life. The idea of hauntings from those who passed bordered on lunacy. The Bastia had no stories like that, but as chaotic as the concept was, there was something about the possibility of life after death, beholden to where one faded into eternal darkness, that allured him.

How many hauntings had he committed his enemies to over the years?

He would venture to say none, but maybe the humans perceived dimensions he could never fathom.

A smile curled his lip at the thought of humanity having the upper hand at anything. That smile faded when his comm chimed.

Viar switched it open and stood before the monitor.

"Captain, I have been granted access to attend the hearing on Mars. Director Igvi has requested that I provide testimony to what I have observed on this ship. I wanted to inform you that I intend to do as the Litar director has asked, with the added benefit of keeping an eye on the mercenary. Do you have any objections?"

Viar considered the question. He wasn't a willing participant in Confederation affairs, but his lieutenant made a valuable point

DAVE ALEXANDER

about keeping an eye on Cushing. "Do it and report back to me regularly."

"I will, sir. Also, I wanted to inform you that I interacted with the humans. It was not intentional, but I saw an opportunity to share our ideals and I took it."

Viar winced. Nra wasn't an emissary, he had no grounds to speak with the humans, but convincing them that the Bastian way was the correct way might prove valuable. Pleading to their humanity was supposed to allow them to empathize with others. Perhaps that was useful in this case. "How did they respond?"

"The female was quiet. The mercenary was objectionable, though I was countering his argument."

The remark made Viar chuckle to himself. "Be safe, Lieutenant. I do not trust these people."

"Neither do I, sir. I'll send word when I can."

Viar closed the comm and sank back into his seat. Lieutenant Nra would be the first Bastian to step foot on a planet in the Sol System in three decades. There was much riding on this, many opportunities to fail. He wondered if he made a mistake sending his junior officer to the field, but it was too late to second guess himself.

All he could do was wait.

Then again... Captain Viar grabbed the comm and made a ship-wide announcement. "All hands report to their stations and assume a defensive posture."

Within seconds two of his officers ran onto the bridge. "Is there an emergency, sir?" Ensign Bri, the youngest member of the ship's wardroom asked upon entering.

"No emergency," Viar replied. "This isn't General Quarters. I just have information that leads me to believe we need to be ready for anything. Assume your station and keep your eyes and ears open."

262

OBLIVION'S DAWN

"Yes, sir," Bri said before jogging over to his console on the other side of the bridge.

A minute later the bridge was fully manned, each officer assuming their duties and giving commands to their departments. Weapons and engineering were mustered and ready to go at a moment's notice. Other departments were in place and preparing for orders.

The waiting game had begun, and Captain Viar wasn't going to fall into the same trap his father had. The moment the humans struck first; he would annihilate them.

THIRTY-THREE
GCS VERITAS

THE AIRLOCK CYCLED OPEN, REVEALING A FOUR-MAN SQUAD armed for a siege rather than a simple prisoner transport. Three of them were Litar, one human, though he quickly looked away when Tella caught his eye.

"Ambassador Spar, I am Sergeant Ezure with the Galactic Confederation Guard. We are here to escort your crew to the citadel to prepare for the hearing."

Tella had already prepared, changing into dress robes provided by the ship. They were the wrong color, a shade of green beneath her station, but would suffice. It beat the gray coveralls she had worn before. "Thank you," she said, moving to allow the team to enter the *Veritas*.

Ezure faced her as their team continued towards the bridge. "Director Igvi advised us to use restraints on your prisoner. Will that be a problem?"

"Not at all," Garret said from around the corner. He stood with his arms extended downward, his wrists touching. "Just be careful with my left side. I was injured before the ambassador rescued me."

Ezure gave a curt nod and moved to Garret, pulling manacles

264

OBLIVION'S DAWN

from their belt. Garret didn't make a fuss over it, but his eyes shouted betrayal each time she looked at him.

The other three guards returned with Lieutenant Nra. "Sergeant, the rest of the ship is empty. Lieutenant Nra, emissary from the Bastia, will return with us," said one of the Litar guards.

"Affirmative," Ezure replied. "Lead the prisoner into the elevator first. Bind him to the bulkhead before the ambassador and emissary join us."

"Yes, Sergeant." The three guards ushered Garrett into the elevator. Tella watched from inside the ship as he was shoved into a corner and bound to an eyelet welded into the frame of the structure. The human guard kept glancing back at Tella, the attention making her nervous.

"How long will we be confined to the elevator?" Tella asked. It was more a question to distract her from what was happening than mere curiosity.

"Half an hour," Ezure answered. "Initial descent is quick, but it slows significantly for the last six thousand meters."

Tella nodded politely and stepped away from the guard. She eyed Nra, wondering what was going on in the Bastian's head. He obviously held opinions he mostly kept to himself, but he had revealed sentiments not unlike those the humans held regarding Garret's actions. There was hypocrisy in what he'd done, regardless of how he justified it.

She wondered if the Bastia and humans would have been allies if things were different. Perhaps they were more alike than either of them wanted to admit.

"Ambassador?" Sergeant Ezure said.

She turned to see he and his team were waiting. She entered the elevator before Nra, then the airlock closed and began its descent.

Her nerves ravaged her mind. There was no commotion inside. The guards were quiet. Garret sulked in the corner, and

265

DAVE ALEXANDER

Nra was his typical, stoically reserved self. There was no one she could confide her fears to. Only the lonely descent to the place she feared to tread.

Several times she considered asking questions of the guards, to try and learn more about them and their jobs, but the heavy gear and masks covering their lower faces only served to make her feel further isolated from the people within arm's reach.

Finally, the elevator slowed to a stop and the airlock opened. The citadel rose prominently before her. The only structure higher was the dome necessary to preserve life on this colony world. She stared in awe, having never seen such beauty before. The citadel on Earth was a hovering monstrosity, while this one on Mars was reminiscent of the ancient temples of Earth. She recalled the rebuilt kingdoms of Egypt she had explored as a child. The pyramids and temples had hieroglyphs etched into the stone and she recognized the influence here; those these weren't merely etchings, but also paintings and embellishments so striking she wished she could linger and examine the stories depicting in the stonework.

"Ambassador, we need to clear the elevator," Sergeant Ezure said, stirring her from her thoughts.

Tella quickly stepped out and waited for them to usher Garret from the elevator, giving them and Nra a wide berth. Two of the guards escorted Garret away, leaving half their team with Tella and Nra.

"We have been instructed to lead you to your own quarters for downloading," Ezure said.

"Downloading?" Tella asked. "We already did this on the ship."

"Standard procedure, Ambassador. The Confederation wants an updated download before the hearing."

Part of her wanted to resist, but there was no use. She was as much a prisoner to the Confederation as Garret was at this point.

266

OBLIVION'S DAWN

It was only her station that gave her the freedom to not be escorted in restraints. Strangely, the same courtesy was extended to Lieutenant Nra.

Tella was escorted away, turning to watch as the human guard led Nra in the other direction.

"Where are they taking him?" Tella asked.

"There are many holding areas in the citadel that allow for downloading and debriefing. We try to keep everyone separated for security reasons."

"You think one of us will try to escape?"

Ezure made an expression similar to a human shrug and said, "We've encountered many situations. Preparedness is key in all endeavors."

Tella agreed and continued quietly along. She watched others move about the citadel. An overwhelming population of Litar crowded the lower levels with a scattering of humans and she noted a couple of Veshnians. In the upper levels, she saw a pair of Af'shai looking over the balcony in her direction.

"Why are there Af'shai on Mars?" Tella asked.

Ezure stopped walking, turned, and confronted her. "Do not mention their presence," they said forcefully. Litar typically didn't display anger, but there was a flash in their gaze that was unsettling. Was it Tella's inquiry, or the presence of the Af'shai?

"I'm sorry."

"All is well," Ezure stated before continuing down the corridor. They ushered her into a small room. It was like stepping back onto the *Veritas*. A lone medical cart sat in the center of the room with several mechanical arms protruding from the ceiling. "Do you require assistance situating yourself?"

"No," Tella answered.

"Very well. Someone will be along to retrieve you for the hearing after your download is complete. Please wait patiently."

Tella stepped into the room as Ezure closed the door behind

DAVE ALEXANDER

her. The locking mechanism clicked. There was no mistaking that she was stuck here until she complied with their orders.

"I may as well get to it," she muttered as she lay on the medical cart. "AI, begin downloading procedures for Ambassador Tella Spar."

The arms moved overhead, guiding a connector to her cerebral port. A moment later, the port engaged, and brilliance flashed before her eyes. Unlike most composites, ambassadors were awake for downloading. The effect was like playing images in her head at light speed. Every moment or so flashed a scene she recognized, while others were too vague to remember.

Her early life felt like someone else's memories. Then there was her inclusion into the GC, her ranking up to ambassador, her first missions, then the recent memories. Every thought, every sight, every perspective recorded like it was a movie played back before her.

She saw Garret in the visions and wondered what drew her to him in the first place. He was a monster, and she knew it. He could have been lying all this time, manipulating her into leading the Bastia to Sol.

If that was true, then the download would reveal it, not from her perspective, but from his. Tella clenched her jaw. The truth would be revealed soon.

Very soon.

Archea, Mars

The guards led him into a white room and placed him on a medical cart, binding him to it with straps and chains. Despite his protests, they worked in silence, double-checking each latch to ensure he would not be able to get free. One guard spoke to the other in hushed tones before ushering themselves out, locking the door behind them.

"Is all this really necessary?" Garret asked. He stared at the black dome protruding from the ceiling. He suspected it was a camera to monitor him, so he glared at it in hopes the person on the other side would see how ridiculous this was. "I'm bound up tighter than a baby in a blanket and you still locked the door? Talk about paranoid."

"Begin downloading procedures for Garret Cushing; aka Steven Chancey," a voice said over the intercom.

Garret startled as the mechanical arms moved. "This isn't very personable," he quipped, but no one was laughing, least of all him.

One arm settled on his forehead and shoved him back into the medical cart while another plugged the cable into his cerebral port. The system engaged with a flash, then darkness.

He came to under a dim light where shadows danced before his eyes. He blinked several times, fighting to focus on the movement before him. Eventually, he saw it, but it unnerved him all the more.

"He's awake," one of them said. He had never been in the presence of Af'shai before, but he'd heard the stories. They were once mistaken as gods. It was easy to see why as brilliant light shone from their bodies. Just looking at them caused his eyes to well as if he were staring into the sun.

"This is certainly a violation of regulations in the composite program," the other said. "They were correct in stating that it is Bastian technology. I have no doubt about that."

"What should we do about it?"

"Let him testify, then ensure he is properly recycled."

"I'm right here," Garret protested.

"Silence, human." The Af'shai to his left clasped a hand to

DAVE ALEXANDER

Garret's mouth and continued. "I can inform Director Igvi of our discovery. They would like to know."

"Certainly. We must also check the progress of the Bastian's download. We can determine if the same technology is used on both of them or if this human is another one of their experiments."

"Very unsettling how they test on lesser species." The Af'shai looked down at him and removed their hand from his mouth. "I understand your species experiences fear of the unknown, but we have concluded that your existence is a breach of protocol and will be dealt with properly. It was very considerate of you to turn yourself over to us."

"I didn't turn myself over for this," Garret shouted as he tugged at his restraints.

The Af'shai looked to one another as Garret struggled to get free. It was useless. The one who had been to his left glanced back at him. If they were human, then Garret might think it was a look of remorse. For all he knew, it was pleasure at his coming demise.

"Go ahead then, recycle me. Bury the truth and throw it away like you do everything that makes you uncomfortable. Your people caused this. You sit atop your thrones and lord over these *lesser species*, but you're just like us. We're all just carbon."

"So aggressive," the Af'shai said. "Your pain will be over soon."

They stepped out of the room and left Garret to stew in his hatred. He swore under his breath and stared up at the black dome. "You treat me like an animal, but I'm a human. I have rights within the Confederation whether you acknowledge them or not. What you're doing is wrong."

His voice cracked and he clamped his mouth shut. He couldn't defend himself any longer. They were doing what he had done more times than he could count. Why should they listen to someone like him?

OBLIVION'S DAWN

Garret cleared his throat and fought against the tears welling in his eyes. He didn't want to break down, but this sense of powerlessness was overwhelming. He had spent so long thinking he was on the right side of history that realizing the truth felt like he was slowly dying.

The lock shifting drew his attention to the door as two guards entered. "It's time," one of them said as the other moved around the medical cart and began unlatching his restraints. "We'll keep you in a holding cell inside the courtroom until time for your testimony. If you act out or try to cause a disturbance of any kind, you will be removed. Do you understand?"

Garret nodded and agreed. The last thing he wanted was to be alone with his thoughts. This was a welcomed reprieve.

The guards helped him to his feet and led him out into the corridor. He glanced to the upper balconies, feeling a presence over him that he couldn't quite see.

"Face forward," the guard behind him said.

Garret complied, keeping his eyes moving side to side as he walked. Every wall was adorned with etchings into the marble. Many depicted ancient stories from Earth, but some showed histories of the different species comprising the Confederation. They stopped before a scene of the Litar Revolution, an event that ultimately led to their inclusion in the Confederation.

The doors opened to reveal a large semicircle courtroom. Seats were arranged on the outer rim for the directors and judges. The open space before them was where he would give his testimony.

The guards ushered him inside and made a quick turn to the back of the room where a single-person cell waited with the door open.

"This hasn't been used in years," a human guard standing outside of the cell said as Garret was led in. "Let's hope we can

DAVE ALEXANDER

get the doors back open to let you out again." It was meant to be a joke, but it fell flat, even with the other guards.

"The hearing begins shortly," one of the guards who led him to the courtroom said before closing the cell. "Remember, don't make any disturbances. Stand when the directors enter the courtroom."

"I've got it," Garret replied. "My stepfather was once a director of the Galactic Confederation."

"Hmm," the human guard scoffed and turned his back. A move that at any other time would have gotten the man killed. A move that still might, once all was said and done. If the Af'shai wanted to recycle him then why not take a few lesser species with him?

He shook the thought from his head. This wasn't who he wanted to be.

The war in his head was getting to be too much as the man he wanted to be fought the man he'd been. Something had to give.

Garret resigned himself to his fate. He'd tell the truth, then accept what was coming. He may not receive redemption, but he would be damned if he let evil be the last deed of his despicable life.

Guards escorted Director Cantor to the courtroom through a series of tunnels separated from the main corridor. He was shocked to see he was not the only human on the panel for the hearing. It appeared that Director Igvi employed multiple species on his staff, a concept that never crossed his mind.

The guards led him to a seat just to the right of Director Igvi. The Litar director would be the last to show up, though there were two seats open to the left of center as well. Had this been Cantor's hearing he would have filled it with military leaders, but those

OBLIVION'S DAWN

seated along the far sides of the semi-circle all appeared to be civilians.

Cantor looked down from the perch and sought General Treff. No one was in the audience, but movement from the dark side of the room revealed a single-person cell. He was too far away to make out the person's features, but he was more than certain that was Garret Cushing, the man who'd united the Sol System if he was to believe the propaganda he'd heard while waiting on his meeting with Director Igvi.

"All rise," a voice called from behind him. He was already standing, so he assumed a rigid, upright position as if he was in a military formation. A hand touched his shoulder, and he stole a glance to see Igvi take their place next to him. The other two seats were taken by a species he'd never seen in person.

"Af'shai?" Cantor whispered.

Director Igvi gave a polite nod to answer his question before asking everyone to be seated.

Cantor couldn't help but stare. The Af'shai had been confused as angels and demons throughout human history. Many times, they covered themselves to keep from being discovered, wearing suits that gave them a close approximation of human appearance, though at seven feet tall and rail thin, they still looked inhuman. Here they didn't have to hide, and it was both amazing and terrifying to see them.

"Thank you everyone for gathering here," Director Igvi announced. "We will be hearing the testimony of a human named Garret Cushing. I'm told that he has an alias of Steven Chancey and is the stepson of former Director of the Galactic Confederation, Artimus Chancey. Mr. Cushing has been wanted across the galaxy for his involvement in acts of terrorism. He has come to us today to turn state's evidence and reveal whom he has been working for.

"I trust everyone will allow Mr. Cushing the opportunity to

DAVE ALEXANDER

speak freely and withhold judgement until the hearing is finished?" Igvi scanned the panel, and each member affirmed their ability to comply before the director continued. "Guard, will you please lead Mr. Cushing before the panel?"

Cantor watched the mercenary exit the cell. Garret walked with a slight limp and held his side as he moved across the room. Ambassador Spar had mentioned an injury, but Cantor suspected this was part of the show, an attempt to garner sympathy when he deserved nothing short of a slow execution.

The guard stood behind Garret, weapon held at the ready. If the mercenary so much as moved without consent, he would be dead. On the far side of the room, the double doors opened, and a squad of guards led Ambassador Spar and the Bastian emissary into the courtroom. They took seats on either side of the aisle while the guards assumed a security posture around the room.

Cantor tried to make eye contact with Spar, but either she hadn't noticed, or was actively avoiding his gaze. He suspected the latter, but he would deal with her later.

"Mr. Cushing," Director Igvi said, "Are you ready to give testimony to support your claims that the Sol System is under threat of attack?"

"I am," Garret answered.

Director Igvi canted their head to the left as one of the Af'shai whispered something into their ear. Cantor followed their head movements and tried to discern what was being said, but all he noted was that Igvi appeared to agree with whatever the Af'shai suggested. A moment later, the Litar director looked to Garret and asked him to begin.

274

THIRTY-FOUR

GARRET'S TESTIMONY REVEALED EVEN MORE THAN HE HAD TOLD Tella on the *Veritas*. The allegations that Artimus Chancey had allies within the Confederation who knew he was still alive stirred gasps from the panel of judges. Tella watched their faces, some shocked, some several shades paler than normal, and some with their jaws clenched tightly.

It was Director Cantor who held her attention as Garret continued his testimony.

"My stepfather has overseen the appointment of each human director within the GC since the attempt on his life. Once he joined the Bastia, he needed people he could trust to make decisions to further their cause. It was no coincidence that his successor was a member of his staff. With three directors in close succession afterwards, each vetted for the cause."

Cantor glared at Garret. He wasn't one of the successors mentioned by Garret, but Tella was certain that the mercenary's testimony was bordering on hearsay. If he kept rattling the cage, they may dismiss every claim. That would leave them worse than before.

"Hold on," Cantor interrupted. He held a hand up and leaned

275

DAVE ALEXANDER

towards Director Igvi, whispering to them while everyone else waited.

Director Igvi consented to whatever Cantor had said before speaking to the crowd. "This testimony is growing more convoluted by the minute. My colleague has suggested that we review the downloads for confirmation of what has been said." Igvi looked to a member of their staff and continued, "Begin the validation process now."

The staffer darted away and exited through a door behind the panel. Tella watched from her seat and wondered how long this would take. They had already interrogated Garret for nearly four hours. Surely a recess would be called soon.

Director Cantor cleared his throat and spoke, drawing eyes from the other judges. "I need to say something." He stared deadfaced at Garret, his eyes boring into the mercenary as if he was looking into the other man's soul. Cantor narrowed his eyes and spoke, "I suspect your testimony is an attempt to usurp our authority in the GC, to force our resignation from the Confederation. Otherwise, you could have told this story to any of the allies. You chose to come to Sol to give this testimony. Why?"

"Director, I'm not sure..." Igvi began, but Cantor cut them off with a raised hand.

"This line of questioning is necessary for us to get to the root of the problem. Let's drop the politics and get to the source of our concerns, shall we?" Cantor replied. "What is it, Mr. Cushing? What brought you before us?"

Hushed whispers formed upon the panel. Shock and awe filled the faces of the judges as Cantor seized control of the hearing, a sign of disrespect to his Litar contemporary. Tella watched, unnerved by what she witnessed, the breakdown in protocol.

"I needed you to hear it directly. The threat is in your system, not any of the others. They want to destroy humanity," Garret

OBLIVION'S DAWN

said. "You don't think the other allies would take this seriously, do you?" Garret shot back.

"That sounds like an excuse, not a reason," Cantor replied. "I think you manipulated my ambassador and used her authority to lead the Bastia here. I think you're working for Artimus Chancey, not against him."

The panel gasped at the accusation, but Garret stood unshaken by it. Both men stared at one another, their shoulders lifting and falling with each deep breath. Tella wanted to intercede but speaking out of turn would find her in contempt. She was in enough trouble as it was.

"You don't know what you're talking about," Garret said, his voice raised enough to stir the guards. They approached him slowly, but he stood defiantly and continued to stand his ground. "I think you know your ascension to Director of the Galactic Confederation was because an outside entity intervened. I think you've been in contact with someone who feeds you advice to act in their favor. I think you know you're a fraud, and you know fate has a special plan for you once the Confederation knows what you've done."

"Enough," Director Igvi shouted as they rose. They put a hand on Cantor's shoulder and pleaded with him to take a seat. Meanwhile, the guards seized Garret and led him back to his holding cell.

"We've had enough testimony from Mr. Cushing. I believe we will all agree that what is best for the Confederation is to have his composite recycled and any records of his existence erased. All in favor?"

A chorus of "ayes" sounded from the panel.

"You're making a mistake," Garrett shouted as the guards led him to his cell. "You need people like me to help in the war that's coming. You can't fight it alone!"

Tella watched as the guards threw him to the floor of his cell

277

DAVE ALEXANDER

and slammed the door shut. She cut her eyes to Director Cantor and wondered if any of what Garret had said was true. Had he been put in his position by an outside entity? If so, then that meant the humans were compromised. Their exclusion from the Confederation would be imminent. Their destruction would be their own doing.

"Ambassador Spar," Director Igvi said. Tella looked at them as they continued, "Will you please come forward and give your testimony?"

Tella rose and answered, "Yes, Director." She moved to the center of the courtroom and swore in.

"I need to know your side of the story in terms of why Mr. Cushing sought asylum on your vessel, why you chose to grant it without authorization, and what transpired while he was in your custody."

Tella took a deep breath. If they dismissed his testimony, then what more would they glean from hers? Unless they were trying to trap her into saying something that would compromise her further. She couldn't let that happen. If there was any hope of saving lives, then she had to insist they take this situation seriously. Tell formed her words carefully, looked to the panel, and began.

Perspective changes everything. The mission on Bala was a failure for both the ambassador and the mercenary, but it ultimately drove them together for another cause. To hear her tell it, one would think he had been on the brink of death when she came swooping in to save him. There was an air of truth to it, but he was hardly helpless, a notion felt by others on the panel if he was reading their faces correctly.

It was anyone's guess which way they would rule. He hoped

desperately that they would reconsider and allow him to help. The chances of that happening were stacked against him, regardless of how well Ambassador Spar spun it.

The writing was on the wall. The human director was a lost cause. As were the Af'shai, though for different reasons. He saw how Director Cantor reacted to his accusations; the man was as guilty as Garrett was for betraying humanity. From the looks of it, the Af'shai witnessed his shift in demeanor too, but didn't let on. Only the Litar seemed to want to continue the hearing and glean more information in hopes for a chance of survival.

If Garret was right, then there was no way to stand against the Bastia without allied support. That would be impossible if the Af'shai believed Cantor was a traitor.

He was, but humanity didn't deserve to go extinct because of it.

"You believe his testimony?" Director Igvi asked.

Garret stared at Tella's back, wishing he could make eye contact with her before she uttered her next words. He wondered if she was resisting looking back. Eventually, she answered, "I do." Her words brought scornful expressions upon the judges' faces.

"Why do you believe him?" Igvi asked, seemingly undeterred by Ambassador Spar's confession.

"I was trained to read people, to determine their motives and the drive behind their actions. Most of his story would lead you to believe he was an anarchist looking to stir trouble, but that was only the effect of his actions. His reasoning was to save his mother. It's a basic human instinct to try and protect those we love. Without that piece of information, I would assume he was a monster. As it stands, I believe he was misguided and desperate."

Garret's jaw went slack. He didn't expect her to defend him to the judges. If anything, he figured she would agree with them to preserve herself.

DAVE ALEXANDER

Disorder erupted from the panel. Arguments swelled amongst the judges to the point the Litar director resorted to banging their gavel to settle the room. As the quiet slowly settled, Tella stole a glance behind her, and he met her eyes. They pleaded with him in that moment, and the only conclusion he could come to was that she had put her neck on the line for him and wanted desperately for him to be telling the truth.

He wanted that too.

He needed it.

Garret gave the slightest of nods before she returned her gaze to the assembled judges.

"Thank you for your testimony, Ambassador Spar. You leave us with much to consider. Before we deliberate, I believe Lieutenant Nra of the Bastian Navy has testimony to bear?"

Garret took hold of the bars of his cell as Nra rose and affirmed his willingness to testify. He had no reason to be considered useful to the court, yet the Litar had invited him. For all they knew, the Bastia could spew lies and cloud the panels' judgement of what they had heard. How would they know if he was even telling the truth?

Tella stared at Garret as she returned to her seat. They couldn't communicate. They might never speak again for all he knew, but he wished beyond anything he would have the opportunity to thank her before the GC exercised their authority. He was as good as dead and had accepted that before he stepped foot off Bastia, but that didn't make it any easier.

Lieutenant Nra swore in, but Garret didn't want to watch the spectacle. He only wanted to watch the person who had put everything on the line for him to be there. The only person who wasn't paid to do his bidding. The only person he knew who believed in him.

He wanted to be anywhere other than that room at that moment. Director Cantor rubbed his clammy hands along his pant leg and tried to look natural, but it felt like every eye was on him. Each time he looked up, another member of the panel was staring, whispering into the closest person's ear.

He could only suspect they were whispering about him, about the testimony Garret Cushing had given, about the fact his own ambassador believed the killer. And now they put a Bastian on the stand. What else was he about to endure before justice could be served?

"Lieutenant Nra," Director Igvi said as the Bastian stood before them. "Would you please state your position within the Bastian military?"

"I am a lieutenant in the Bastian Navy, serving as a communications officer aboard the *BNV Pourgua*."

"What does that entail?" Igvi asked.

"I am responsible for the sending and receiving of communications for the ship. I am also trained in decryption and forensic investigations of media."

"Were you required to investigate any media received by your ship regarding Mr. Cushing?"

"I was not called to do that duty, though I did investigate the request for the *Pourgua* to escort the *Veritas*."

"You took it upon yourself?" Igvi asked.

"I did."

"Why?"

Nra hesitated to answer, his eyes focused forward until he slowly canted his head towards Director Cantor. There was a familiar look in the Bastian's eyes, but it shouldn't be possible. Neither of them had met previously. "I lacked confidence in my commanding officer, and I wanted to verify the message before he accepted it."

"What did you find?"

"The message was fraudulent."

Igvi sighed, then leaned forward to look over the panel at the Bastian officer, "Do you mean to tell me your people agreed to escort the *Veritas* knowing the initial message was fraudulent?"

Nra shook his head. "I didn't report it."

A gasp filled the room. Cantor narrowed his eyes at the lieutenant, pondering what he was getting at. The Bastian just admitted to dereliction of his duties as if it meant nothing. "Why not?" Cantor asked, breaking into Igvi's inquisition.

Nra looked to the human and answered, "Because I've spent years preparing for this opportunity to be here. Once I saw the chance for my people to cross the galaxy and orbit one of your planets, I knew we had to take it."

The room grew cold, withdrawn. The judges shared nervous glances. Some backed away.

"And what did you plan to do with this opportunity?" Cantor asked. His voice cracked with the question.

Nra smirked and moved forward. "Everything Garret Cushing said is the truth. There is an attack planned for this system. Supreme Commander Freist wants to bring destruction to Sol and claim your hytocostic crystal mining facilities. He hopes that by becoming a producer of the resource again, the Bastia will be included in the Confederation."

"Why not seek inclusion without attacking another system?" Igvi asked.

Nra cut his eyes to the Litar and said, "Because the Supreme Commander was made promises by Artimus Chancey after he betrayed his own people. The Bastia get revenge and are welcomed back into the Confederation to fill the void left by the newly extinct humans."

"That's genocide," Cantor shouted. He stood and stared boldly down at the Bastian officer. "We have allies in the Confederation. Two species have heard your intent. This will not stand."

OBLIVION'S DAWN

"It's too late," Nra said. "The plan is already in motion." He looked skyward and Cantor's stomach turned.

He didn't have to see through the ceiling to know there were two Bastian warships orbiting Mars. Bombardment would wipe them out in minutes.

Three of the Litar judges sprang from their seats and moved for the exits, but they were locked into place by an unseen force. Realization flooded the human director as he watched their faces turn in horror. The Bastian was using mind compulsion and had infiltrated the GC. Their own people were now aiding the enemy.

"It was you, wasn't it?" Cantor said.

"What was me?" Nra replied.

"The person I spoke to regarding the situation with Garret Cushing." Anger boiled beneath Cantor's skin. He felt the flames of hatred licking at his heels. He wanted nothing more than to end this with resounding finality, but the only thing that would accomplish was his own annihilation.

"That wasn't me," Nra replied. "That was him." The lieutenant looked back at the cell, right at Garret Cushing.

THIRTY-FIVE

TELLA COULDN'T BELIEVE WHAT SHE WAS HEARING. DID Director Cantor just confess to conspiring with an unknown source about a GC investigation? That screamed treason.

Her eyes fell on Lieutenant Nra expectantly.

"That wasn't me," Nra replied with a turn towards the back of the room. "That was him."

Tella didn't have to look to know he was referring to Garret, but she couldn't stop herself from meeting his gaze.

The mercenary looked confused; his brow furrowed as he stared back at her.

"You have been played, Director Cantor," Nra said with a sneer. There was something about the shift in his voice that was all too familiar. Her realization struck in sync with Garret.

The mercenary leapt forward, grasped the bars of his cell, and shouted, "It's a trap!"

Nra's expression soured. He stomped towards one of the guards frozen in place by his compulsory power and snatched a weapon from them. "You're a traitor to our kind, Garret. Tell Artimus we send our regards."

OBLIVION'S DAWN

With those words, he pulled the trigger, painting the walls with Garret's blood.

Shouts of terror filled the room. The people were powerless against the Bastian as his reign of terror began.

He fired on the judges point blank, scattering their remains. Tella watched in horror while he slowly made his way around the panel. She was caught in his mind trick, locked in position with her hands folded on her lap. She fought against it, her gaze drooping enough to see her fingers touching the wrist communicator that kept her in contact with the *Veritas*. All she needed was an open comm. A final chance to do the right thing.

Tella fought to reach the switch, but it was like lifting herself out of bed as a fresh composite coming to for the first time. Never mind the distracting report of gunfire reverberating around her as the Bastian murderer laid waste to the judges.

Like a miracle from above, her finger depressed the switch, opening a channel to the ship's AI. "Survey emergency and report to Confederation. Send to Bastian ships in orbit," Tella ordered, her voice strained as she fought to speak over Nra's will.

He cut his eyes at Tella. Her breath caught. The wickedness behind those orbs betrayed every fiber of hope that humanity stood a chance. He fired, without looking, killing the Af'shai seated next to Director Igvi. Bluish goo, the Af'shai's blood, trickled down the walls.

Tella's wrist device vibrated softly as the AI used infrared imaging to survey the scene. A double chirp of vibration let her know it was done and forwarded to Captain Viar. She had no way of knowing if Nra was acting on orders, or of his own accord, but she took the leap of faith anyway.

He had to know that the war wasn't sparked by humanity. It was sparked by his own kind. They broke the Tel'stra Treaty. They delivered death under the false veil of peace.

Soon everyone in the Confederation would know.

DAVE ALEXANDER

They never had a chance.

Nra fired another round into Director Igvi and then spoke, his voice sounding like it was underwater. "I've looked forward to our meeting for years, Director Cantor. It's too bad things couldn't have ended differently. You would have made a great martyr."

Nra placed the weapon in Cantor's hand. Tella gasped as her director took it, aimed it at the judges to his right, and fired in rapid succession. Five more Litar lay dead at his feet. His face was frozen in painful contortion. Eyes welled with tears.

"You brought this destruction on them, Director. You were a weak leader. You were unable to control your ambassador. You welcomed a murderer into your system. You betrayed your people and your allies," Nra said as he moved to the center of the room. The only witnesses to his violence were the two remaining humans and the Litar guards standing in the back of the court. "May history remember you well."

With those words, Nra released his captives. The Litar guards drew down on Director Cantor and fired relentlessly. Multiple shots tore through his torso, splattering his remains against the wall.

Tella screamed in horror. She refused to look at the weapons now drawn on their next target. Nra stepped to her side and spoke softly, "Politics is a dirty business. Sometimes you have to clean house to get anything done."

He stepped away. Cleared his throat. And the guards fired.

BNV Pourgua

He didn't believe what he was seeing. He'd been in a lot of sticky situations during his military career, but nothing was as bad as this. In truth, he wanted to exact his revenge, but he wanted to do

OBLIVION'S DAWN

it on his terms. Lieutenant Nra was a lot of things but not someone he would've trusted to send on an offensive strike. Whatever this was, it wasn't on his orders.

Captain Viar stared at the monitor watching the playback. In the past, the Bastia had used their powers of compulsion to preserve peace. What he was seeing was the opposite, and it scared him to death. He grabbed the ship's comm, keyed it, and made his announcement. "All hands, this is the captain speaking, prepare for emergency withdrawal. Repeat, prepare for emergency withdrawal. Man your stations. Captain out."

He eyed the playback as his lieutenant shot the Litar director. It was settled, and in that moment, a silent declaration of war had been made. There was no going back. He patched through to the *Nir and* gave the order to hyper-jump on his mark.

Just like his father before him, Captain Viar was on the run from the Sol System, dishonored. Only this time it wasn't a human's doing, it was one of their own.

The feed shifted to Nra handing the gun over to Director Cantor. He couldn't watch. It was clear what was coming, and he would have no part in it.

"You've betrayed your people, Lieutenant," Captain Viar said under his breath as his crew manned their stations.

"Sir, we don't have enough energy in the hyperdrive to make a full jump," Commander Ull, his engineering officer said. "The *Nir* will be in the same situation."

"Calculate the best jump coordinates and make it happen. I don't want to linger around this planet any longer than I have to," Viar replied. "Where are we on weapons?"

"PDs are good to go, sir," Weps replied from his console.

"What about offensive weapons?" Viar shot back.

"I thought we were evading, sir?"

Viar grimaced, he hated the idea of running away, but he didn't have a choice. "I have to destroy that Confederation ship.

We can't afford to allow Nra off that planet after what he's done. We destroy the *Veritas* and get out of here. Understood?"

"Yes, sir!" Weps called out. The captain waited for the weapons officer to relay the orders to his respective department. They had time, though it was ticking away at an alarming rate. He kept his eyes on the monitor for the inevitable retaliation. They had to deploy something to try and strike back.

"Primary cannon is armed and ready, sir."

Viar set his jaw, narrowed his eyes, and gave the order. "Fire at will."

The dull thud of a warhead exiting the tube reverberated inside the bridge. They were far enough away to witness the explosion without danger. He had to be sure. There was no time for half-measures.

Less than thirty seconds later, the *Veritas* was struck on her starboard side. The following explosion whited out the monitor. A direct hit. Once visuals returned, Viar and his crew watched the hull of the Confederation ship drift apart in pieces.

"Such a waste," he said solemnly. He had placed his hope in having something to show for this mission. Now all he had was his worst nightmare coming true and the shame of his own involvement. "Let's get out of here."

"Yes, sir," Ull called from his console. A moment later the *Pourgua* was outside the Sol System, midway through the Ort Cloud. They were far enough away to be safe, but they could never outrun the news of what had happened.

Viar looked to his personal monitor to see his traitorous lieutenant speaking to the ambassador. Nra stepped away as shadows crept upon the scene. Viar didn't want to look, but pulling his eyes away from the massacre was a childish way of pretending it never happened. He would have to brief his superiors. Not knowing wasn't an option.

The darkness crept closer with only his lieutenant and the

OBLIVION'S DAWN

ambassador in the frame. He expected what was coming with helpless anticipation. There was a finality to death, even for the composites that dulled the soul. He considered saying a prayer for her, but it was already too late, and his faith waned in the midst of such a crisis.

Instead, he straightened, standing at attention for the human who placed service over herself. She was as misguided as all of Sol's children, but she never wavered, even in the face of death.

The guards fired a moment later. Viar's eyes widened, and his heart quickened. There was a void where his sadness should have been. All warriors die in the end. That was the universal truth that every faction within the Confederation agreed on.

In the end, none of them were gods.

EPILOGUE
ARCHEA, MARS

"Three days in holding and zero charges. I guess you can consider yourself lucky," Director Treff said as the Litar guards led her from the cell. "Negotiating your release was the easiest part of my tenure, if you would believe that."

"Thank you, sir, but I don't understand. I expected to be recycled," she replied sheepishly.

Treff sighed, leaning against the wall as she approached. He may hold the office of Director of the Galactic Confederation, but he certainly didn't look the part. He was more grunt than politician. Then again, he was the only person suitable for the job considering the assassinations which took place days prior. "Things changed considering recent developments, Tella. I'll brief you on the way."

He stepped away from the wall and escorted her through the double doors leading out of the jail. It was after midnight and the purple sky over the dome sparkled with starlight peeking out from the abyss. Somewhere, out in the distance, two Bastian ships were in hiding. She learned that much during her stay, but considering the investigators were seeking information from her, she doubted they intended to keep her in the loop.

OBLIVION'S DAWN

They walked quietly together. Two Litar guards followed closely but kept enough distance for them to speak without being overheard. "Lieutenant Nra wasn't who you thought he was," Treff said, his voice barely above a whisper. "The Af'shai were too focused on Garret Cushing to take the time to review the download of the Bastian. If they had, they would have noticed something startling."

"What was it?"

"At a certain point in time, they were the same person," Treff answered.

"What?" After everything she'd learned about Garret, this didn't seem possible. He had admitted to using more than one composite, but never did he mention being the composite of another species. Her heart raced at the bitterness of his betrayal. "He was using me."

"That's actually not accurate," Treff replied, pulling her attention to him. "The truth appears to be much more controversial."

"How so?"

Treff led her to the edge of the city, the dome a mere fifty meters away from where they stood, separated by the churning waters of the Archean Sea. To Earth-born eyes, it was more a lake than anything, but considering the wasteland the planet had once been, it was a stark improvement.

"The Litar and Af'shai have reviewed all the downloads, including yours. They have no reason to believe Garret was using you. It's more likely that there's a rebellion forming on Bastia and that Nra attempted to ignite a war between the factions."

"Was he successful?" Tella hated to ask, but she had to know. Regardless of blame, she was culpable. She had led them here.

"No. Calmer heads prevailed. The Af'shai bore witness to what had happened and relayed their findings to Supreme Commander Freist."

Tella shuddered when she heard his name. He may have been

291

more an ally in that moment than at any other point in history, but days before he had attempted to kill her. Justified, or not, it was hard to forgive and forget.

"Humanity is safe, then?"

"For now," Treff confided, "but that's subject to change."

Tella looked to the grizzled old man expectantly.

He turned to her and continued, "I have an assignment for you, and it was part of the release agreement." His tone had shifted from positive to remorseful, and his expression did little to settle her growing nerves.

"What is it?"

"You're needed on Karnack, but it isn't a diplomatic mission."

"What is it then?"

Treff turned away. He stared out over the rushing waters as he prepared to answer her, each second a lifetime before he finally broke his silence. "You're being sent to find the real Garret Cushing."

"I thought he *was* the real Garret," she replied.

Treff shook his head. "As I said, things have gotten a bit crazy while you were locked up. The Af'shai believe you know him better than anyone. They want you to go and find him, get him to turn himself over to the Confederation."

"For what purpose? The real Garret Cushing would be an old man by now."

Treff let out a sigh and looked her dead in the eye, "They aren't telling me anything more than that. But believe me when I tell you that humanity's continued inclusion in the Confederation hinges on you doing this."

Tella looked away. The last thing she wanted to do was the bidding of the Confederation. Being recycled seemed the better option at this point. "Service over self," she whispered indignantly.

OBLIVION'S DAWN

"What was that?" Treff asked.

"Nothing." She looked back at him and asked, "When do I leave?"

The story will continue in Blood Lines!

THANK YOU FOR READING OBLIVION'S DAWN

WE HOPE YOU ENJOYED IT AS MUCH AS WE ENJOYED BRINGING IT to you. We just wanted to take a moment to encourage you to review the book. Follow this link: **Oblivion's Dawn** to be directed to the book's Amazon product page to leave your review.

Every review helps further the author's reach and, ultimately, helps them continue writing fantastic books for us all to enjoy.

Also in series:
Oblivion's Dawn
Blood Lines
Artifacts of the Gods

Want to discuss our books with other readers and even the authors? Join our Discord server today and be a part of the Aethon community.

Facebook | Instagram | Twitter | Website

You can also join our non-spam mailing list by visiting www.subscribepage.com/AethonReadersGroup and never miss out on future releases. You'll also receive three full books completely Free as our thanks to you.

Looking for more great books?

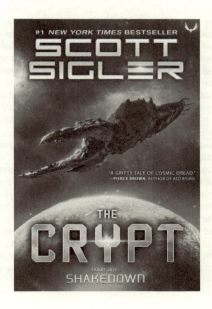

DAVE ALEXANDER

The only way out is to die... Few know the warship's actual name. Fewer still know what it really is. And almost no one knows of its unique ability, an ability that could tilt the balance of power if not outright win the war. But everyone has heard the rumors. Rumors about the worst place the Planetary Union Fleet can send you. Rumors of a ship with an eighty percent crew mortality rate. In these hushed, fearful whispers, the ship does have a name. People call it "the Crypt," because those aboard are as good as dead. The PUV *James Keeling* can do something no other vessel in existence can do — slip into another dimension, travel undetected, then re-emerge onto our plane and surprise enemy targets. But the thing that makes the *Crypt* unique also makes it a nightmare for those onboard; interdimensional travel causes hallucinations, violent behavior, and psychotic breakdowns. *Keeling* could be the Union's greatest weapon, a game-changing asset that can defeat the bloodthirsty zealots of the Purist Nation, the Union's mortal enemy. If, that is, the brass can find the right crew. But with those dark rumors traveling at lightspeed throughout Fleet, sailors with connections, with favors to call in, or those with careers on the rise pull any string they can to avoid being assigned to the *Crypt*. The brightest and best shield themselves from this top-secret craft, yet the brass *must* send it out on critical missions. As the war drags on and casualties pile up, Fleet crews the ship by assigning the worst of the worst. If you are convicted of assault, fraud, cowardice, theft, rape, murder — or you cross the wrong Admiral — you may find yourself aboard the *Crypt*. Most are given a choice: serve a two-year stint on the Keeling and have your record expunged, or be executed for your crimes. Welcome to the PUV *James Keeling*, where the only way out... is to die.

Get Shakedown Now!

OBLIVION'S DAWN

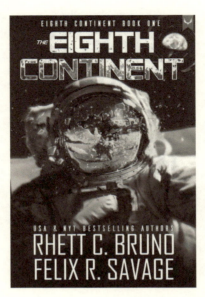

"This stellar near-future tale masterfully fuses SF thrills with an enthralling mystery." —Kirkus Review **A lowly construction worker on the Moon is Earth's only chance...** Nick Morrison always wanted to be an astronaut. When a startup company recruits him to build a lunar launch system at the Moon's south pole, Nick gladly leaves behind his troubled life on Earth— but Nick doesn't know that the company is in financial and legal trouble. Deprived of support from Earth, the team on the Moon must figure out how to survive on their own. Worse yet, there's another base at the lunar south pole, run by a ruthless contractor who has big plans for the Moon... and for Earth. Nick's team just so happen to be in the way. **Join them in their mission to stop the conquest of the Moon and Earth in this new Science Fiction Survival Thriller from Nebula Award Nominated author Rhett C. Bruno and NYT bestselling author Felix R. Savage. It's perfect for fans of The Martian, Artemis, and For all Mankind.**

Get The Eighth Continent now!

For all of our science fiction titles, check out www.aethonbooks.com/science-fiction

Made in United States
Troutdale, OR
01/15/2024